THE PLEASURE OF A KISS

"What, my lordship, have you been wondering all evening?"

"Whether your lips really do feel like rose petals or I just imagined that."

He could see she remembered the kiss as well as he did. The hunger in her eyes was indisputable, but something battled with desire.

"You should not speak to me so."

"I cannot seem to help myself."

"What can you possibly be thinking?"

"I think you are unlike any woman I have ever met. You hold contrary views. You speak to me as if you are intimidated by no one. You intrigue me. Surely you would not begrudge one kiss. What harm could that do?"

She leaned down to him, whispering, "Curiosity can be fatal. I don't know why I'm doing this."

Then she touched her lips to his . . .

BOOK YOUR PLACE ON OUR WEBSITE AND MAKE THE READING CONNECTION!

We've created a customized website just for our very special readers, where you can get the inside scoop on everything that's going on with Zebra, Pinnacle and Kensington books.

When you come online, you'll have the exciting opportunity to:

- View covers of upcoming books
- Read sample chapters
- Learn about our future publishing schedule (listed by publication month *and author*)
- Find out when your favorite authors will be visiting a city near you
- Search for and order backlist books from our online catalog
- Check out author bios and background information
- Send e-mail to your favorite authors
- Meet the Kensington staff online
- Join us in weekly chats with authors, readers and other guests
- Get writing guidelines
- AND MUCH MORE!

**Visit our website at
http://www.kensingtonbooks.com**

Never Too Late

AMARA ROYCE

KENSINGTON BOOKS
KENSINGTON PUBLISHING CORP.
http://www.kensingtonbooks.com

KENSINGTON BOOKS are published by

Kensington Publishing Corp.
119 West 40th Street
New York, NY 10018

All Kensington titles, imprints and distributed lines are available at special quantity discounts for bulk purchases for sales promotion, premiums, fund-raising, educational or institutional use.

Special book excerpts or customized printings can also be created to fit specific needs. For details, write or phone the office of the Kensington Special Sales Manager. Attn.: Special Sales Department. Kensington Publishing Corp., 119 West 40th Street, New York, NY 10018. Phone: 1-800-221-2647.

Kensington and the K logo Reg. U.S. Pat. & TM Off.

eISBN-13: 978-1-60183-117-0
eISBN-10: 1-60183-117-X

First Electronic Edition: May 2013

ISBN-13: 978-1-60183-208-5
ISBN-10: 1-60183-208-7

Printed in the United States of America

To my husband

ACKNOWLEDGMENTS

My journey toward publication began several years ago, and many people have bolstered my every step.

To my agent, Jessica Alvarez, thank you for your tremendous enthusiasm, insight, and encouragement. To my editor, John Scognamiglio, thank you for being so easy to work with and for believing in my work.

Thank you to the wonderful members of the Compuserve Books and Writers Forum—especially to forumites Diana Gabaldon, Joanna Bourne, Beth Shope, and Kristen Callihan, all exceptional novelists and excellent teachers of the craft of writing. Very special thanks go out to forumite Barbara Rogan, also a novelist, editor, and former literary agent; I had the pleasure of taking one of her online writing courses, offered through *Writer's Digest*. Barbara's teaching and feedback have been tremendously helpful, and she continues to be a valuable source of encouragement and guidance. Thank you as well to past and present forumites, too numerous to name, who have helped me hone my skills and grow as a writer.

Thank you to the online writing forum at the Absolute Write Water Cooler. In particular, thank you to Absolute Write's creator, MacAllister, for creating and maintaining such a wonderfully informative and diverse playground for writers.

To my dear friend Chris A., thank you for all you do to help me stay sane.

To my parents and my in-laws, thank you for your seemingly bottomless well of love and support and free meals.

Finally and most importantly, to my husband and my son, thank you for your love, encouragement, acceptance, love, humor, affection, love, indulgence, patience, and even more love. Thank you for knowing what I need before I do. You two are everything to me.

Chapter One

London, June 1851

Evans Principle 1: Customers must, at all times, be treated with civility, no matter how uncivil they may be.

If she hadn't been dusting the reading nook so beloved by customers, young and old, Mrs. Honoria Duchamp, owner and proprietress of Evans Books, would not have heard the cruel comments about her from some society mum shepherding her daughter to matrimonial slaughter. Now it echoed in her mind: "Did you see that woman, Margaret? Did you? Take a close look at her and at this cramped, suffocating little shop. This is the best you can hope for if you don't marry well. Do you think that shriveled-up mouse of a woman wanted this menial life?" The mother's sharp voice had grown shrill toward the end of this little speech. *It just goes to show*, she thought, *nothing good can come of dusting.*

If she hadn't been feeling particularly content right then, the comments likely would have wafted through her mind with no more impact than a falling nettle in a forest, just one more lifeless wisp. This time, though, the cruel depiction of her as a cautionary tale sliced through her equilibrium. What she'd seen as enough was seen by others as cramped and suffocating. She felt small, her ambitions lacking. It felt almost true.

"You see, Margaret"—the mother's voice cut through the bookshelf between them, interrupting her self-reflection—"do you see why I harp on you about finding a good match?"

"Yes, Mother." Resigned flat tone. Honoria quirked her brow. Ah, yes, all too common a conversation in the advice section. She could almost picture the young lady; they always wore pale clothes, always wore their bonnets primly, always sported pristine white gloves that meant they couldn't actually handle any of the books themselves, for fear of muss.

An older couple approached the register to purchase a stack of periodicals so she went to take care of them. The husband, all business, made pleasantries about the weather, but the wife, her plump figure swathed in gray worsted, looked with kind eyes at Honoria and reached out to pat her left hand while she wrote out the bill of sale with her right.

"Don't you take those careless words to heart, dearie." The wife's touch was gentle, warm. "My niece lost her man in a railway accident two years ago, and with two little mouths to feed yet. She's remarried now to a kind older gentleman who wanted companionship. 'Course she's only one-and-twenty yet."

"Ethelyn, must you?" At the husband's low chiding, the woman withdrew her arm. "No one needs to know your family business."

"Oh, bother. Freddy, I'm sure the missus could do with a kind word or two. Now, dear, keep in mind you have a lovely face, regardless of your age. Don't lose hope!"

One couldn't lose something one never had. Honoria was quite content with her single life; she'd never hoped for a husband, at least not since taking over the family business. She deflected the conversation adroitly and professionally as she recorded the sale in the ledger. "May I interest either of you in this tract about abolition or perhaps this new commentary on art by Ruskin? Both are quite well written and informative. Here is a fascinating anonymous article on child labor." She fanned a selection of pamphlets on the counter.

Stressful as it could be, owning a bookstore had its advantages. Aside from the financial independence, meager as it was, she was constantly surrounded by the one thing she loved. Words. Knowledge. Countless worlds and lifetimes. The eternal truths and fantasies of humanity. All bound in paper and leather and stacked two stories high. The printing press was, she was sure, the most magnificent invention of the modern world. The customers she'd inherited from her father trusted her professionalism and helped to build her clientele and her economic stability. While she could avoid participating in the social world, she couldn't prevent it from entering her Greek Street storefront.

The husband gruffly said, "No, thank you," as he collected his change, then gave his wife his arm as she bid a good morning and glanced back one last time, sympathetic, as they walked out. Of course, the woman meant to be comforting, but even such well-intended condescension had long since grown tiresome. She watched the two stroll blithely out of view, so charmingly a couple even as they bickered, and started sorting the most recently received titles stacked behind the counter.

"Now take these books," said the anxious mother from the back corner. "We'll study them tonight. Tomorrow you'll work on your vocal and piano lessons. We must prepare for the season. What was that book Mrs. Nesbeth suggested? Something about letters. *Ladies with Letters? Letters for Ladies?*"

The woman's raised voice, nasal and piercing, suddenly filled the shop. "Miss! Oh, miss, we need your help over here."

She stifled a groan as she made her way to them, anticipating which volume regarding letters they might possibly want. The daughter, Margaret, held a stack of five advice manuals to her chest, as if they could coalesce into a fairy godmother, complete with pumpkin carriage and princely suitor. A pretty girl, probably around age seventeen, with fine ash-blond hair and brown eyes—and, yes, fetchingly dressed in pristine white frock, bonnet, and gloves, the young miss looked hesitant and yet curious. She noticed the girl's eyes roaming other corners of the store, perhaps for more interesting fare.

"Miss, do you have *Letters for Ladies?*" This from an extravagantly coiffed older woman, clearly young Margaret's high-strung mother, dressed in the newest fashions but somewhat awry. Like a painting ever so slightly askew, the woman's clothing seemed . . . off. Perhaps it was the garish yellow or the excess of blonde lace, trying too hard to appear refined. "My neighbor highly recommends it for all young ladies of good breeding. I would assume any smart bookseller would have a copy, but I can't seem to find one."

She swallowed hard. *The customer must always be treated with civility, even if said customer is a pill, a massive, chalky pill to be choked down with gall!*

"I believe you may mean *Letters to Young Ladies* by a Mrs. Lydia Sigourney, It was a very popular volume for several years, but so many other more recent books have taken over the shelves. We should have a copy, though, along this wall," Honoria explained as she examined the shelves methodically. She'd grown accustomed to relaxing her eyes ever so slightly, not reading specific titles but seeking appropriate patterns of lettering and coloring. By the time she got to the bottom shelf, the mother behind her was audibly exasperated.

"There is one more shelf, madam. See, up there, recessed just so. I believe some of our older ladies' guides are up there. I'll just be a moment." She fetched the wooden ladder from the back of the store and climbed up, forcibly reminded that she'd never been quite tall enough to reach that shelf, even with the ladder. It had been where her father shelved texts not suitable for her as a young woman. Still, she stretched her body as far as she could reach, from the tips of her toes to the tips of her fingers and found she could just barely hook the top binding of some items, some laced with fine spider webbing. In this position, though, she could not see what she was feeling, couldn't read the titles and reach them at the same time.

The door chime announced a new customer. She parroted the usual greeting without looking. "Good afternoon. If you seek something in particular, I will be with you shortly, as soon as I have finished helping these gentlewomen. In the meantime, please feel free to explore." Her eyes were intent on counting the number of books on the shelf up to her prey. She then followed the count with her fingers.

There it is! "I'll have your book for you in just a moment, madam."

Stretch just a bit more. Every inch of her strained to reach, inching closer to the spot where she could hook the top of the book and yank it out.

"Would service in this establishment be quicker if I assisted?" A male voice, deep and smooth, disrupted her focus. She heard the ladies gasp behind her.

Without ceasing her efforts, she replied, "No, no, sir. Please don't trouble yourself. I will be right with you. This will take but a moment more."

One tiny hop ought to do it. Stretch and hop. *Yes!* She felt the book slip easily away from its neighbors.

That final exertion, however, put her off balance. As the book gave way, the momentum of her pull made her lose her footing. She grabbed for the ladder but found only air. Her hands slipped down shelves without purchase. As she fell headlong toward the ground, she heard a tiny scream and was so startled, all she could do was flail her arms and legs, her eyes shut tight. She'd be lucky if she didn't crack her skull open on the floor. Wouldn't that be good for business?

Her breath slammed out of her upon impact. Except she felt not the hard, unyielding wood. Unyielding, yes, but ... warm ... and enveloping. She opened her eyes to find herself looking at disheveled but otherwise finely clipped black hair atop a man's head. She'd landed, it seemed, in a pair of strong hands, and her ... *bloody hell* ... her bosom had landed square on the man's face. *If he wears spectacles, I've surely blinded him!* She could feel the warmth of his breath, even through several layers of cotton and wool.

"Margaret, avert your eyes!" Poor Margaret's mother lunged to block her daughter's view.

Honoria pushed against the man's shoulders, very firm and broad shoulders, to disentangle herself but couldn't find purchase on the ground until he lifted her away and set her down firmly. For a moment, flushed with mortification, she couldn't speak, although a string of unutterable curses ran through her head.

"My stars!" she said, grasping at the first acceptable epithet that came to mind and trying to recover gracefully. "I ... thank you, sir. I'm deeply sorry. How clumsy of me." She focused on brushing dust off of her skirt and found she couldn't bring herself to look at the man's face. Her chest tingled from the impact. She caught the mother's horrified expression and felt an inexplicable bubble of laughter she had to tamp down. Really, the fall was ridiculous but hardly cause for the woman's scandalized alarm.

"I am always pleased to be of service to a lady in need." The man's deep voice dripped with sarcasm. He bent to pick up the *Letters to Young Ladies*, which had fallen out of Honoria's grasp, and held it out to Margaret's mother. "I believe this is for you?"

"Thank you, sir. Hmm, it's rather slight." The woman was curt but then looked at the man more carefully, her eyes seeking something. "My lord, I believe we have some friends in common."

"Is that so?" The coldness in his voice could not be mistaken. Apparently, he was not here for random conversation and barely tolerated the distraction. But he was clearly too well-bred to give a cut direct.

"Yes, indeed, sir. Are you Lord Devin? Who was at the Wenthrope dinner last Thursday?"

"I am indeed Lord Alexander Devin, at your service, madam." He made a polite bow to the mother and then to the daughter. Reputed to be a recluse, the Viscount Alexander Devin's presence at a society dinner and now at her shop was unusual, to say the least. While Honoria didn't give much credence or attention to scandal sheets, she tried to keep abreast of a wide range of timely subjects and potential clients of the ton. "I apologize," he continued, "but my memory fails me. Whom do I have the pleasure of addressing?"

"Oh, I don't think we were formally introduced, your lordship. I am the wife of Mr. Arthur Hayman, and this is my daughter, Margaret." The Hayman family obviously needed all the etiquette advice they could find; Honoria was embarrassed for them, especially since they didn't seem to perceive their egregious faux pas. Instead, there was a smooth curtsy from Margaret. The girl's demeanor had transformed. Like a once-listless puppet set dancing by its master, she came to life, with a delicacy to every motion and a faint gleam in her downturned eye. "She's ever so talented. She can sing nicely and her needlework is quite fine." Surely, next, the mother would be showing off her daughter's teeth. Margaret's face remained politely impassive, but Honoria noticed the undisguised interest in her coy glances at his lordship, in the tilt of her head and the flutter of her lashes.

And why wouldn't the girl be interested? Such matches between an older gentleman and a young girl were ordinary, if not expected. Of course, most girls like Margaret wouldn't want a septuagenarian, but even if Lord Devin were, as she estimated, ten years the girl's senior, he was a fine specimen of manhood in its prime. He was the definition of a strapping young man—notably tall, broad-shouldered, lean, his face appropriately pleasant and inoffensive. And, of course, he was a viscount, highly prized on the marriage mart. Upon quick assessment, she guessed Margaret's obvious response to him was not unusual. Here was yet another girl building a Cinderella fantasy in her head. It would be sweet if the story weren't so unlikely. Many a girl wove such fairy tales for themselves only to find the pumpkin carriage was moldy and the prince was a toad. Or worse, they learned the only reality was the ash heap—no prince, no godmother, just a castle fashioned from dust.

To his credit, Lord Devin didn't seem to respond in any way to the girl's feminine wiles. He maintained a consistently superior, mildly sardonic tone and demeanor. Normally, she denigrated such lordly behavior, yet she could swear she glimpsed humor in his eyes when he glanced her way. Yet the mother and daughter either didn't notice or steadfastly remained undaunted. Then he looked at her directly with a glint of combined mischief and entreaty. She repressed a shiver as she recalled the warmth of his body against hers and responded to his tacit request, though not as he might expect.

"Pardon my interruption." She had to get back to the business at hand. "But, madam, would you like me to bring your books up to the register for you? So you can continue your conversation unencumbered." Receiving an affirmative response, she turned to Margaret. "These are all lovely, but perhaps you might also be interested in more entertaining reading. I have here a few titles that are currently popular, including the newer edition of *Wuthering Heights*, the one revealing the identity of the Bell authors." The girl's eyes finally tore away from the strapping gentleman and glinted with genuine interest at the reference to *Wuthering Heights* but her mother intervened.

"No, my Margaret doesn't have time for frivolous reading, I assure you. Ours is a Bible-reading home," the mother said. "As it is, these prices are steep for honest, upstanding families who have serious financial responsibilities." More snideness. Honoria prided herself on being a reasonable businesswoman, striving to meet every customer's needs, whether enlightening or entertaining, and at a reasonable cost; she would endure personal affront but would not let insults to her business go unchallenged.

"I agree, madam. I do strive to keep prices as low as possible and yet still make some kind of living. It is my policy to charge no more than one percent above the publisher prices. It's a terribly difficult business." Honoria hoped she kept the venom out of her tone as Margaret's mother turned her attention back to Lord Devin. She raised a brow fleetingly at him and received an amused tilt of his head as he squared his shoulders to defend himself against the maternal onslaught. As she wrote out the sale back at the register, the little group's voices ranged and flowed, the mother's voice always the loudest.

"Well," said the mother, finally sputtering to an end of her verbal dysentery, "Margaret, come bid Lord Devin a good day. Sir, I do hope you find the ideal gift for your mother. That shee-hair-a-zod, is that German? It sounds quite interesting." As soon as they'd taken their leave of him, the mother ushered her daughter to the register to collect their purchase. The mother gave what seemed like an inappropriately casual wave of her fingers at the gentleman as they pushed out the door.

The click of the door latching suddenly, inexplicably, made Honoria uncomfortable. She was preternaturally aware of the Viscount Devin, the only remaining customer, striding to the register. He was surprisingly young, perhaps twenty-five or twenty-six, but then she caught herself—why should that be a surprise? What, from their limited interaction thus far, would give the impression he was older? His barely restrained disdain for everyone around him, perhaps? Not that such behavior suggested true maturity, just a level of assumption she associated with older men. His black hair still slightly disarrayed from their collision, she felt the impulse to smooth it down. But as she glanced down at her hands, wondering where the devil that thought came from, she noticed the not-so-fine lines on her knuckles, the bagginess of her skin, and she balled up her fists and slid them beneath the counter. Immediately, she berated herself for such vanity and forced her hands to grasp a ledger and place it softly on top of the counter. *Really, Nora! What can you be thinking?*

She looked up at his face as he arrived, standing before her with an air of ownership and expectation, as if all the world bowed to his will. As if anything he wanted were his for the taking. Her breasts tingled anew, her skin remembering the contours of his face. She was shocked at her response, unfamiliar and unwelcome. A chit like Margaret could behave fancifully, but that a woman of forty should react in such a way! The human body could be so wayward and pathetic. *Get a grip, Nora!*

It was nearly dinnertime. She hoped the young gentleman wouldn't take long. She still had plenty to do in the back. Obligatory curtsy, professional smile, placid tone. Onward.

"My lord, if you don't mind my overhearing, if you are interested in the Scheherazade stories, I do happen to have a copy of Edward Lane's *One Thousand and One Nights.* As you might imagine, I couldn't stock the twelve-volume French version."

"The Lane version will be fine. Thank you, Mrs.—?"

By this time, he'd reached the counter, and she had to tilt her head back to look up at his face. Yet her eyes didn't focus on him, not when her instincts warned her to quell the silly emotions fluttering through her.

"Mrs. Malcolm Duchamp, my lord," she said, addressing the light fixture beyond his head. "I am the proprietress here. It is my pleasure to serve you. I'll be right back with your book."

Before she could step from behind the counter, he said, "If it truly were your pleasure to serve me, you would have come to my aid back there."

He glanced behind him to follow her gaze, making her self-conscious about her avoidance of him. How rude of her. When she finally looked directly at him, her cheeks warmed at his eyes and his words, yet another unfamiliar sensation. All the air seemed to be sucked from the room. It would be a relief to leave his presence for a brief reprieve.

"Such services are not in my purview. I would happily recommend books to enlighten and entertain; I could perhaps see if there are any specifically regarding how to avoid matchmaking mothers."

"I could think of other, more entertaining fare."

Despite his lack of inflection, she read innuendo in his statement but quickly dismissed it as her own oversensitivity based on unfortunate experience. His behavior was really beyond reproach.

"I'll get that Scheherazade." She made a hasty retreat to the back room.

When she returned with the sumptuously bound volume, he asked, "Duchamp? How did you come to be attached to Evans Books?"

His query surprised her, adverse as he supposedly was to idle chatter. She couldn't imagine he would be interested in the lineage of a common bookshop.

"Duchamp is my married name. My father, Sir Samuel Evans, was the owner and operator of Evans Books until he died twenty-two years ago. I served as his assistant for many, many years before taking over the business myself."

"I see. How unusual for a baronet to go into commerce." The distaste in his voice was clear. No titled gentleman in his right mind would stoop to the level of a common merchant. "And you run the shop yourself? Independently?"

Hairs at the back of her neck bristled. She nodded, concentrating on writing up his purchase, trying to mask her reluctance to delve into her family history. If he openly denigrated her father, their business acquaintance would be short indeed.

"You don't employ any help? What of your husband? Does he take an active role? Does he approve of your activities?"

She shook her head at the rush of questions, at the audacity of his inquiry, having difficulty focusing on the numbers in front of her and adding them for the third time in a row. When she managed to separate his questions into individual pieces, she said, "I fail to see how my shop could be of such interest to you, my lord. I can assure you that I run it impeccably. I have a delivery boy in the afternoons. That is my only help, but it is quite manageable for me. As for my husband and his approval . . ." Here she worked very hard to temper her annoyance at his impertinence and presumption. After all, it wasn't unusual, given her circumstances. "My husband passed many years ago."

"My condolences." He did not, however, apologize for his forwardness. "How interesting," he continued, as he picked up his purchase and turned the volume in his hands. "This is a handsome edition of Lane. Have you read it?"

"Yes," she said, "I read a copy when they first arrived. One of the unparalleled pleasures of this business, I suppose."

"What did you think of it?"

Surprised by the question, simple as it was, Honoria looked up at him and noticed for the first time how strikingly green his eyes were, like new oak leaves in spring. She forgot his question. When he repeated it, his demeanor indicated it wasn't an idle question; he wanted an answer. Every day, she offered recommendations based on individual purchases, but no one stopped to ask her what she herself read or preferred. It was her role to steer conversations with clients; being on the receiving end left her unnervingly open to the unexpected. It took a moment for her to compose a moderate response.

"Yes, well," she said, hesitatingly, "it's so very fantastical. So much variety and exoticism." Lord Devin grimaced for a moment, so quickly she thought she might have imagined it.

"You don't find the fantasies extreme? Unrealistic?"

How can we really tell what is unrealistic? she thought. Some children have seen horrors no one should ever see, that no one would ever believe. Unrealistic they might seem, but true nonetheless. She shuddered but kept these thoughts to herself. Instead, she responded, "Well, of course. They're intended as such, to catch the attention of a jaded king. What binds them to our world, as I'm sure you know, is Scheherazade herself. That is, the legend of such a storyteller, one with the creative power to deflect the vengeance of a ruthless king with simply her words—what a dream such a gift would be."

She looked out the shop windows, lost in thought.

"But?" Lord Devin prompted with an open palm. It was terribly kind for him to indulge her in such conversation, when he surely had more important business and powerful people to attend to. It must be such a bore for him. She couldn't imagine why he lingered here in idle literary conversation. The gliding motion of his hand distracted her. His long, graceful fingers, encased in pristine gloves, seemed so out of place here.

"Oh, but the brutality. So much of it against women and children, powerless and weak."

"You contradict yourself. You just said Scheherazade herself is a paragon of cleverness and ingenuity. Isn't that power in the end?" Lord Devin focused on her with an intensity she couldn't interpret. Those spring eyes were darkening to the emerald of summer grass. It had been a long day, and obviously her fancy was running away with her.

"Yes, but how sad that the heroine must use such trickery to protect herself." Again, feeling discomfort in his presence, she slipped back into her professional persona. That was when she realized she hadn't finished writing up his receipt. No wonder he hadn't left. *How much of a flibbertigibbet am I today?* "Shall I wrap this for you and deliver it directly to your mother?"

"Have it delivered to me at Devin House in Eaton Square. I would like to give it to my mother in person."

"Very good, my lord." Accustomed as she was to customers being curt and overbearing, she gritted her teeth nonetheless at his orders. The trouble was she didn't think he was being rude or inappropriate, and yet his tone rankled her anyway. "Will there be anything for you? Might I interest you in one of these abolitionist pamphlets? It is edifying. Come to think of it, this might be a reasonable base to balance out Mr. Lane's rather acidic view of Negroes in *One Thousand and One Nights*. I highly doubt his tone toward that group is true to the original story."

"Of course, please add that and this labor treatise to my purchase. I'm curious. Are these bindings done in-house?" He glanced around the shop.

"Yes, we do offer bookbinding services. The machinery is in back. Mostly, we handle minor repairs. We can also do limited printing orders, mostly signs and pamphlets. Why do you ask?"

"My family has some books that have seen rough usage and want fresh binding."

"If you bring them in, I would be happy to estimate the cost of re-binding."

"Just so," he replied. At the completion of the transaction, he added, "I am pleased to see you have recovered easily from your little fall." Amusement lit his eyes for a moment, or perhaps she just imagined it.

"Yes, thank you, my lord." *My boy would be more likely*, despite the strange little flutter in her belly and that now-embarrassingly re-curring sensation in her nipples, as if they had a memory of their own. These unusually extreme pitches of emotion unnerved her. These silly manifestations would subside, she was certain, after his lordship disappeared. "I am completely fine. Your arrival was fortu-itous."

"I hope I can be of service to you again someday, Mrs. Duchamp." He stood still for a moment, looking at her intensely, if inscrutably. Then he bowed and took his leave.

Now what was all that about? she thought, as she locked up and went in the back to square the accounts and start the printing press.

"Make the woman's acquaintance," Mr. Withersby had said.

Well, I have certainly done that, Lord Devin thought. Upon enter-ing, he hadn't expected to do more than scan the shop and get a gen-eral impression of its owner. Unobtrusive, subtle, distant. Instead, he'd become abruptly and intimately acquainted with her ample bosom before he even formally knew her name. *Bloody hell*, he'd thought as her body careened at him. He could still recall the faint scent of lilies that wafted from her. He could still feel the delicate weight of her in his arms. And on his skin.

"Investigate and neutralize," Mr. Withersby had said.

Lord Devin still needed more time and information to comprehend why there would be a need to neutralize such a harmless, albeit lovely, matron. She might be able to convince customers to drop an extra penny or two they hadn't planned to spend, but she was no threat to the future of British society.

Two days prior to the bookshop encounter, Lord Devin had found himself in the dark, smoky, heavily appointed office of Mr. Withersby, attorney-at-law. He abhorred this dank building, this increasingly seedy district, and this man, this sniveling excuse for a man whom he'd enabled to claw into the Devin family's stronghold.

"You have a job for me?" he said as he barged into the office. He didn't care if Withersby was otherwise occupied, whether with client for business or, just as frequently, with some skirt for pleasure.

"No time for pleasantries today, Lord Devin? Have a seat."

"I do not take kindly to being called like a dog, Withersby. You called; I came. I do not want to be here any longer than necessary." He remained standing, glaring down his nose at the short, stout, spectacled solicitor, who resembled a woodchuck, with his beady eyes and pointy face.

"Quite right, milord." Withersby stood and went to the mahogany sideboard to pour himself a brandy. He swirled the dark liquid in the tumbler. "I have a client who complains of a nuisance, and I want you to take care of it."

"What kind of nuisance are we talking about, a thorn in the paw or a spear in the side?"

"Oh, to be sure, it's a mosquito, my good man." He waved a hand around his head by way of illustration. "Tiny. Distracting. Mildly irritating. But it's proving annoyingly difficult to swat."

"Hard to believe such a miniscule nuisance, as you called it, would require special attention." Lord Devin recalled the last "mosquito" Mr. Withersby sent him to swat; it turned out to be a peer with outrageous bestial impulses that needed to be curbed. It was an unpleasant encounter. He knew there was much more to this story and hoped to high heaven that this pest didn't prove to be as messy or distasteful. "I am sure you have plenty of flyswatters to hand. More to the point, I am sure you have expert pest exterminators who would make quick work of this without blinking an eye. Why not give this job to one of them?"

"Considering this particular little fly, my clients would prefer the situation be handled with a certain finesse and exactness. My usual workforce is a bit too blunt and heavy-handed for this kind of project. We need a cunning spider who can set a fine but sticky web."

"Do tell," Lord Devin said flatly. He quickly tired of this discussion and the annoying insect metaphors. He resented the hell out of this perpetuated obligation and made no efforts to disguise his feelings.

"Have a look for yourself." Mr. Withersby returned to the desk, set down his glass, and slid a thin envelope from a pile on his desk.

Lord Devin took the envelope, weighed it in his hand, and removed its contents: a single sheet of paper. Previous assignments involved much bulkier documentation. The smooth cream page had few lines written on it, taking up less than half the page. He scanned the simple dossier and looked at Mr. Withersby in open surprise.

"Of all the— Is this a joke? This is your mark? A mosquito, indeed." Several things seemed wrong with this assignment. First, he had never targeted a woman before; it seemed beneath him. Second, she hardly seemed worth targeting. "Your client wants to harass a lowly widow? A widow who runs a bookshop? You can't be serious. She can't possibly require this kind of attention." The page provided a brief biography, physical description, and a rough schedule of her weekly activities. "For God's sake, the woman is entombed in a bookstore and attends a weekly knitting group for orphans. Are you saying this meek mouse of a human being is a danger to the realm?"

Withersby shrugged.

"My client has his reasons."

Lord Devin couldn't make sense of it. He perused the sheet again for more weighty information. Then a new and exceedingly distasteful thought occurred to him.

"You mentioned that the case requires finesse. What exactly do you mean?"

"This isn't, as you so charmingly suggested, an extermination. Nothing so extreme or crass. I do have several associates who could perform such a task easily and efficiently. But removal of this particular pest would not, my client believes, solve the underlying problem. Hence, the objective is to have this woman disgraced publicly, her judgment and integrity completely discredited such that her connections and opinions are likewise brought into question."

"You will need to be more specific about how I am expected to accomplish such public disgrace," Lord Devin stated. Then the most absurd thought occurred to him. "Hold! You want me to seduce her? A forty-some-year-old bookselling widow, who is probably as dry and papery as her wares?"

Mr. Withersby guffawed for a full minute, losing his breath and turning purple.

"The look on your face, man! As if you were a maiden about to be sacrificed to a barbarian horde. No, Lord Devin, nothing of the sort." He continued to chuckle as his coloring returned to normal. "Make her acquaintance. As you see in the dossier, my client believes she may be printing and distributing incendiary materials. Combined with the proposed legislation, her alleged work begins to pose a significant threat to my client's industry. Investigate and neutralize. If possible, get the woman not only to desist but to renounce prior work. If sedition charges could be brought, so much the better."

"Hundreds of crackpots spout outrageous ideas regularly in Kennington Common. What difference can this one woman's voice possibly make?"

"Yes, well, apparently, putting things on paper makes a difference. And these inflammatory materials have been making enough of an impression to spur demonstration and to raise alarms. That's all I can say at the moment. So?"

The question hung in the air, as if Lord Devin had a choice in the matter. Of course, he would do it. Just as he'd done the other odd jobs Withersby had thrown at him. He would do anything to protect his brother's reputation, to protect his family from disgrace and scandal, and Withersby well knew it. One of these days, though, Withersby would go too far in these assignments. Lord Devin just needed more time to plan a way to circumvent Withersby, a way to make his threats impotent.

"My patience is near its end, Withersby. I shall do this, but I am tiring of these games."

"Do this well, and perhaps it will be the last."

"Perhaps? That is not good enough."

"It will have to be. I'll be sure to keep you abreast of your brother's . . . jaunts. I'm sure Andrew would appreciate your conscientious concern for his . . . well-being. If photographs are available, I'll pass them along as well."

Lord Devin clenched his jaw and gave a curt nod. He resented the hell out of Withersby dangling his brother at him. He resented his brother's supposed jaunts and indiscretion almost as much. After all, if it weren't for his brother's recklessness . . . But that kind of thinking wasn't productive. He would sever this commitment to Withersby one way or another.

"We're done here, milord. I'm sure you know the way out." Withersby slumped into his leather chair and reached for a stack of files without looking at him again.

The dismissal rankled at him, but he had nothing more to say and didn't want to perpetuate the meeting. He left the door open behind him.

And so, now here he was. Introductions had been made. He recalled her open conversation with him. Her composure impressed him. No shy, tittering ingénue. No haughty, challenging debutante. No fawning. She'd been irked by his impertinent questions, certainly, but she showed no doubt or self-consciousness. No pretense. No excuses. *Is it a function of her job or a result of her maturity*, he wondered, *that she speaks to each and all as an equal, mindful of their interests?*

He was surprised too by the physical appearance of this Mrs. Honoria Duchamp. The file described an average woman, brown hair, brown eyes, medium height and build, past middle age, unremarkable in every way. He wasn't prone to the effluvium of the day's popular romance novels, but there were marked differences between the basic one-sheet and the flesh. The woman before him had porcelain skin, mahogany tresses with hints of chestnut pulled back into a tight chignon, and intelligent, piercing eyes, eyes that dimmed when she spoke of her father. She'd felt light in his arms, movable as a chess piece. And her form, what he could see and feel of it, was slim and taut, except for her . . . ah, those breasts. He could still feel the warmth and weight of them against his skin. She had the body of a full-fledged woman, not one of a girl on the threshold of womanhood. No sign of shriveling or age, just a bit of dust from that pesky upper shelf. Just updating the file with accurate observations, he told himself.

He picked up the abolitionist tract that had been delivered with his mother's book. Perhaps it would hold some clues.

Reading didn't distract his mind from its cataloging of Mrs. Duchamp's finer attributes. Instead, the dry scent of the parchment reminded him vividly of the shop.

Chapter Two

Evans Principle 2: Every interaction is an opportunity. Choose your responses productively.

Slowly, Honoria climbed to the third floor, her thoughts only for her bed and her clothing weighing her down more than usual because of her tiredness. In her mind, alongside the catalog of titles she'd ordered, tomes she'd repaired, and print jobs she'd completed, she cataloged the little pops and aches up and down her body that she hadn't known in her youth. Tonight, her vertebrae and hips cracked with each step and ached from her stooped posture at the printing and binding machine. She caught herself as she tripped on the top stair. It was past midnight, and she wondered if she'd be able to scrub the ink stains off her hands. At least this week's print run was complete. She would need to arrange some interviews as fodder for next week's; the factory girl she'd intended to profile fell into a press and now no one would talk with her there.

Reliable Minnie, her only servant, really her only family along with Minnie's brother, Erich, warmed a plate for her supper. To her exhausted mind, the beef was indistinguishable from the potatoes, except by texture.

"Minnie, do I have anything special on my schedule for this week?"

Honoria needed to plan her time carefully. She'd drafted a new tract but needed time to edit it before setting and printing. Wednesday tended to be the quietest day in the shop so she should have some time available.

"Miss Honoria, this week is a bit busier than usual. The hospital today, as usual, then the orphanage on Tuesday, new inventory arrives Thursday, and the Needlework for the Needy this Thursday evening as well. I think there are a few visits due as well, to Mrs. Danson and the new Mrs. Leventon. And here are some calling cards you really need to return."

The array of calling cards made her itch. Her largest group of customers was made up of upwardly mobile mothers, landed gentry, and newly rich wives of merchants seeking the key to marrying a peer of the realm. She certainly wasn't an expert, but many such women were reluctant to show their eagerness by frequenting the shop. Instead, their requests for a visit were thinly veiled sales calls. Lots of talk about who was seen with whom and who would be at what party and which fine young woman would be best suited to which upstanding gentleman. Then which books had been recently recommended as *the* book to have on propriety and decorum and marriage. It rankled her. She had serious things to worry about here. At least the shop would be, as usual, a stabilizing influence amidst the social flurries. It also supplied reliable topics of conversation.

"Oh, and this note arrived for you a few hours ago."

The fine vellum caught her attention. Still, the words within surprised her.

Dear Mrs. Malcolm Duchamp,
The pleasure of your company is requested at dinner this Thursday evening. My son informs me that you are knowledgeable about publishing, and I have several friends eager to meet you. I do hope you are able to attend.
Cordially yours,
Lady Rose Devin

"Why didn't you give this to me earlier, Minnie?" *God's frogs!* She looked at her assistant carefully. Minnie was always a diligent worker, but she seemed distracted lately. Even now, her clothes were a bit disheveled and her hair appeared hastily tucked into her cap, long strands poking out haphazardly.

"You were busy, Miss Honoria," the girl responded matter-of-factly. Minnie and her brother were the only ones who still addressed her as they had in childhood, and she appreciated their rare familiarity.

Her mind raced as she reread the invitation. It had only been a few hours since she'd made Lord Devin's acquaintance. Why would she be invited to something like this? What sense would it make to invite her? And how could she possibly accept? The prospect of wooing new clientele offered some little appeal, but the parallel prospect of trying to charm total strangers brought on a wave of nausea. It was exhausting. Of course, she couldn't attend. The Needlework for the Needy Association had its regular meeting that evening, and she was expected. Easy enough. Sustenance secured and loose matters organized, she sent Minnie home and dropped onto her bed still fully clothed. A pair of jade green eyes floated in her mind as she drifted into sleep.

Chapter Three

Evans Principle 3: Never allow customers behind the curtain. They don't need to know how the sausage is made.

Lord Devin strode into Evans Books impatient and irritated. Blackmail from an amoral solicitor aside, he wasn't accustomed to his wishes being thwarted. Invitations to his mother's salons were an honor not to be refused. He'd orchestrated the invitation expertly, hinting at the cache of having a bookseller amid the writers and leaving the shop's business card on the entry table. He was subtle, damn it, but apparently subtlety didn't work on Mrs. Honoria Duchamp. So here he was to try the direct approach.

"Mrs. Duchamp, what a pleasure to see you again."

She looked at him for a moment as if trying to remember him, but she waited a few seconds too long for him to be convinced. He was a lord, after all, and, without bragging, he could say with confidence that people tended to remember him.

"Lord Devin, how kind of you to stop by. Did your mother like her birthday gift?" Oh, she remembered him just fine. He knew well enough the signs of a woman who wasn't indifferent toward him. The glint in her eyes, the way her body canted away from him ever so slightly, the way her voice became overly bright. She wasn't indifferent at all, but she was attempting to hide it.

"Yes, she was quite taken with it. She has grand ideas of dressing as Scheherazade for her next masquerade ball. Actually, she is threatening to dress as Aladdin."

She smiled patronizingly and responded, "Well, I'm sure those aren't her only options from such a wide array of characters. What can I help you with today, my lord?"

"Ah, you are all business. What a relief. My mission is twofold. First, I have here some books in dire need of repair."

"Let me have a look." As she reached for them, her hands slid across his gloved ones. That same electric current he felt when she fell into his arms ran through him. She must have felt something as well because she jumped as if bitten. Then she focused her attention almost too fastidiously on the books in front of her.

"These aren't so bad. A little glue and stitching and they'll be fine. Would you like me to make an estimate of how much the repair would cost?"

"No need. Whatever it is, I am sure it will be reasonable for your services. The cost does not signify."

She looked at him curiously but didn't comment, and then she wrote out a note and tucked it into the top book.

"I'll be right back. I'm just going to put these in the repair queue. Feel free to have a look around and then we may discuss whatever your second mission is."

As he watched her walk away, his fingers itched to touch her, to grab her firmly about the waist, and pull her against him. It was damn disconcerting. After a moment's consideration, he decided to follow her into the back room to continue their conversation, particularly since he couldn't tell how she would respond to his second request. It was also an excellent opportunity to fulfill his investigative duties.

He walked through a short, dark hallway and found himself in an office taken up by a massive partners' desk made of oak, the kind of desk that seated two people facing each other. Books and vellum pamphlets haphazardly covered one side completely, leaving only one side usable as a writing surface. The room had two doors, as well as stairs leading up to the second floor. He took a guess and proceeded through one door farther to the back of the building. In this second room, he found a printing press. Still, no Mrs. Duchamp. As he turned to go back to the office, the door smashed into him, striking his forehead first, knocking him back a few steps.

"Oh, my goodness! Lord Devin, is that you?" She rushed up to him and touched his forehead, where a welt was no doubt growing. "I'm so sorry!" Her brow furrowed. "Wait, what are you doing back here?"

He scrambled for an answer, distracted first by her gentle touch, sparking a heat all out of proportion to the actual physical contact. Then he was distracted again by her hand's abrupt and much regretted removal.

"I had more questions about the repairs. You did say I should feel free to look around."

"I beg your pardon, my lord, but you may not be familiar with the etiquette of commerce. The back room of any establishment is rarely meant for public access." He sensed tension beneath her sardonic chastisement. "These questions couldn't wait until I returned?"

"Quite right." Yet he could not seem to think quickly enough.

She waited.

"Well. They seem to have slipped my mind. Perhaps they were knocked out of my head by the door." It was perhaps unfair of him to play upon her guilt, but he needed to shift her attention.

Immediately contrite, she brought her hands together as she came toward him again. "Oh, again, I'm so sorry about that. I am usually the only one here, and I tend to move quickly in the back office. I never expected . . . are you all right? We should go back to the front room where you can sit down."

"I am completely fine, I assure you. I shall survive." Everything in her demeanor clearly declared she wanted him out of this part of the shop. Seeing an intriguing opportunity, he pressed his advantage. "Perhaps this little mishap will incline you to grant me a small favor."

"That depends on the favor." She took a small but obvious step away from him.

"Well, in trying to find you, I found the printing press. I am curious about the mechanics of this printing machine. I have never seen one in action. Might I prevail upon you to give me a demonstration?"

As she looked over at the press, her forehead creased and her mouth twisted. He could see anxiety written all over her face, suggesting his suspicion about her printing activities was correct. Yet he felt an unnerving impulse to reach out and stroke her cheek to relax her tensed features.

"I suppose that would be fine. It will take me a few moments to reset the machine, though." She hurried to the side with the letter blocks and removed a tray of text. "It's not very modern. It's just a flatbed hand press, and it can take quite a while to complete a basic copy order."

"Oh, you need not change the printing on my account," he said as he came up behind her. "I do not intend to read the results; I would simply like to see how the process works."

"This is a special order so I need to protect the author's privacy and intellectual property." Her hands moved quickly. "In recent years, probably due to the increasingly broad dissemination of print material, the law has become very strict about copyright." She tucked the set type into a low drawer behind her, locked it, and pocketed the key.

"That applies more to competition between British and overseas publishers than to individual vanity printing, does it not?"

She tucked her knuckles under her chin, looking thoughtful, but it seemed that in the second before her hand moved, her brows raised in surprise.

"Such legislation goes through Parliament, of course," he said imperiously by way of explanation.

She nodded and said, "That is the economic foundation of the laws, but my clients are also quite sensitive about their work. They come to me because they know I will protect the integrity of their property." Still looking at him strangely, she brought out a tray of print blocks and slid it into the machine, presumably some standard template. It took a bit of effort for her to start turning the crank. He offered to assist, but she kindly declined. Once the dial was in motion, she spun it more steadily as the machine churned out a few printed sheets. She took the first sheet and clipped it to a rope along the back wall.

"As you can see, printing is not really all that impressive, at least not on this small a scale," she said, raising her hands at her sides briefly.

"On the contrary, when you consider that copying used to be done entirely by hand and take years, this is a wonder of the modern world.

And you are a modern prophet." While she scoffed at his assertion, he walked over to examine the newly printed sheet, which put him in very close proximity to her. It was the first page of a handbill for a ladies' reading group. He was suddenly taken with the idea of reading this page very, very carefully, particularly as he stood so close to her he could feel the heat of her body. He turned to her, so close he could smell the odd combination of lavender and a bit of dust in her hair. Different from before. What dictated the scent of her?

"Tell me, Mrs. Duchamp, if you do not find this process all that noteworthy, what do you find impressive?"

"What— I—" She seemed a little dazed, but she didn't move away from him. "I don't know. What do you mean?"

He leaned in closer, spurred by impulse, and pressed on. "What impresses you? Anything. A book, a person, an idea . . . What do you see as impressive in this world?"

"What a heavy question. So very serious." Her eyes cleared; her whole being snapped back into place. "I'm sure there are many things that impress me. A good Beaujolais, I mean really good. Carolers in harmony. Factory children playing Kick-the-Can on a rare holiday. Someone defending a helpless stranger simply out of human decency. Honesty, valor, fairness . . . all these things and more have the power to strike me dumb with awe."

"I am reassured to hear it. I was afraid that perhaps you might not have the capacity for awe." Seeing a flash of hurt in her eyes, he expounded, "No, I only mean your reactions are so even-tempered, I wondered if anything could make a significant impression on you. I wondered if I could possibly make an impression on you."

At that, she backed up a few steps and rubbed her hands on her skirt.

"I'm sure I don't understand your meaning, Lord Devin. You must make some impression on everyone who encounters you. Peers of the realm tend to do that, as if bred into the role."

He couldn't stand this strange interplay any longer. He needed to get this distraction, this nuisance, this *whatever it was* out of his system as directly as possible. So he did the most logical thing: he closed the distance between them and touched his lips to hers.

It was swift, a mere brush of their lips, but the electric tingle from that light touch ran through him. How he'd gone from a simple printing demonstration to this far-from-simple complication, he couldn't puzzle out. Her eyes widened too, as if she felt a similar shock. He stood there for a moment, looking at her intently.

In that moment, she had enough time to recall the first time she'd kissed a man. Mr. Ranseed was the butcher's son, an excellent match, both sets of parents agreed. The third time he'd come to visit her at home, somehow they'd been left unchaperoned. They were taking a walk in the countryside, talking about some innocuous topic or other, like the weather or, no, they'd been talking about feed, about what grasses are most conducive to good beef, and suddenly he'd butted her up against a tree and begun kissing her. That was all, just his mouth against hers, but it was clammy and horribly intrusive. Startled, she just stood there, letting him probe with his tongue and wondering what all the fuss was about. He seemed agitated and eager, but whatever he was doing with his mouth felt awkward and unnatural. She decided three things immediately: *1. I do not enjoy kissing Mr. Ranseed. 2. I am not inclined to allow him such familiarity again. 3. I will not marry him after all.*

Of course, looking back, it didn't much matter whether she'd enjoyed what he was doing. She was a headstrong, arrogant, and naïve maiden; she came to understand later that she would have gone through with all of it. She would have allowed him such familiarity, and much more. She just wouldn't have enjoyed it. She would have married him, without question and without hesitation, because that was what their families had agreed upon. That was what her parents required from a dutiful and honorable daughter. That arrangement best suited both fathers in building solid mercantile alliances.

She wouldn't have had the selfishness or strength to break the commitment.

But one month after their encounter, the weaselly Mr. Ranseed did just that. He ran off and eloped with a hat shop girl. His parents were mortified and apologized abjectly to Honoria's family. They offered to make amends with gifts of beef and venison, but the damage ran much deeper than commerce. It wasn't emotional or economic. No one else in town would have her, but she and her father could never figure out why.

In the span of a moment, before Lord Devin's lips touched hers again, she had enough time to recall all of this and to compare it with the present moment. If that wet, awkward fumbling by the butcher's son could be called a kiss, then this—what was happening now—

could not in any way be defined as something so ordinary as a kiss. This was a conflagration, an electric explosion—when all he'd done was brush his lips against hers. After the initial shock, his mouth returned to hers, his tongue teasing the edges of her lips to coax them apart. And, with conscious decision, she responded. She slipped her hands around his neck and nestled them in his hair. Her lips moved freely with his. Her breath mingled with his, hot and urgent. This didn't feel like an intrusion at all. It was exploration, it was play, it was heaven.

It was wrong. Very, very wrong.

She broke away, shaken. Dallying with a young viscount—what could she be thinking? Rumors circulated about the pliability of widows. She couldn't allow herself to become that story.

"Oh, my." She quickly backed away until she was against the press. Her breathing still erratic, she folded her arms in front of her and strove for composure. He stepped forward as if to follow her but halted immediately when she raised a hand, palm out, to prevent him. "If I were younger," she said, "I'm sure I'd feel flattered by your interest. Well, flattered and then indignant. I suppose slapping you in the face would be the right thing to do in this situation. I'm guessing, though, that no young lady could resist your charms."

"Why do I get the feeling you do not mean that as a compliment?"

"Oh, certainly. You seem quite the expert on seduction, and I expect you're generally successful."

"I am not an 'expert on seduction,' by any stretch," he replied dryly. "This definitely would not be a good example of seduction, at any rate. 'May I see how your printer works?' is, after all, so flirtatious it must be used in ballrooms across the land."

She smirked but maintained her original conclusion.

"Then why did you do that?"

"Do *that*? You mean, kiss you?"

"Yes, that. What did you hope to accomplish?"

"I rather hoped we would both enjoy it. I know I did, and I suspect you did as well. Am I wrong?"

She kept silent but felt a telltale blush spread up her neck. Prevarication would be futile; her response was obvious. She'd long ago dismissed the passionate embraces in fiction as just that: fiction. So she had no way to catalog the sensations she'd experienced. He smirked in return but said nothing.

"Really, it was . . ." All the words she couldn't say came flooding back to her . . . conflagration, explosion, *heaven*. "It was . . . unusual. It was also unacceptable and entirely inappropriate. I'm sure you've got fresher prey available."

"Again, what flattering imagery. Do you really imagine I see you as prey?"

"Don't you? Perhaps as a trophy to boast to your chums about. Widows are so frequently assumed to be easy pickings . . . desperate for affection, free of entanglements, already experienced. . . . I know how men like you view women like me. I've fended off enough attentions from men bound and determined to convince me that being their mistress is my right and my due."

He bristled. She wasn't far off the mark. Several of his friends at the club had boasted of such conquests. Widows made convenient mistresses and tended to cost less to maintain than actresses and opera singers because inheritance made them self-sufficient. Being lumped in with such a tawdry lot didn't sit well with him, though. He didn't target women; they came to him freely or not at all.

He gave an undignified yelp as something orange and furry leapt onto his shoulder.

"Jupiter! That's uncalled for." She reached for the striped tabby and carefully disengaged its claws from Devin's fine coat.

"Jupiter? Can I assume there must be a Janus nearby as well?"

Surprised, she responded, "Why, yes, but he usually stays in the back room. He seems to find the printer comforting."

He reached out to pet the now-sedate cat in her arms.

"I assure you I am no cad, dear lady. I do not collect women, which sounds like a troublesome and unpleasant sort of diversion. And I have never had to force my attentions on a woman. I have never had to convince her to entertain my affections. Do not mistake me for all the cads who have thrown themselves in your path."

She patted his cheek with her hand, a gentle pacifying act that had the opposite effect. So he already was furious when she said, "Not so obviously, perhaps. But you are accustomed to getting your own way. I don't believe you've been truly tested. Yet. You wouldn't force an unwilling woman, of course. You're a gentleman. But how far would you go, or perhaps have you gone, to twist a woman's *No* into *Yes*?"

Her words distracted him, confused him. He'd never forced a woman, never coerced a woman. Women didn't just fall into his bed;

they leapt into it eagerly. Immediately, a heady blond actress and a redheaded former scullery maid came to mind as quite literal examples. He wanted to say as much but realized he couldn't possibly, not to her.

He simply said, teeth clenched, "I assure you that I have not and would not accept a woman's company without her complete and express desire. The very idea of coercing a woman's attentions is abhorrent. I shall not even comment on the evil of physically forcing a woman."

"That's good to hear. I think you'll understand then when I say it's time for you to leave."

He scowled but responded, "Of course. I expect you will contact me when the books are restored."

"Lord Devin, no apology?"

What the devil? Apologies were not part of his vocabulary.

"For what?"

"Why, for taking liberties, sir. You wouldn't treat a woman of your station so cavalierly." She didn't look offended but simply expectant.

"My dear, I am sorry if you feel offended by my actions. I can assure you they shall not be repeated if they are considered unwanted. But that was far from cavalier. And I would not have you delude yourself into thinking it was a casual salute. I meant it, and I would do it again if you were willing."

"I am not your dear, Lord Devin. That is a disingenuous apology, and what you describe will never happen. Nothing you could offer would convince me to stoop to whoredom."

Well. Definitely an unusually serious conversation.

"As you wish, madam."

"Wait! You were here for two purposes. Am I to understand both are now completed? Were you so sure of my low morals that you came here intent on seducing me?"

"No." He turned slowly toward her. "No. This moment may not demonstrate it, but even upon our brief acquaintance, I hold you in high regard, Mrs. Duchamp. What an unfortunately timed reminder of my second task, which must now be rather unwelcome. My second task today was to convey a message from my mother. She was deeply disappointed when she received your news of a prior appointment. She keenly wishes for your attendance at dinner."

He saw the suspicion in her eyes and continued. "Here is a letter from her. I had nothing to do with this, but I assure you she is extremely eager to introduce you to her circle of writers. She is a devoted patron to these authors. It would mean a great deal to her and to the other guests if you could at least make an appearance."

She took the envelope he held out and considered his statement. Shaking her head, she said, "As I explained to your mother, I have other commitments that evening."

He didn't believe a word.

"Well, if it would make a difference to your commitments, my dear, I can certainly find myself otherwise occupied. My mother's invitations to these events are highly selective, and rather famously unorthodox. She would value your presence highly."

"But she doesn't even know me."

"But I know her, and I think I know a bit about you. She is deeply invested in the success of her associates. And you will enjoy their company."

She faltered. It would indeed be a great opportunity to build the shop's clientele and perhaps develop acquaintances with renowned authors. "As I said . . . I am otherwise engaged."

"If your plans change, please do consider my mother's invitation."

As she stared up at him, she felt herself nod slowly. This would not end well.

Chapter Four

Evans Principle 2 Redux: EVERY interaction is an opportunity. Do not leave any opportunities unexplored.

How she ended up here, in a finely appointed guest bedroom in Devin House, laced into a gray silk ball gown that surely cost more than six months' revenue, seemed impossible. She'd said no to the invitation, to begin with, but there was no real prior engagement. Lady Devin's special request, conveyed more heavily in the note her son delivered, seemed so reasonable, so accommodating. Thus, despite some internal quaking, she'd penned a brief note stating her prior plans were postponed and she would be honored to attend dinner.

A note from the presumed leader of the Needlework for the Needy women conveying extreme disappointment and an urgent need to meet had given her pause. But she could reschedule such a meeting easily. By the time she'd arrived at Devin House, she'd had quite enough of correspondence for the day, if not for the week.

Then there was Lady Devin.

Honoria had arrived at Devin House at the appointed time, only to find she was, in fact, unfashionably early. It really had been a long time since she'd socialized in *society*. Lady Devin charmingly brushed off her faux pas with an airy hospitality. When the butler presented her to Lady Devin, the first thing that struck her was how very different the lady looked from her son. In sharp contrast to Lord Devin's dark hair and green eyes, his mother was all lightness. Hair the color of enchanted straw haloed her head in an elaborate coiffure, accented with beading. Her movements carried an ethereal grace, enhanced by her pale skin and delicate features. She and her son did share the same lithe, statuesque build, but she carried herself regally whereas her son's demeanor was more rigid and exacting.

"My dear, it is such a great pleasure to meet you." Lady Devin greeted her and clasped both her hands as if they were already lifelong friends. The hostess's hazel eyes bestowed warmth and welcome. "Do you not love the energy building in the air this evening?"

Such a statement would have struck her as odd if she didn't know exactly what Lady Devin meant. She hadn't consciously thought of it, but she'd certainly felt a palpable electricity in the air when she arrived and climbed the stairs to the front door—a sense of infinite possibility and indefinite promise. It wasn't just an interest in meeting writers and potentially finding a group of like-minded bibliophiles. There was both more weight and more lilt in the air. She wondered how Lady Devin knew, but she simply answered, "Yes, it's a lovely night."

And from that moment, Lady Devin continually amazed her with pronouncements and observations and revelations that were at once intensely personal and brilliantly cosmic in scope. It was impossible not to feel like the lady of the house was one's closest friend. Fleetingly, she thought Lady Devin must have been quite the source of drama in her time—presumably the heart-seizing belle of her season, universally sought by the most prized bachelors and just as universally despised by her competition. And yet, from just their short acquaintance, she knew without doubt that no one could do anything but adore Lady Devin, such was her consummate charm and disarming intensity.

So there was Lady Devin. And then there was the dress.

When Honoria had first entered the house and saw the gilded mirrors and lacquered furniture, she felt so completely out of her element. Surreptitiously eyeing Lady Devin's gown of burgundy satin, she realized her wool jacket and skirt were sadly inappropriate for the occasion. Nothing could be done about that, though. She didn't own any gowns or finery. Minnie took sewing jobs to supplement her income, but it wasn't fair to add to her workload by asking for frivolities. These pragmatic wools and cottons were all she needed in her daily life—not to mention, all she could reasonably afford. But then Lady Devin did the most extraordinary thing.

As they made their way to the drawing room, she grew increasingly self-conscious about her banal appearance. She was dressed for work, hair in a tidy bun, and when other guests arrived, she would stand out as dross amid flax. She fingered her high collar, feeling constricted. Even the luxurious settee on which she found herself seated made her stand out in stark unpleasant relief.

"Mrs. Duchamp . . ." Lady Devin leaned toward her, which struck her as exceedingly unusual.

"Yes, Lady Devin?"

"Do you have siblings?" What an odd question, such a non sequitur.

"No, my lady, I was an only child."

Lady Devin nodded and said, "I had a younger sister, Melina. We were very close. She passed away ten years ago, and yet sometimes I feel her loss as if it were yesterday."

"I'm so sorry," Honoria responded. She well knew the keen, and sometimes, shockingly sudden stab of grief—the imagined comment or look, the thought that said loved one would have so enjoyed this joke or that novelty or a fleeting moment. The momentary forgetfulness sometimes made it seem as if said loved one would be right around the corner.

"From one grieving widow to another"—Lady Devin tilted even closer, laid her hand on Honoria's arm, and whispered—"would you be willing to indulge my fancy just a bit?"

She startled, curious but wary.

"If it is in my power, I would be happy to consider it."

"When we were girls, my sister and I adored dressing up in our mother's finest frocks, and she gave us free rein, even setting aside gowns that were practically new for our amusement. We spent so many afternoons giggling and preening together, pretending we were princesses. I miss her giggling terribly."

Honoria nodded, wishing just a little that she had a taste of such a lifestyle. Not just a sister to play with, not just the gowns for play-things—she wished briefly for the life of leisure and luxury that made such play possible.

"And so, here is my request . . . and I hope you perceive its sincerity: Would you indulge me in an evening of dress-up?"

So there was Lady Devin, who managed to convince her that borrowing a dress was not an act of charity from the hostess but rather an indulgent favor *to* the hostess.

Honoria hesitated. She schooled her face to mask her ambivalence—on one hand, she should be offended by the offer of charity and the insult to her appearance. On the other hand, she really wasn't dressed properly . . . and it didn't really feel like the offer was made out of charity. And, if she were being completely honest, she really, really wanted to know what it felt like to be dressed befitting the London ton. She was fairly sure it must feel heavenly.

And then, again, there was the dress.

"I feel a bit like Cinderella, all done up by her fairy godmother, even though I'd be better cast in the godmother role," she whispered to her hostess before Lady Devin went to greet other guests. Not for the first time in the past hour, Honoria puzzled over how she'd ended up here. In Lady Devin's guest room. Being dressed up like a china doll. Not that she'd had a serious chance to say no. Her proud yet futile resistance of the offer was ignored and finally subsumed by this remarkably gorgeous gray silk, the color of storm clouds. She chided herself for being so easily swayed, but really it was the most extravagantly lovely fabric she'd ever encountered. The full, bell-shaped skirt flowed like cool water through her fingers. The dress shimmered like fine rain and made her feel, even with all the layers of crinoline and petticoats, as though she floated. She felt so exposed, though. The neckline of this gown, according to current fashion, was much lower than her usual serviceable attire with collars up to her chin, more befitting a widowed bookseller. And she was laced in so much more tightly than she would choose; she was sure she'd crack a rib if she tried to take a deep breath. The corset added significantly to the sensation that her bosom could pop right out of the top of the dress. When one of the maids went to powder her shoulders, it felt embarrassingly intimate. She wrapped her shawl tightly around herself and proceeded to join the party.

By this time, several of the guests had arrived and had overflowed from the drawing room into the main hall. Honoria descended the stairs slowly, growing more uncomfortable and ungainly with each step. As she neared the bottom, she was startled by the sudden appearance of Lord Devin at the foot of the stairs, facing away as he spoke with a stately older couple. And, of course, startled, she would have to get tangled up in the skirts of her borrowed gown and trip halfway down the stairs. As she pitched forward, she thought, *Ah, yes, this is how it is. Greeting London's literati by pitching myself headlong into their midst. Can I not hope for one unabashed evening?* But then the oddest thing happened. For the second time in their very brief acquaintance, as she braced to slam into the floor, Lord Devin caught her. It was not nearly as spectacular or intimate as his first rescue. He simply turned and extended his hand to her as if their movements had been choreographed; it was all she needed to anchor herself. In fact, quite possibly all anyone else saw was that, with her hand in Lord Devin's, she lightly danced down the stairs.

Safely on the ground floor, she greeted him cordially, trying to level her breathing.

"Good evening, Mrs. Duchamp. What an honor for you to grace us with your presence," he said, ever dryly. Then he kissed her gloved hand before blessedly releasing it. The electric tension was still there, transferring even through their gloves. The sensation immediately brought to mind their last encounter, and she had to school her face as she tamped down the little zings shooting through her. He continued. "It is a pleasure to see you looking well. May I introduce you to Lord Tennyson and his wife?"

Lady Devin, the dress, and now Lord Devin himself . . . with a dash of literati sprinkled into the mix. Any woman would be swept off her feet, even one who prided herself on being too old for such stuff and nonsense.

And so began a lively evening of sparkling conversation and wit, such as Honoria had never experienced before. It was difficult to avoid feeling like a sycophant in the presence of such literary luminaries. Lord Tennyson turned out to be every bit the erudite gentleman and attentive husband he was rumored to be. He and his wife exchanged frequent glances, and she wished she could interpret them, at once sad and intimate and encouraging.

Until they were all seated at the table, she had trouble keeping track of who was who. She'd observed carefully how the assemblage followed a delicate order of rank as they entered the dining room. Only when they were all together was she able to get a sense of each individual character. The only person with whom she was already acquainted was John Chapman, publisher and fellow bookseller. They maintained cordial acquaintance as his offerings were more specialized than hers. He'd told her excitedly at dinner that he was starting a new venture, a periodical called the *Westminster Review*. Astutely, Lady Devin seated him near essayists, including Mr. Thomas Carlyle.

Honoria was impressed by Lady Devin's choice of seating arrangements overall. Clearly, she'd planned with an eye toward lively, thoughtful conversation. Essayists were seated around Chapman near one end of the table, poets claimed the center on both sides of the table, and she found herself flanked by novelists and poets on the other end of the table. She ended up seated between Lord Tennyson and novelist Edward Bulwer-Lytton, who began a swiftly moving discussion about the purpose of literature. This was clearly an ongoing and potentially heated debate between them. She noticed Lady Devin had judiciously placed Lord Tennyson and Mr. Browning a reasonable distance apart and remembered, as everyone else there likely knew too, that Mrs. Browning had been considered the favorite for poet laureate the previous year, but Lord Tennyson had been named Wordsworth's successor instead. It would have been such a crowning achievement for Browning, not only because her work deserved such honor but because it was exceedingly rare for the title to go to women. Of course, as gentlemen, no sign of animosity or discomfiture showed between them. Still, distance made sense. Honoria wondered if Tennyson's presence was the reason for Mrs. Browning's absence.

She could feel Lord Devin's eyes on her. Silly and juvenile as it seemed, she was fairly certain it wasn't her imagination. At first, when she felt the occasional prickles on her skin, she glanced at him surreptitiously and noticed swift movement of his head in other directions. Then she avoided looking at him, but her skin tingled every so often. Her lips remembered the soft touch of his; every forkful of food became an unbearably sensual exercise. Periodically, the hair on the back of her neck stood and sent a slight shiver through her. Eventually, she noticed Lady Devin was watching him not very subtly, as were the few pairs of young feminine eyes arrayed around the table.

It was easy to interpret the interest of the young misses, but she was afraid of what Lady Devin might see.

When the poets around her turned to the subject of love, she felt telltale warmth wash over her skin and struggled to keep from looking in his direction.

"Surely love for one's wife, if indeed it is a love match, is far different from love for one's friends, even bosom friends," said Mr. Browning. It was easy to see how smitten he still was with his wife.

"All relationships are unique, to be sure. But there are some friends with whom one shares perhaps a deeper affection than marital love," Lord Tennyson replied quietly. The murmurs and nods suggested that everyone at the table was as familiar as Honoria with his masterpiece *In Memoriam*, written in honor of his dear friend Arthur Henry Hallam. The two had been close, and anyone present could see how deeply the loss still affected the great poet. "And there is a difference between fresh, naïve love and love that has been tested by fire and blight and been strengthened like steel." Here he looked conspicuously at his wife, who seemed to be fighting back tears.

"I think we can agree there are those, whether lovers or friends, who we simply cannot live without," Tennyson continued. "There are those who make our world. Oh, the world exists before them and possibly long after them, but their love gives us life and meaning and wholeness."

Honoria felt painfully choked by this barrage of sentiments. Who talked like this at dinner? What struck her keenly was the quiet awareness that she had no such person, whether lover or friend. She knew her work held meaning, but could she truly say she *lived*? When her hand stole up instinctively to worry the button and lace that normally covered her neck, she was surprised to feel only bare skin. That notch, that warm, soft hollow at the base of her throat, reminded her sharply of the gown's low neckline.

Again, she felt a warm flush spread along her face and shoulders, along with a prickling sensation of being observed. Feigning casualness, she looked in the direction of Lord Devin, intending to focus just past him, at the doorway. Instead, she found herself caught in his dark, open gaze. He made no pretense of accidental or fleeting eye contact. Instead, the intensity of his expression deepened into an almost elemental entitlement. His eyes seemed focused on her hand, on the spot where her fingers touched her throat. She froze under that riveting stare, momentarily unable to breathe, unable to see anything in the room but him, unaware of anything or anyone else. When she recollected herself, she quickly moved her hand back down to the table. His eyes briefly tracked the motion and then lingered again at her neck before meeting her eyes. Something about him reminded her of Jupiter—the way the tabby would crouch, belly nearly brushing the floor, body contracted, just before springing on his prey, whether it was a hapless intruding mouse or a ball of dust. She was shaken and tried hard to mask her tumultuous emotions, but, from across a crowded table, he'd somehow established a commanding intimacy without even touching her. She knew she ought to feel offended by his presumptuousness, but that didn't help to quiet the hot licks of some undefined emotion skittering across her skin, particularly in areas caught by his eyes.

"Mrs. Duchamp, perhaps you can shed some light on the female perspective." Lady Devin cut into her thoughts. The lady's kind eyes begged her to speak up. "The gentlemen here seem quite sentimental this evening, do they not? Do you think love is a necessity in marriage?"

She felt thirty pairs of eyes on her then and wished she could faint dead away instead of responding. No such luck.

"In deference to my fellow guests," she replied as she looked around the room, "I certainly see the appeal of a love match. It makes marriage so much more tolerable, I'm sure. So much more meaningful, as Lord Tennyson has said. Yet I suspect the ideal of star-crossed lovers drawn inexorably to each other, despite all obstacles, despite all reason, is fundamentally dangerous."

Silence.

Lady Devin stepped in to mend the breach, and Honoria had the strangest sense that they understood each other entirely in this matter. "We women are more practical than we are given credit for, don't you think, gentlemen?"

Mr. Browning nodded to her but then looked back at Honoria and prompted, "Dangerous, you say? How so?" he asked without accusation or affront, so it was easy to respond to him directly.

"It has to do with how expectations are shaped. Girls take these romantic fantasies and will not be content without them. Yet the function of marriage has historically been political, not personal. The entire history of British rule has been about establishing powerful alliances and protecting the English throne through political marriages. And those times when a monarch has given passion precedence over politics have been disastrous." She continued in this vein with greater vehemence and detail, even as she saw one young miss barely hiding a yawn with her napkin. "And so here is my concern—when we train girls, and boys too, to expect that marriage is founded in a love match, we obscure how marriage weaves them into our social fabric. To put it more bluntly, marriage makes them hypnotized cogs in the machine." When she finally stopped and caught her breath, she realized just how severe she sounded. "Present company excluded, of course. I didn't mean anyone here was . . ."

She abruptly shut her mouth as she realized all of the married men at the table were, in fact, in marriages of love.

"Sounds like you're fond of Karl Marx and his bosom friend Engels." This from a gentleman across the table whose name she could not recall. He sounded accusatory.

"I have read their work, yes, and I find it thought-provoking."

"Tell me," the unnamed man continued, "do you not feel complicit then in your own role as merchant? Do you not actively feed the machine by parting customers from their hard-earned shillings?"

It seemed no one would step in. But then, at least no one else was on the attack.

"I am as much a cog as anyone, I admit. But I strive to spread knowledge, to foster learning, to perpetuate the history of civilization. Until someone makes it possible to give such knowledge away freely and still feed and clothe and house themselves, I suppose I have to accept my place and my limitations within the current system."

Having stated her situation so baldly, she felt a tremendous opportunity to shift the group's attention to real, serious problems.

"We are not animals at the mercy of our instincts. We are rational and spiritual beings, with both the privilege and responsibility of building a society better than the one before us. We can only do that if we know where we are, who we are, how we fit. If we know what goes on around us."

"Of course, but—"

"Tell me, sir. Do you know how many children have died working in the Featherbury factory this past year alone?"

"I—no, but—"

"Twelve in just these past six months. More than half of them were the age of five. They should be clinging to their mother's skirts and playing Ring around the Rosy in a field. Instead, they died in a dark, dank dungeon—starved, filthy, beaten, and choking from ash." She stifled a cry and realized her voice had risen sharply. She was near hysterical. "My deepest apologies to Lady Devin and to all of you for introducing such unpleasantness into the evening. I hope you may understand somewhat my reluctance to speculate about fanciful notions of love when I am preoccupied with matters so very different."

"Nothing to apologize for, dear Mrs. Duchamp," Lady Devin announced graciously. And her statement was enough to shake the others loose of the dark turn of discussion. They turned to Marx and Engels and various assessments of these radical theories.

" 'From each according to his ability, to each according to his need.' Pshaw!" said the gentleman who could not be named. "If that were the case, I'd be entirely useless in this society, unless whistling, tying a cravat, and riding a horse count as abilities to sustain a nation. London society is not meant to be productive."

He laughed at himself, and many at the table joined in, nodding and adding their own useless talents. She gradually slipped into more ease.

"Have you heard Mr. Marx's view of our beloved Great Exhibition?" he asked the table.

"I heard he denigrates it as an obscene spectacle of English commodification," an essayist responded from the far end of the room. "My impression is that he objects to the way the Exhibition treats the labor and ingenuity of so many nations as a sales opportunity."

"Heathen!" said another. "That Exhibition shows the world how very advanced and all-encompassing England is today. No society has progressed as far as ours. And no society embraces and celebrates the achievements of other nations as exuberantly as ours does."

"Spoken like a well-oiled cog in the machine." Honoria, who'd remained silent through this part of the discussion, glanced up from her plate as her words echoed back at her. Lord Devin, for whatever reason, had joined the fray by parroting her words. "Well, you must admit," he continued, "Sir Dawson is not wrong in that assessment.

That's exactly the purpose of the show—to display to the world what great advances and trappings of wealth England has wrought and how superior England is to the rest of the world."

"There's nothing to be done, then, but go and see it," Sir Dawson responded. "One cannot determine the Exhibition's success or value without firsthand experience."

"What a splendid idea!" Lady Devin spoke up from the head of the table. "We should all take a tour of the Great Exhibition! Oh, Mrs. Duchamp, do say you'll join me."

What could anyone say when Lady Devin focused her gentle hazel eyes and embracing manner in their direction but "Yes, of course, Lady Devin. I would be delighted."

Chapter Five

Evans Principle 5: Beware of extravagant offers. They come with hidden costs that are often too dear.

"Darling Alex," Lady Devin said as everyone rose from the dinner table, "everyone else here has seen the library before. I am certain they would all understand if we indulge Mrs. Duchamp's professional interest in the special editions. Be so kind as to give her the tour."

No one demurred, although a young Miss Spenser looked longingly toward Lord Devin, then at her mother. No, such a proper girl of the ton could not be so forward, could not make her matrimonial aspirations so blatant, even though it must be clear every marriageable girl in attendance had to have her eye on his lordship, by necessity. Significantly, no one called into question his escort of Mrs. Duchamp to the library without a chaperone. Her age and station put her outside of concerns about maidenly propriety; theirs would be a purely business interaction, as his mother made clear.

The library was what one would expect of such a house, and Alex knew its secrets would be irresistible to a bibliophile like Mrs. Duchamp. Bookshelves lined three walls, ceiling to floor, and were completely full. Decorative paneled columns on each wall broke up the visual monotony. A writing desk and chair stood between the windows on the far wall, and a heavily upholstered settee sat askew in one corner. Two long tablelike display cases ran perpendicular to the windows. The room was lit only by sconces behind the desk.

"This is inappropriate, you know," she said. Yet she appeared drawn to the nearest display case, captivated by the sight of leather and parchment. "You should not be here with me, unaccompanied, in a dark room, no matter what your mother said."

When she described it like that, he could imagine all sorts of inappropriate reasons exactly why he should be here with her in this dark room, lit only by a few candles. It was also conveniently out of earshot from the evening's festivities. He could see her comment was an idle one, though; she made no move to open the door. She knew all too well this was a business matter between a lord and a merchant, best handled behind closed doors, just as everyone would perceive it. So he shifted his thoughts to business, particularly in light of her dark observations at dinner about the Featherbury deaths. He'd given the sample printed sheet from her shop to Withersby to demonstrate his meager progress. It was time for him to do more extensive archaeology of her professional work, but he had to do so delicately, or she'd startle and bolt like a cat.

"I did not think you would come this evening," he admitted wryly, as he stood at a corner shelf pouring brandy. Silently, he held a glass out to her.

She gave a tight smile, shook her head, and said, "I was given to understand that I didn't have much choice." She tilted her head as she added, "Very adroitly implied, I should say."

"True, but you do not seem the type to cave to the demands of others."

"On the contrary, my profession, like most commerce, inherently defers to the demands of the customer. I am at the mercy of customers on one end and suppliers on the other. Of course, I have to cave in some areas."

"So, if you would agree that you caved to the invitation, why the change of heart when you were so clearly not interested in attending?"

"Your mother's request, for one. I am not foolish enough to offend a viscount and his lady mother by rejecting an explicit invitation. My curiosity, for another. Why little old me? What could I possibly bring to such an occasion that would warrant said invitation? And, of course, I am a businesswoman first. To sit at a table with some of the finest living writers of our time, how could I ignore that opportunity?"

"My mother has taken a liking to you, as I suspected she would. You two are kindred. I could see she was shaken to the core over those factory children you mentioned. I would not be surprised if she convinces many of her friends to contribute to the cause, however ineffectually."

She looked at him for a long moment, skeptical, before returning her attention to the displays, fingertips on the edge of a display case to balance herself as she leaned in.

"Anyone not made of adamant would be shaken," she said. "Lady Devin is very kind and altogether exceedingly generous and gracious. She does seem so familiar . . . in the best possible sense." She trailed off, confused at her own susceptibility to this family. "I'm not so sure I acquitted myself well professionally with the guests, though."

Her progress along the display case was arrested. Her eyes focused sharply, and she leaned close to the glass top.

"Are these Blake illustrations authentic?"

He nodded.

"They're beautiful. The pairings make such a thought-provoking contrast . . . the Lamb and the Tyger . . . the chimney-sweeps." She continued to follow the line of the display, observing each piece carefully, appreciative of the obvious care taken with all of them. Without looking at him, she added, "I'm sure your mother makes everyone feel favored. She seems to have a special gift for making guests feel she is entirely in sympathy with them."

"True, but she is really quite selective with her inner sanctum, metaphorically speaking." He could see her trying to extricate herself from the discussion about his mother and let her go. He stood and shifted topics, delving ever so delicately into his mission. "How did you know about the children? One hears about random accidents, but you had very specific information, even down to the children's ages."

"I am fortunate that some investigative journalists trust me to publish their work anonymously. Those tracts you purchased, for example. You may have guessed that the authors use noms de guerre and pseudonyms for their subjects to defend against retribution."

"How do you know then that these authors are . . . forthright?"

"I know them personally, not just by name. I know and admire their legitimate work. I know and trust their characters. They are sincere, upstanding citizens, devoted to aiding the weak and defenseless."

He believed her. More than that, he wanted, he realized sharply, for her to talk about him with that same unwavering faith and admiration. Even as he tried to shut down her work. Here she was essentially explaining outright a process by which she could attack prominent manufacturers. She made no pretense otherwise. This hypocritical snare left a bitter taste in his mouth that the brandy couldn't wash away.

"This map is beautiful!" she said, her attention riveted to the wall display.

He groaned inwardly. The map was impossible to miss, large as it was, and positioned so centrally—behind the desk, between the windows. Upon entering the library, most people noticed it first. A bookseller, on the other hand, would naturally be drawn to the displays. He still hated the map, but his mother loved it. His siblings cherished it. Everyone who saw it marveled at it.

"Ah, yes, the map."

"You disagree?"

He shrugged. "It is just a map."

"What do all these dots represent?" Leave it to her to scrutinize it so intently.

"Those are pinholes my father made. He used to put pins in to note the places he visited."

"But there are so many. He couldn't possibly have traveled to all these places, could he? It would take years."

"He was an explorer for as long as I can recall. When I was younger, I suspected he was Ponce de León reincarnated, still seeking the secret to immortality. He wrote monographs about some of his travels. They are housed on the shelf over here, along with notebooks he kept on each of his journeys." The shelf he pointed to was filled with irregularly shaped volumes, some immaculately bound and others worn, with oversized objects poking out the top. Most people would be impressed by his father's body of work. Suddenly, he didn't want her to be one of them.

"Have you been to any of these places?"

He laughed mirthlessly. "No, I had no interest in following my father's shadow. I leave that to my brother and sister."

"Where are they these days?"

"My mother has not told you about them already? I suppose the opportunity has not yet arisen. She is ever so fond of relating their adventures. Amelia is married to an Italian baron and now living happily in Florence. Before they had children, they traveled every summer. Mother tries to visit them at least twice a year."

"How lucky for your sister to marry so well."

"Yes, lucky."

"You disapprove?"

"As you said, Amelia was fortunate to find someone so compatible and indulgent."

"And you disapprove." Tenacious little thing.

"They are married and have been together happily for more than six years now. He treats her well. I have no complaints."

"Hmm." She seemed about to press further but then shifted. "And where is your brother?"

"Ah, Andrew. Unlike Amelia, he has no ties or responsibilities to slow him down. He follows the wind."

"How does he afford to be a nomad?"

"Well, much like a traditional nomad, he travels light and makes the most of available resources. He has a modest living and seems to fall into grants from various societies—historical, cartographical. Sometimes he travels on assignment, but most of the time he appears able to wander the globe for pleasure."

"Again, how . . . lucky."

"Hmm."

"Where is he now?" she asked as she traced the line of pinpoints running from London to Pakistan to Hong Kong.

"He does not keep us as informed of his movements as I would like. Last I heard, he was in Amsterdam." Without conscious intent, he too reached up. Crossing over her arm, he put his finger on that city. It was the first time since pulling out all those pins that he actually touched this record of his father's obsession. As fresh anger and frustration swept over him, he couldn't breathe. She took her hand off the map slowly and touched his arm.

"It must have been awful for you all, your father dying so far from home. While your mother helped me prepare for dinner, she told me how shocking and devastating it was to her."

He closed his eyes, unable to speak.

"I'm sure he wouldn't have wanted it that way," she continued. "I'm sure, given the opportunity, he would have wanted one last chance to see you all, to say good-bye."

He turned on her, unable to keep his silence.

"You have no idea. He had every opportunity. Every. Opportunity. To be with us. To be a family," he ground out as he loomed over her. "Over and over, he chose to leave. He never wanted to stay."

"I—I'm sorry," she said, barely audible. She took a few steps back. "I spoke foolishly."

As if he hadn't heard her, he barreled on, focusing his attention back on the map. "He had a wife and children who idolized him. Caesar himself could not have received a warmer, more extravagant welcome from his subjects. After she turned four, Amelia wept for days every time he departed again. Andrew was more of a man about it; he would retreat into his studies and athletics. Mother strove to put on a happy face, praising her errant husband as a man of the world." He picked up a letter opener and began turning it in his hands as he moved toward the bookshelves, aimless but needing to move, needing to distance himself from the map, from the conversation.

"What did you do?"

"What?" he asked coarsely as if just noticing with irritation that she was in the room.

"When your father went away on his travels, what did you do? You said your sister mourned and your brother distracted himself. What about you?"

"I did whatever I was supposed to do at the time. When I was of school age, I focused on whatever skills I needed to eventually take on the role of viscount. When my studies were complete, I simply took on as much of my father's duties as I could. I was running the estate under his title well before he died."

"It sounds like you didn't have much time to pursue your own interests."

He looked at her directly as he said, "My family is my most fundamental *interest*."

She stared back into his eyes and nodded. "Sometimes we have no choice but to sacrifice ourselves for our families, for the greater good."

"I do not consider it a sacrifice. I consider it my vocation."

"What would you do, though, if you didn't have these responsibilities? Don't misunderstand me—your devotion to your family is noble, it's unutterably admirable, and it's all too rare. But consider, just for a moment, what you might do if you were beholden to no one? If you didn't have to worry about your siblings and your mother? Where would you go? What would you want to be? What would you want to do?"

"Such idle speculation is a waste of energy. It is dangerously fanciful."

"My father didn't think so," she replied coldly. She turned and went back to the nearest display case. "After my mother passed, he became extremely reflective and philosophical."

No good can come of that, he thought, but thought better of saying it aloud.

"As much as he loved the bookshop, he'd originally wanted it as much for my mother's sake as for his own. After she was gone, he held on to it in her memory but didn't want me saddled with its keeping. He didn't want to dictate my future. Every few months, he would ask me, 'What would you do if you could do anything without reservation?' It became a game, actually. I started with reasonable education and travel goals and eventually embellished wildly, sometimes just to see his reaction. At one point, I wanted to be an inventor of the male version of a corset. And then I wanted to be a mortician. And then I wanted to be a harem girl."

"A harem girl?" He stared at her as illicit images of her flesh wrapped in sheer scarves flashed through his mind.

"So that I could lead the harem in a revolt and subvert the entire Persian ideology of women, of course."

He snorted, his imagination firmly tamped down, and thought briefly of the profile from Withersby. She was certainly intellectually and philosophically capable of producing subversive documents, and she had the machinery and wherewithal to print and distribute. But that wasn't necessarily a bad thing. The turn of their discussion had diverted him from his mission; he needed to regain focus, but her voice kept drawing him to the dark corners of his mind, to questions—and emotions—he'd ruthlessly suppressed.

"So," she said softly, "what would you do . . . if you could do anything without reservation?"

He shook his head.

She waited.

Seconds stretched out to minutes.

At first, he refused to consider the idea. But she simply watched him with those doe eyes, soft, sympathetic, somehow familiar. She watched him and she waited. And when he truly thought about what he wanted to do, what he would do if he had no responsibilities, no obstacles, no rules, only one answer came to him. It had nothing to do with exotic places or dazzling careers. It had nothing to do with Withersby and his clients or even with the Devin family. It had to do with this room and this moment and this luminous woman in front of him. He walked toward her slowly, tentatively, at first, but then more confidently as he found his voice.

"What would I do if nothing stood in my way?"

She nodded.

"What would I do if I had no one to answer to and nowhere to be?"

"Yes, in your wildest, freest dreams, what would you do?"

He was close now. One more step, and her skirt would brush his trousers. He could see smile lines on her cheeks, the promise of joy and approval. Her eyes, open and frank, narrowed slightly at his approach. Her lips, full and lush, seemed on the verge of spreading in glee.

He took one last step toward her and said, "Assuming there were no objection . . . what I would do, in my wildest dream, is kiss you."

She backed away, her brow furrowing, but he noticed the change in her breathing. Faster, shallower.

"Don't toy with me. I was being serious," she said. He was almost certain he heard something very unladylike whispered under her breath as well. She walked toward the door.

"I am not joking. That is what I want to do."

She halted and looked at him, a rather unwelcome look. "Stop. I was wrong to be so forward, so presumptuous as to ask you about your deepest desires. I had no right to ask such intimate questions, and I am duly chastised. There was no need to be snide. It's best I return to the party."

"Wait! Please. I was not being snide or sarcastic."

She still looked like a bird about to take flight. He gestured to the chair nearest her.

"Please," he repeated, "if you will sit, we can talk seriously."

She sat stiffly, perched on the front of the chair, a hand to her throat.

"It was not at all my intention to offend you or chastise you. My answer was sincere."

At that she stood again. He continued hurriedly. "But if I am honest with myself, there is much I want to do with this life that has nothing to do with the viscountcy. I cannot give time or energy to such indulgent dreams because I *do* have responsibilities. Besides, you said yourself that your answers turned outrageous. You never actually said what you truly wanted to do."

She sat back down, all but slumped into the chair. She wasn't the only perceptive person in the room.

"No. You've caught me. I haven't seriously considered the question in years. I have responsibilities too. The bookshop is but the most obvious one, and it forms its own circular argument. I need to run the shop in order to be financially independent. Only if I am financially independent can I pursue some fantasy path. But if I were to pursue some dream, I would have to close the shop and therefore be unable to afford the dream. For me, such dreams are a trap packaged in a paradox."

Again, the room was quiet for a few moments. He fervently wished he could see the thoughts streaking through her mind, reflecting in the swiftly changing expressions on her face. It was a reverie he felt should not be disturbed. When she finally looked up at him, he changed the subject.

"I've been remiss," he said, maintaining his distance. "I meant to tell you earlier your dress fits most becomingly. There are extra panels in the bodice, I believe."

She looked at him askance, offended. Well, at least that got her attention. Her eyes were no longer distant and glazed.

"I only mean panels added for modesty, not size."

"You mean the neckline was originally lower than this?" *Impossible*, she thought. With her shoulders and neck exposed so, she constantly feared she might fall out of the top as it was. She had observed that it was more modest than any of the other ladies in attendance, but she still felt as though, if it were any lower, well, her nipples would undoubtedly pop out.

"The original owner was not so magnificently endowed in that area."

She wasn't sure what to make of this soft, docile Lord Devin. Where were the sharp edges, the sardonic comments, the cocked brow? She wasn't accustomed to niceness from him, and she certainly wasn't accustomed to compliments from anyone. So even this inappropriate one made her feel special, if only for a moment. Heat spread through her.

"You look radiant this evening," he added.

Her face burned; it was a wonder she didn't spontaneously combust.

"You shouldn't speak to me so." She got up and moved to the far side of a display case, clearly putting even more space between them.

"Whyever not?"

"You know perfectly well why, young man." She looked at him pointedly.

He cocked an eyebrow then but seemed to take her meaning, as he moved back to the settee.

"You seem to be enjoying yourself with my mother's writer friends. She does love to show off her writing circle."

"They're a lively bunch, aren't they? I'm surprised to find myself espousing such a contradictory stance on the love issue, but I enjoyed their open exchanges," she replied with a smile. "It's always fascinating to see where authors get their inspiration, how they piece ideas together, what they see in the world that we easily miss or forget. They're a special breed. Maybe that's why so many of them are in love with their wives."

"Do you truly believe love is not important in marriage?"

"I don't think it's a requirement, no. I'm sure it can develop over time, but I think what many young people take as love is really just physical attraction, which fades. Or infatuation, which likewise cannot be sustained. Those aren't qualities upon which to build a lifelong commitment."

"And financial stability is? Or, no, political power. That is what you said about the British monarchy—using marriage to empower and perpetuate the throne was the most effective motivator. How does it work for us lowly folk who have no political position to maintain?"

"Well, first of all, do not be disingenuous. You do have a viscountcy to maintain. Don't tell me your parents didn't drill into you the importance of marrying well to continue the Devin line. Don't tell me your brother doesn't struggle with his position as the second son, having to establish himself or rely on his older brother. He will eventually want a wife, and it would be best for him to find a financially advantageous match."

"That sounds mercenary."

"Call it what you will. This world is not easy for those without means. I think it is especially hard for those who were raised accustomed to an easy lifestyle but then left to fend for themselves."

"Like you? Is that what happened to you? Your father was a baronet. Surely, you would have been raised as a lady."

"I'd rather not talk about me. Suffice it to say, for many people, marriage must be about security, not about something so fickle and fleeting as emotion."

"I would wager that several people tonight would claim their affections for their spouse are far from fleeting. And attraction is a much more powerful, visceral force than money. Many of them, in fact, work hard to support themselves financially. They effectively separate their emotional inner lives from their professional outer ones."

She nodded, but her face remained noncommittal. Unconvinced, she was done with the conversation and would soon move to return to the other guests. He needed to shift her attention.

"So," he began, "I've been wondering something all evening."

"The current price of tea in China? Currently, it depends on the importer." That had been a brief subject of debate at the dining table, one she clearly had no patience for, if her dismissive tone was any indication.

He chuckled and replied, "No. My curiosity does not extend to commerce this evening."

"Politics, then? Who will be the next prime minister?" She'd made her way to the far end of the room again, close to the door. But she hadn't left. Her continuing presence had to be an encouraging sign.

"No, now stop pacing like a frightened cat and come here to me a moment." His tone was unmistakably authoritative, but he sat on the edge of the settee, a supplicant, arms extended, waiting to see if she would come to him of her own accord and take his hands.

She did walk to him, but placed her hands on her hips, looking not a little like a beleaguered nursery maid.

"What, my lordship, have you been wondering all evening?"

"Whether your lips really do feel like rose petals or I just imagined that."

He could see she remembered the kiss as well as he did. Her arms fell to her sides, hands balled into fists. The hunger in her eyes was indisputable, but something battled with desire.

"You should not speak to me so."

"I cannot seem to help myself."

"What can you possibly be thinking?"

He couldn't very well answer that. If he gave voice to his increasingly erotic thoughts, she'd surely flee the room like a cornered rabbit.

"I think you are unlike any woman I have ever met. You hold contrary views. You speak to me as if you are intimidated by no one. You intrigue me. Surely you would not begrudge one kiss, one meek, cordial little kiss? What harm could that do?"

She leaned down to him, whispering, "Curiosity can be fatal. I don't know why I'm doing this." Then she touched her lips to his softly, chastely.

"Ah, rose petals . . . soft, velvety . . . but also warm and supple." He exhaled the words against her lips. They were every bit as delectable as he remembered.

She raised a brow and asked, "Do your lips often touch rose petals?"

The pulse at the base of her neck belied her sardonic tone. When he felt her start to pull away, he gently grasped her elbows, just enough to hold her there without making her feel trapped. And she stayed. God in heaven, she stayed. He kissed her again and ran his tongue lightly between her lips, testing, requesting access. When the tip of her tongue met his, a stab of lust ran through him, straight to his groin. One hand reached up to the nape of her neck to pull her closer, to open her deeper to his kiss.

Her hands braced his shoulders, not pushing away but rather gripping tightly. So she wasn't immune to emotion. Still, this was not enough. He needed more. He wanted to explore every inch of her and wanted her to ravish him in kind. His mouth slid along her jaw, his tongue darting out in teasing forays as he made his way to her ear. He took her earlobe in his mouth and sucked ever so gently. She gasped. When he used his teeth lightly, she shivered, her hands now massaging his shoulders, as if restless and seeking stable ground. *Good. More of that, please.*

"This means nothing," she whispered, followed by a whimper. "Physical sensation is fleeting."

"Then we should take what we can get." His mouth returned to hers, with all its heat and sweetness. If he kept her mouth occupied, maybe he could quiet that skeptical corner of her brain. Through layers of silk and cotton, he felt her nipples tighten against his chest. He slid his fingers across one, and she moaned into his mouth.

Yes, the perfect height. He'd known it the moment they walked into the room. Sitting here, he was perfectly level with her most excellent breasts. And suddenly he was determined to lavish attention on them, to taste them, to learn her exquisite texture and weight and scent.

His mouth traveled down her neck, nibbling and licking, as her cool skin was warmed by his lips and breath. His lips pressed against the hollow at the base of her throat, that spot he'd been obsessed with all evening. He tasted her pulse there. His hand caressed her collarbone, drifting lightly across her in concert with his mouth. By this point, she was practically lying horizontally upon him, her posture dictated by her corset.

She panted softly and said, "I don't know why you would want someone like me. Silly, really."

"I have never wanted anyone like you. Let me clarify—I have never wanted anyone as much as I want you right now." He couldn't stand it. In a swift motion, his roaming hand dove under her neckline and slipped a generous breast free of her clothes. So soft, so pale, so full. He would show her how seriously he desired her.

His mouth captured a rosy peak, causing her to shudder and gasp, "Oh, my!" *Yes.* The sensations rocketing through him were unspeakable, his erection struggling against his trousers. He sucked more of her into his mouth and teased her taut nipple with his tongue. His hand caressed the other breast, nails gently raking back and forth across the tip. She arched her back, giving him greater access as she moaned and ran her hands through his hair.

Then abruptly, with a hard shove against his shoulders and a loud smack of suction broken, she was gone.

"Stop this!" She'd pulled out of arm's reach, red-faced and breathing heavily. She turned her back to him and fussed with the front of her dress. When she faced him again with her face a bright and blotchy red, she was fully covered and more composed, but just barely.

"What are you doing? I am old enough to be your mother," she said, furious. "This is your mother's dress, for heaven's sake. And you would suckle me like a babe? What is the matter with you?"

"Clearly, I must correct several erroneous assumptions," he replied calmly. "First, you are younger than my mother, as I believe you have already estimated. Second, I believe this dress rightfully belonged to my sister, Amelia. And perhaps most importantly, can you not tell the obvious differences between the practicality of feeding an infant and the decadence of engaging in a distinctly carnal act?" As Honoria sputtered insensibly, he continued. "The pleasure that spiked through you just then . . ." His eyes dared her to contradict him. She did not. "That's undeniably a carnal pleasure, one common to lovers in the heat of passion. In no way could it be confused with maternal care or infantile craving. I am rather surprised and disappointed that your husband, may he rest in peace, never performed such a service for you."

Honoria gave him her back, silent.

"I am sorry," he said, instantly chagrined. "How vulgar of me. I would never dishonor your husband's memory, Mrs. Duchamp." He wanted to go to her, embrace her in apology, but her shoulders were forbidding. He added softly, "I only mean it is not such an uncommon act. If anything, it is a common, simple way to derive mutual pleasure. Forgive me if I overstepped my bounds."

Still well out of reach, she gave him a tentative, sidelong look and said, "We should return to the parlor."

He sighed heavily, almost laughing at himself as he did so. For him to sigh like some heroine in a penny-mag! Her emotional baggage was heavier than he'd surmised. And he couldn't completely account for why he wanted her, but undeniably he did. He would get what he wanted eventually, he was certain, because he was reasonably sure from her reaction that she wanted it too. His friends had occasionally joked about the pliability of widows, experienced yet neglected, and he trusted this one would be swayed eventually, not because she was a widow, but because of whatever current ran between them. Why he felt the need to persist, he couldn't really begin to consider.

"I apologize, Mrs. Duchamp, for my . . . what did you call it previously?"

"Taking liberties?"

"Ah, yes, 'taking liberties.' Sometime in the future, you'll have to explain to me how exercising our liberties is a bad thing." When she opened her mouth to argue, as of course she would, he immediately added, "But I still haven't shown you the work we came for." He strode to a corner shelf, slid open a false panel, and pulled out something wrapped in velvet. He went to the desk to unveil the contents.

Of course, she came to stand next to him. Of course, she bent down to get a closer look at the gold leaf on the illuminations.

"Can that be real? Is that truly a First Folio?"

"It is indeed and verified by the Royal Shakespeare Society. They have been trying to convince the Devins to part with it for over a century."

Of course, as she leaned over the bound parchment for a closer look, he could see far down her truly spectacular décolletage, which he knew would haunt his dreams.

"It's breathtaking," she whispered reverently.

"Yes, it is." He agreed, but he wasn't referring to the manuscript. The view from his vantage point did steal his breath away. In point of fact, as he thought more and more about the way her body responded to his kiss, he knew she wasn't indifferent to him. He wasn't ready to give up, and he knew she appreciated directness.

"Honoria, I want you."

"Mrs. Duchamp to you. I'm right here. What is it?"

Woman, is your obtuseness natural or deliberate?

"No, I mean, I desire you."

"I gathered that a moment ago, Lord Devin," she replied archly.

So . . . deliberate then. Maddening siren.

"But we can't always have what we desire," she continued primly. "Surely you've experienced some rejection, some privation in your lifetime. Haven't you?" At his amused nod, she continued. "After all, children don't get candy or toys whenever they desire—some things just aren't good for them."

His temper flared at her condescension.

"Do not dismiss me. I am a grown man, fully aware of my desires and motivations and of what is or isn't good for me. And what—who—I desire is you." His eyes held her own, direct and unblinking.

"Why?" she asked, her voice dubious.

"Because you fascinate me. You intrigue me. You excite me to a degree I have never experienced before. If you knew me, you would understand how significant that is. And I want to know you."

She shook her head and said, "I don't engage in dalliances. Bad for business."

"I do not either," he said. And it was true, after a fact. He'd had fleeting encounters with amenable women, but he didn't keep them. This was different. "But I have a proposition for you, one that I think would be mutually agreeable."

"Any propositions you have don't interest me," she said, coldly. "I don't want your money, and I am no one's mistress."

"Ah, but I was not thinking of money." He looked down at the exquisite manuscript before them, ran his hand along a page, and heard her gasp in surprised understanding.

"The Folio?" she said, incredulous. "You would trade the Folio—God only knows how much it's worth—for a night with me?"

"Based on our recent experience, I can say with certainty that one night would not be enough to satisfy either of us. But, yes, that is the basic idea."

"And how would you explain such an exchange to your mother or to your brother? Or to anyone who knows your family owns this? That you handed over possibly the most valuable English document in history besides the Magna Carta for *that*?"

"Well, of course I cannot make known the whole circumstances. As viscount, this belongs to me, not to my mother or my brother. It is mine to dispense with as I wish."

"You don't deserve to own it if you would trade it so carelessly."

She began to flip through the Folio's pages gently, silently. He considered it a good sign. When she got to the end, she closed the volume with a light touch.

"No, thank you."

"Pardon?"

"No. I'll admit your offer is tempting. This is a dazzling work of art, one that probably belongs in a museum. And I would be a fool not to take possession of it, whether for my own pleasure or for the tremendous income it would provide." She smiled wistfully for a moment, and then her face turned serious, brows knitted. "But just as you don't deserve to own it if you'd make such a tawdry trade with it, I wouldn't deserve to own it if I bought it so shamelessly."

"But it is priceless."

"So am I," she said with conviction. "I know my worth. I won't be bought."

He was stunned. He'd been so sure she couldn't resist the offer. And, if he were being honest, his pride stung just a little. But he had to admire her self-possession, and so he took the mature course of action.

"Well," he responded, "surely, you understand I had to try."

She looked at him surprised, and perhaps a little amused, as if to say, "*That's all?*"

"Really," he added, "I think we would both find such an arrangement incredibly enjoyable, but if you are not interested, then that is all there is to say."

"Thank you," she said tentatively, "for being such a . . . gentleman about this."

They both laughed at her choice of words.

"I hope this does not mar our acquaintance, Honoria. I enjoy your conversation and would like to continue our association."

A few seconds passed before she conceded, "Talking seems innocuous enough, *my lord*. Of course, then, we can maintain our acquaintance. You may visit me at the shop, as you choose. But I have provisions."

"Oh? You would dictate terms for our association?"

"Given our recent, uh, encounters, I think that's wise. The shop is my life, and I cannot risk anything that would lower my credibility or professional reputation. So here are the terms: You shall not take such *liberties* again. You shall not speak to me as if I am one of your paramours. In all interactions, you shall treat me as a professional."

"Let me amend your terms thusly: I will not take any liberties you do not freely give. I will not flirt with you or compliment you in an insincere manner. I will treat you as a respected compatriot. In return, you will not be skittish around me."

"Skittish?"

"You look ready to bolt at any moment. I am not so threatening, am I? You enjoy my company, do you not? So allow yourself to relax. I will not press you for anything you do not wish to give. Do not fear me."

He could almost see her mind turning the words over, weighing them on invisible scales.

Finally, she said, "That is acceptable. Now we really must rejoin the other guests." She nodded her head once as a final stamp of her decree and then quietly walked out of the room, leaving the door ajar.

Stupid, stupid, stupid. He'd acted like a green boy, confronting tits for the first time, pawing like an uncontrolled beast. He was more talented at the art of love than this. He hadn't been this awkward about sex since his first time; by God, even his first time had been more careful and moderate than this, smoother by nature, if not by design. He should probably count himself lucky he didn't prematurely release himself, to top it all off.

He thought offering the Folio was a stroke of genius, impossible to refuse. And yet she did just that. In his state, he would have promised her anything. He knew her rejection should not bother him as much as it did. He could easily find a plethora of other women, including several tractable widows, who would accept a much lower offer. He knew, too, that he was acting just like a child, desiring the forbidden object that was even more tantalizing because it was out of reach. But his want was so damn strong. He could still smell her, still feel her under his hand, still hear the small sounds of pleasure deep in her throat.

And yet he had just agreed he would never again seek any of that. She had the right of it, though, he realized. As he replayed the moment in his mind, he knew it was dastardly of him to pursue her in light of Withersby's orders, even though they were orders he didn't want to fulfill in the first place. If he could get out from under the man's thumb, well, he couldn't even start down that path. . . .

As he returned to the party, a servant delivered a small, folded note.

Lord Devin:
Tick tock. Tick tock.
—Mr. A.

And here was the one thing he needed to make the evening a complete travesty, as if he'd conjured Withersby with his thoughts. What would he do about this mission? He could not allow Withersby to destroy her livelihood. If indeed she were the author of those pamphlets, what could she possibly have brewing that would be so devastating to Withersby's client? Everyone knew the problems of child labor, everyone knew the horrors of slavery, and yet these didn't rent asunder any major industries. She could, and clearly did, print reformer pamphlets, but what could she possibly print with such devastating anticipated effects?

Chapter Six

Evans Principle 6: There's always more than one person to please. Consolidate your efforts but never compromise yourself.

"So where were you last week, Honoria?" Predictably, that would be the first thing Marissa would ask. The tenacious Mrs. Marissa Clarke always dove headfirst into whatever question preoccupied her. Some might even say she resembled a bulldog, with her stout, solid body and her snub nose. One could never say Marissa gave them the wrong impression. People saw exactly who she was and what her intentions were; she saw no need for finesse or tact. Such subtlety was the job of the sisters, Mrs. Helena Martin and Mrs. Elizabeth Addison, the same Helena and Elizabeth who sat across the room by the picture window, ostensibly minding their knitting. They'd appear so even if they were eavesdropping; such was a skill they'd mastered as children in their father's study.

"A business opportunity arose," Honoria explained, "a dinner hosted by Lady Rose Devin, and I thought it would be an excellent chance to make some new connections. The guests were among the country's most touted intellectuals. I made sure to offer them my card in hopes of having them do public readings at the shop. I suspect one or two might even be open to disseminating our more controversial work."

"Speaking of which," Marissa replied, "I think Helena has new information for us from a visit with some Bethnal Green children. But that can wait. How did you come to be acquainted with Lady Devin?"

"By chance, really. Her son Lord Alexander Devin purchased a book from Evans as a birthday present for his mother. I suppose he must have mentioned the encounter and she must have thought it would be conducive to have a bookseller among the book authors."

"Sensible enough. Seems peculiar, though. How often does one make a purchase at a shop and think to make the seller's personal acquaintance? Sure, we all know the shopkeepers along your row and at most establishments who can garner us access to information, but we've cultivated those acquaintances purposefully."

By now, Elizabeth had given up the pretense of talking needlework with Helena and piped up, "Marissa, you seem to be leading us to a particular conclusion. What is it?"

"I was simply testing your hearing, dearie," Marissa shot back with a sly grin. But then she added, "It seems unlikely the Devin family would take an interest in you, Honoria, so suddenly. I don't know why, but my gut feels unsettled about the invitation and abrupt familiarity."

"What familiarity? I attended a dinner with thirty other guests." She felt a need to keep silent about the events that transpired in the Devin library. Familiar, indeed. Marissa's forwardness was due in no small part to her keen intuition; her instincts were nearly unnatural in their accuracy. Why should this time be any different?

"It's not like you to be secretive, Honoria."

"I'm not being secretive. There is very little to say about the event. I attended dinner; I conversed on a wide array of topics with several well-known writers, which was quite an honor. And I hope I made enough of an impression on them that I can call upon them in the future to help further the success of the shop. As I said, it was a rare business opportunity I felt I could not decline."

This time Helena inserted herself into the discussion with "Strange as it may seem, I agree with Marissa. I know what it is! The invitation was based on Lord Devin coming to your shop for a book. That in itself is rather unusual. Moreover, you've said nothing about your dealings with Lord Devin. Something must have happened to garner enough of his attention that he had his mother invite you."

This was too much.

"Ladies, there is really very little to tell about dinner or about the Devins. They are lovely people, and I was uncommonly fortunate to be rather randomly invited. Let us not get caught up in trivialities. We have work to do."

True enough. Whether they were genuinely dissuaded or simply acceding to her obvious desire not to talk further about the subject, Marissa went to get some knitting out of a basket in the corner. Honoria inwardly breathed a large sigh of relief and made her way toward where the other two ladies were seated, stopping to pick up her satchel along the way. Each of the women placed their yarn projects on their laps, pieces large enough to hide the notepaper on which their reports to the group were based. If anyone happened to make an unscheduled visit, they could easily secret their work away in their needle projects between the butler's announcement of the visitor and the actual presentation of said visitor in the drawing room. Even when they met at Honoria's more humble abode, they maintained the pretense of knitting or needlepoint and occasionally even finished some of those projects as they worked through more important strategies. Helena's interviews took precedence this evening, and they quickly moved far away from discussion of Lord Devin, his mother, and the peculiar dinner invitation, although Honoria's thoughts didn't stray far enough from them.

Chapter Seven

Evans Principle 7: All that glitters—well, you know the rest...

The glass and metal structure, at once encasement and centerpiece of the Great Exhibition of the Works of Industry of All Nations, gleamed as sunlight broke through the clouds. Awestruck by its effulgence, Honoria marveled, openmouthed, like a child. It was massive yet delicate, imposing yet ephemeral. The building suited the elaborate name of the showcase.

"What do you think of it, Mrs. Duchamp?" She didn't miss the note of amusement in Lord Devin's voice. In fact, he seemed to be perpetually amused by her or perhaps by life in general, a sardonic amusement.

"It is lovely," she admitted. "Breathtaking, even. Quite a feat of architecture and engineering. I expect it to collapse like a house of cards or shatter if a stiff breeze arises. It's amazing."

"I agree," he replied. "It is a jewel. The exhibits within are equally spectacular. I would be honored to serve as your guide."

"Oh, Alex, you must make sure she sees the textiles from Turkey and Greece," Lady Devin added.

"But what do you wish to see, Lady Devin?" she asked. "Since you have both seen many of the exhibits before and everything is equally new to me, I would be happy to explore sections new to you."

"That is too kind of you, dear." Lady Devin moved in front of her son to link arms with Honoria, reinforcing the sense of little girls at play. What an odd pair they must make, a regal lady and a nobody. "Let us seek out a newer world!"

Exactly as he said, the interior of the Crystal Palace was as astounding as the exterior. Colors and smells she'd never experienced before, a mishmash of sensations, bombarded her. Everything bathed in golden sunlight. The wave of humanity entering with them directed their path, rushing them through the entryway and ultimately depositing them in the West Hall.

A photography demonstration drew their attention immediately.

"I have heard about this," said Lord Devin. "It is a remarkable new process for making multiple copies of an image—rather quickly too."

In fact, the photographer showed off images he had taken and developed there at the Exhibition. A few of the more interesting ones, such as a view from the exterior, were available for purchase. When the photographer offered to take their portrait, however, she immediately shook her head and deflected the question. "Perhaps you would like to have a portrait of yourself and your son, Lady Devin?"

Lady Devin murmured to her son, who spoke in professional tones with the man and handed him a calling card. The two men shook hands, and Lady Devin led them farther into the hall.

A massive panel display of art competed with a Far Eastern porcelain display for their attention, both of them in the shade of a tree, around which the building must have been erected. As they rounded a corner, they found themselves again in a crush of people, this time waiting to glimpse what was assumed to be the most highly prized gem in the world: the Koh-i-Noor diamond. When would she get another opportunity like this?

The diamond turned out to be disappointingly unremarkable. Large, certainly, but not especially attractive. For all she could see, it looked like a large chunk of dirty glass.

Lady Devin stopped to speak with a tall couple but urged her son to take Honoria farther into the international displays.

Near the overblown hunk of rock, bright color and delicate movement from the Chinese alcove caught her eye. A lovely girl who she could only guess must be Chinese stood in front of a display of porcelain vases, her voice carrying over a small group of tourists obviously charmed by her. The child's long braids stood out against her pale robes, embroidered with exotic flowers and birds. As Honoria moved closer, she was struck by the girl's articulate erudition. She wanted to ask about the bronze statues at the end of the neighboring display because they shared motifs with some of the vases, but before she could get the child's attention, she felt Lord Devin's hand at her elbow.

"Have you found something of interest here?"

"These displays from the East are lovely. That child, though, is even more fascinating. I do not see her parents, though they must be close by."

"I shall have to point her out to my mother. She lent a few items to the collections here and has more at home that she wants to be appraised for authenticity. Perhaps the child's parents can be of some guidance."

Though the sight of the exotic child nagged at her without clear cause, she was equally struck by an undertone in his comment.

"Was your father often in the Orient?"

"My father was everywhere. I have no doubt he was often fleeced when he traveled, particularly in Asian countries where he did not speak the language. He was overconfident and easily impressed."

"Excuse me for stating the obvious, but you seem to talk rather flippantly and disdainfully about your father."

He dipped his head, and she watched the tips of his ears turn pink before he responded.

"You have noticed that as well? I can assure you I do not normally talk about my father at all, much less so derisively. Certainly not to someone outside the family. And yet with you, it simply slips out. I find myself saying the words before I have had proper time to censor myself. It is unaccountable. Suffice it to say that I disapproved of some of his choices. And now it seems only fair then that you reciprocate—you have said little about your family, but it has always been with a tone of wistful happiness. Tell me about them and why you adored them so."

He'd unknowingly found the right key. She didn't have much opportunity to speak of her parents, less and less opportunity as time passed. And *adoration* was such a mild word for what she felt toward them.

"My father's family was landed gentry," she began. "My grand-father held a baronet but wasn't much of a land manager. As the second son of an estate in decline, my father didn't have much to live on. Between the modest income supplied by his brother and the modest dowry from their marriage, my parents made do. But when it became clear my uncle was not only inept at management but actively gambling away what little he had left of the family legacy, my father decided he wanted to set out on his own. I understand they had quite a row over it—a baron's son turned merchant. Apparently, not for the first time, they came to blows just before my parents married. My uncle was furious about the shop, even though he couldn't really afford to interfere. My father loved books, and so he got it in his head that he wanted to open a bookshop and make it his legacy. My mother was supportive, in her own way. And, in truth, I think he fastened on to the bookshop precisely because he was so in love with her. She was an aspiring poetess, you see. She spent much of her time at her escritoire, and I think deep down he dreamed he would one day be able to feature her poetry in the shop. He would have so enjoyed showing off her work."

Lady Devin had rejoined them during her recounting and studied her face for a moment. "Were your parents Mr. and Mrs. Samuel Evans?"

"Yes." She knew from the tone what was coming next.

"Your father was a grandson of the Earl of Eastwick?"

"Yes," she responded quietly.

When Lord Devin finally found his voice, he said "You are a great-granddaughter of the Earl of Eastwick?"

"I am." While such logic should go without saying, he seemed to have particular difficulty incorporating this information into his view of her.

"How is that possible?"

Lady Devin answered for her. "Your grandfather would have been the earl's third son, correct? He had quite a colorful reputation, if I may say. And your father was his second son."

"Yes, Lady Devin. A second son of a rather profligate third son.

My uncle inherited a lesser title and little else. Fortunately, my father already had a vocation in mind, even if it was deemed beneath him."

Yet another alcove housed a fascinating dance troupe made up of women costumed in scarves and tiny silver baubles that jingled as they swayed. Her initial shock at the amount of exposed skin she saw was subsumed by the graceful frenzy of the dancers. Translucent colors swirled in circles and snakelike arcs as their bodies undulated.

"They dance with such abandon. What must it be like to move so free of inhibitions?" she said, without thinking.

At her ear, Lord Devin whispered, "I do believe, Mrs. Duchamp, that you would be quite something if you dropped your inhibitions. I, for one, would pay to see your emotions run wild."

She looked around askance but saw Lady Devin in another conversation out of earshot. "What if your mother heard you speak so?"

"Absent of context, she would most assuredly agree." He grinned. The upstart had the nerve to grin, as if he'd won a game.

She continued watching the dancers and whispered back, "Don't bet on it."

When his mother rejoined them, Lord Devin asked about how Honoria came to run the bookshop.

"It wasn't until after my mother's death that my father and I moved to the quarters above the shop. My uncle had washed his hands of us, and there didn't seem to be any point to keeping our country house. It was too expensive . . . and too painful." She scanned the crowd, needing a moment to regain her composure. "In any case, through my father's diligence and industriousness, the shop slowly became a solid enterprise. It has never grossed more than six thousand pounds per year, and those were years of feast. These days, it runs . . . somewhat . . . lower than that. But it's stable and currently self-sustaining."

"Why have you not hired staff to help you run the place?" Lord Devin asked. "Surely your messenger Erich is of an age when he could start to be of more use?"

"It is my responsibility," she said simply.

He looked at her sharply but then nodded.

"You would not trust anyone else to protect it. And you would feel as if you were shirking your proper duties if you handed it off to someone else." His eyes said he knew exactly what that felt like. She stared at him.

"Exactly. My father entrusted me with his legacy. He passed on everything he knew to me, and I cannot betray that trust." After a pause, she added, "Erich and Minnie are my responsibility too. Their parents predeceased mine. My parents made a promise they would be taken care of. He is free to pursue whatever career he chooses. I would not yoke him to the shop."

Despite young Lord Devin's consistent attention to his companions, it was difficult to ignore the parade of fine young ladies who brightly acknowledged him. Young ladies in elegant silks and finely wrought lace, intricate brocades, and expensively modest jewelry. Young ladies who seemed more interested in Lord Devin than in the wonders of the world displayed around them. Some young ladies who went so far as to flout convention by greeting him themselves, even though they were escorted by their fathers, brothers, or some other male who was responsible for conveying acknowledgments. Goodness, even she knew that the male companion responds to greetings on behalf of the accompanying female. Only someone insensible, veritably blind and deaf, would miss the tacit message being conveyed—Lord Devin was highly prized marriage material, and the women he escorted were not part of that picture. Yet he acted immune to their fans and coy smiles and pretty curtsies, responding to each greeting with equal solicitude.

"What do you think your father would have thought of the Exhibition, Mrs. Duchamp?" he asked kindly.

"He would have adored it. I'm sure he would have seen this as walking through worlds of books come alive. He was always so curious. My mother too would have loved all this; I'm sure she would have written whole journals full of observations about the contraptions, the styles, the artwork, the cultures. She would have wanted to capture sight and sound. She would have been particularly fascinated by the photographic equipment, although I hear it can be as much a curse as a blessing. What of your father, the world traveler? I can only assume he would have felt quite at home here in the midst of all this multinational chaos."

"Indeed."

"Would you care to expand on that?"

"My father most certainly would have had an active hand in planning and executing this extravaganza." He didn't say it admiringly. His tone said, in no uncertain terms, that this was not an avenue open to travelers.

"Well, as astounding as this whole extravaganza seems to be," Lady Devin interjected, "I would greatly appreciate a bit of fresh air."

"Are you well, Lady Devin?" She took the other woman's hand, noting her taut posture.

"It is nothing to speak of, Mrs. Duchamp." Lady Devin lowered her voice. "This building. It gives me the sense of a birdcage. It may be a giant cage, but it is still a kind of prison."

"This way, Mother." Devin led the way with authority, dividing the crowd with his stature and purposeful stride. It was as if the world truly did bow to his whim.

When their little group returned to the dazzlingly massive Central Transept, however, a circus show was in full swing, drawing a wall of onlookers impenetrable even to the great Lord Devin. Colorful jugglers spun and crossed the floor in intricate patterns, attending only to the balls they tossed in the air. Dancers wove through their paths. And then, the main attraction drew all eyes toward the sky: a trio of tightrope walkers suspended high above the crowd made their way across an impossibly fine thread. Two of the walkers supported a bar between them, hooked in some way over their shoulders, while the third walker balanced above them on that bar. They stepped slowly but surely along the rope, which trembled from their movements.

"Can you persevere, Mother?"

"Of course, my dear."

Still, Lady Devin's pale skin had developed a fine misty sheen. Honoria gripped her hand, as if to transmit her own strength. She was distracted though by sharp gasps from the audience. She followed the eyes around her up to the tightrope, where one of the performers wobbled dangerously.

"What a foolhardy risk," she said.

"That is the career they have chosen," Lord Devin responded, his eyes likewise riveted above. "Presumably, they train regularly to maintain peak performance. They accept the risk."

"I could never do something so dangerous."

"Could you not? I wonder if you do not do so every day."

She tore her eyes from the spectacle above to stare at him.

"Whatever could you mean by that? I don't put myself at risk."

He looked at her fully.

"You are a single woman, running your shop and living on your own. Your fortunes could change at any moment. Sales run dry. A careless fire could leave you with nothing." *Damn it, woman, you spread truths people want to kill you for. Of course you put yourself at risk.*

She replied as if she'd heard what he did not say. "One cannot live as a prisoner of fear. We do what we must because it is the right thing to do, because we could not conceive of living a life without it."

"There are many things you could—"

Whatever he'd been about to say evaporated as danger sparked above. The audience gasped as one. The highest tightrope walker, the one being supported by the others, had slipped and now gripped the bar with one hand, dangling and jostling against the rope. The walker behind him tried to offer a hand but was too far out of reach, kept at a distance by the bar he shouldered. Unable to assist him, his partners focused on trying to stay balanced as the rope swayed and jiggled. The walker in peril tried to catch at the rope with his legs, but that caused them all to shake more violently. He tried to grasp the bar with both hands to pull himself up, but it wouldn't work. If he could not stabilize himself, all three were at risk of plummeting. As he continued to struggle, the clouds that had been drifting randomly over the building all morning broke, releasing a wash of light that blinded the upturned audience. There was no way to see what was happening to the tightrope walker right then—no way to know whether he inched closer to safety. Only sound conveyed the truth: a woman's high-pitched scream and an awful, dull thud revealed his fate.

The chaos afterward was horrible. The crowd scurried in contradictory directions with people colliding and stumbling, children crying. Someone barreled into Honoria, as she tried to make her way toward the fallen performer. The impact nearly knocked her down, but Lord Devin caught her awkwardly.

"Honoria, what are you doing? We must get out of this crush!"

"That man needs help!"

"I am sure his people are helping him!"

"More hands make light work," she was fairly yelling now over the crowd.

"Do you have any medical experience? If not, you will only be in the way. You are endangering yourself, not helping. We must get to safety. And we need to get my mother out of here." With that, he lifted her by the waist and carried her, struggling like a wild cat in a sack, along with the escaping crowd until he could veer into a quiet alcove. So many people had rushed into the hallway to see what the fuss was about, while the people already in the transept were stampeding out, that some exhibits were nearly empty.

The moment he let her down, she moved to return to the crowd, but he held her arm steadfastly.

"You don't have the self-preservation instinct God gave a goose," he said impatiently.

Abruptly, she turned on him and swung her reticule at him hard. But the weight in her hand felt terribly wrong.

"Oh, my God! Oh, God!" She began scanning the floor frantically. There was no sign of anything.

"What is it? What's wrong?"

"My reticule! Look, it's been cut! Everything is gone."

He examined the purse. The bottom had been slashed from end to end, and now the purse gaped open, empty.

"What are you missing?" Lady Devin was at her side immediately.

He watched her mentally list her belongings, her head nodding as her fingers counted off items. Then her eyes opened wide and she said, "My keys! Oh, no, my keys to the shop are gone." He watched in fascination as she talked herself calm. "The thief can't possibly know where I live. I carried nothing today with my name or address on it. The fan and the mirror could fetch some coin, but the keys will be useless. Won't they?"

Lord Devin stilled. Could this be more than a common pickpocket? Could this be the work of Withersby and his lot? Did Withersby have other crews on this job? If so, then someone was currently on his way to the shop with the keys and nefarious intent.

"Mrs. Duchamp, I have a presentiment that we should get back to Evans Books and see it secure. If you wish to see more of the Exhibition, I can gladly escort you another day, but I think it is best if we return you immediately."

His words did not have a calming effect. She began looking around like a cornered animal seeking even the smallest avenue of escape. When she took his proffered arm, she ceded control and allowed him to part the crowd with his imposing presence and furious energy. He couldn't have erased the scowl from his face if God himself ordered it. Once outside, Lady Devin came round and put an arm over her shoulders. "It will be all right, dear."

He hoped his mother would be proven correct, but he had serious doubts.

Chapter Eight

Evans Principle 8: Sometimes dips in productivity can't be avoided. Accept it. Dust yourself off. Start fresh with the new dawn.

It would most certainly not be all right. Not a chance. Any hope Lord Devin had that the loss of Honoria's keys was random misfortune died a sharp and stabbing death as the coach pulled to a halt in front of the shop. As he disembarked, he gave directions for the coach to take his mother home and see her safe, and then for his driver to fetch the police. He handed Honoria out of the coach and stood with her for a moment, silently assessing what they could see from the pavement in the fading light of day.

The double doors hung open with only the first few feet of the interior visible. Through the large front windows, some panes of which had been smashed, he could see emptied shelves, battered fixtures, and shredded volumes. Walking into the store ahead of her, he attempted to shield her from the full impact of the destruction. The perpetrators had moved quickly. From the moment they (there must be more than one, considering the widespread devastation) took possession of her keys, they must have raced at top speed to the shop. More than half the shelves were emptied onto the floor, mixing with random torn pages and shredded pamphlets. An acrid odor wafted up from some damp areas, and he didn't want to surmise the liquid source. The sales counter had been chopped up. He was impressed by Honoria's composure; each new devastation showed on her face, but she continued on to survey the wreckage, without a tear or even a gasp.

The building was silent, a small blessing that suggested the culprits were gone. Unable to convince her to remain outside, he made sure Honoria stayed close behind him as they searched the premises, and he was the one to move first into the back room.

The printing press was destroyed. Not only had it been dismantled, but large pieces had been pounded against each other to warp them beyond repair. Twisted, mangled, strewn across the scarred floor. And here was more concrete evidence of human waste than just damp odor. What animals. At least they hadn't set the place ablaze. Could this really be Withersby's men? He knew Withersby used unsavory characters on occasion, but this seemed extreme even for them.

"Jupiter! Janus!" she called, before he could motion her to silence. He wanted to be sure the house was empty.

In the darkening of twilight, he lit some candles so they could check the upstairs. Once he confirmed the upper floors were empty of intruders, she went right to her wardrobe, picking her way carefully through broken glass and porcelain. The scent of lilies was overwhelming. One of the wardrobe doors hung off a broken hinge; as she pushed it carefully aside, she gasped and knelt. From what he could see, the interior was as desecrated as the rest of the building. Urgently, she tossed great handfuls of clothing that had been piled on the bottom of the wardrobe until she revealed a low drawer, one that had been taken out and smashed.

"It's gone," she said, incredulous. He could barely hear her.

"What is it, Mrs. Duchamp? What's missing?"

When she looked up, tears welled in her eyes. Her voice quivered as she said, "My father's signet. I don't know how they knew where to find it. Out of all this"—she waved her arms wildly—"that ring was the only thing of actual value to me. Now it's gone."

"We will find it. I promise you, I will get it back for you." He had no idea how he would accomplish this, and she didn't believe him anyway.

"Don't trouble yourself. It's impossible." He hated the tears streaming silently down her cheeks and leaving dark trails on her skirt. More than that, he hated the resignation in her voice, in her slumped form.

"I will have agents monitor the local pawnshops and jewelers. Whoever took it will seek to profit from it, count on that."

"You are too kind," she said, but her voice sounded empty.

She stood slowly and opened a closet.

The sudden flurry of motion caught him, shocked him, and he froze. A curse escaped him as he realized he'd let his guard down, assumed they'd searched everywhere and the intruders were gone. *Bloody idiot*, he thought, as he stared at the dirty blade now being held against Honoria's throat. He swore to himself that if this scum hurt her in the slightest, he would tear the vermin limb from limb with his bare hands.

He quickly assessed the assailant. Approximately six feet tall, judging by how the doorway framed him. The thug's face and hair were darkened, perhaps with coal dust or ash, to mask his features, but he might be able to recognize the man by the contours of his face ...and by his eyes. Dark, vicious eyes. Alex stood motionless, tense—if he had to let that scum go to prevent Honoria from being harmed, he would. But justice would be meted out eventually.

The hand holding the knife didn't waver. Good. He could reason with a calm, calculating criminal. Someone who felt panicked would be more likely to act impulsively and irrationally; desperation was more likely to result in bloodshed.

"Let her go," he said in a low voice.

The criminal's eyes moved back and forth between him and the door, gauging distance and speed, no doubt.

"Give me back my father's ring!" Honoria blurted. Loudly.

A dark laugh rumbled through the room.

"Sorry, lovey. I ain't got it. My buddy found it first. Long gone, he is."

"Let. Her. Go."

"No, my good sir," came the mocking response in an exaggerated affectation. "I don't believe I shall. I quite like this little lovey in my arms just now."

"If you hurt her, I will kill you," he said, never more sure of a statement in his entire life.

"If I choose to hurt her, you can't do a thing about it, man." The knifepoint bit slightly into Honoria's neck, close to her ear. She whimpered, and the anger in her eyes abruptly turned to fear.

"Release her, and we will let you walk out freely."

"I could just as easily kill you both and walk out freely anyway."

"Perhaps you didn't hear me just now. If you hurt her, I will end you. If I have to rip you apart with my bare hands and with my last dying breath. . . . Harm her in the slightest, and you will never leave this room. Just release her and go."

Just when he thought the intruder was convinced, the man shifted his stance. Honoria gasped and her eyes went wide. Then the man's free hand moved. That's when Alex finally understood what was happening. The hand, that disgusting paw, slipped down her body, stopping briefly to squeeze her breast hard through her clothing, hard enough to bring tears to her eyes, and then moving down lower, unspeakably lower. Honoria closed her eyes and seemed to curl inward visually at the awful intrusion.

"I was promised things, I'll tell ya. Aside from the ring, there wasn't anything worth stealing. Had some fun downstairs but not worth the trouble. I could use some real entertainment tonight."

"Get your hands off of her!"

"I've just had a promising thought." The cur lowered his mouth to Honoria's ear, although he still spoke loud enough to be heard across the room. "I think it's time to lock ol' spoilsport over there in this closet and . . . have ourselves a little party." With the knife digging into the other side of her neck, Honoria couldn't move as he ran his tongue along her ear—a tongue that Alex vowed to cut out at the first possible opportunity.

Honoria looked directly at Alex then, and her eyes went hard. She wasn't going to allow this to continue, but he couldn't tell what course of action she would take. All he could do was be ready to strike.

She visibly relaxed against her attacker, whose response was immediate.

"Oh, so it's like that, is it?" A sinister chuckle. "I'd heard widows were easy sport. Mayhap you have a taste for the danger . . . or for the dirt." The knife lifted away from her neck slightly as the other hand roamed her body again. A hand that would be bloodied and ideally dismembered very, very soon.

"Let me turn around," she said quietly, her hands light on his restraining arm.

"Your man over there ain't too happy about this." The man under discussion was working hard to stifle a growl in his throat and tuck his clenched fists against his thighs.

"He's not my man. I barely know him."

"Don't seem that way right now. He can't be very good if you're so willing to whore yourself so easily." Her eyes closed, as if steeling herself against the thought. Surely she didn't really mean to go through with it! Surely she would move to escape him soon.

"I said I barely know him. Now may I turn around or not?"

"Eager, eh? That's nice. But we'd better figure out what to do about that one first. He sure objects to our plans. In the closet, I think."

"You could just let him go. We won't be needing him."

"I'm not so stupid, lovey. I let him go, and I'll as like find him bashing my head in while I'm bashing your—"

She'd spun in his arms and covered his mouth with her hand. She rubbed up against him. It was a sickening sight. But she'd captured his attention fully, if only for a moment.

Alex took that moment to move in front of the dresser and grab a candlestick. He only had his eyes off the couple for a moment, but he heard metal clatter to the floor. Suddenly the attacker was doubled over, moaning, hands between his legs, and Honoria was kicking the knife away from his grasp. Handicapped as he was, the filthy dog still managed to trip Honoria as she tried to rush away from him. Alex's vision went red as he rushed forward and swung the candlestick hard. The man slumped unconscious, and Honoria scrambled away toward the door, sobbing.

He ran to her, quickly scanned her to make sure she wasn't bleeding or injured, and held her for a moment. Then he ripped off his cravat to tie the intruder's hands behind his back. He could still see the man's chest rising and falling, and he couldn't guess when or if consciousness would return. Better to take precautions. Then he guided Honoria downstairs and they waited for the police.

Chapter Nine

Evans Principle 9: Accept help when it is offered with a sincere heart. Accept it, but don't become dependent on it.

"You will be safe here. In the morning, we can go to the police station to follow up on the investigation." It was well after two A.M. by the time they'd given their statements to the police, who performed a quick survey of the damages and promised a thorough investigation in daylight. "In the meantime, you know you cannot stay here tonight," Devin had said. "Your locks will need to be changed, windows repaired, and I am not at all convinced that these criminals are done with you. Do you have somewhere else to go?"

Her silence had been answer enough. She'd given Minnie and Erich the day off. They would not return until tomorrow, and she could not bring herself to impose upon them in their tiny apartment. She was unable to convince Alex that she would be safe alone, that barring the upper floors would be sufficient. In the end, he had offered to see her settled in his mother's keeping and then depart for his own apartments for her comfort.

And so here she was again at Devin House.

Lady Devin ... Rose ... was so kind. Visibly drained from hours of waiting and worrying, the viscountess retired soon after their arrival but not until she'd made clear Honoria was welcome to stay as long as she wanted and was to have full and open access to the house—to treat it as her own. And Rose meant it. Honoria was struck anew by her genuine concern and hospitality. She owed this woman so much.

Yet here on the brink, in the front hall, she couldn't quite imagine how she'd gather the audacity to make her way through this house, a palace compared with the plebeian home she inhabited. Having seen some of the upstairs during her previous visit made it even worse. She knew exactly how out of place she was here. A maid stood a few feet away, as ordered, waiting to show her to her room. She just couldn't take that first step, an alien in this opulent, foreign land.

"I thank you, Lord Devin," she said. "I am convinced that your intervention adds gravitas to the investigation. The police have much to do, and the officer who took my statement while you were upstairs was, shall we say, less than diligent before you appeared." She was silent for a moment, thoughtful. "Funny how you have entered my life at a time when I have the greatest need of you."

"Funny," he echoed in a tone she could not identify. "Would you like to sit for a moment? Perhaps a drink?"

"Yes, please God, yes." A small measure of relief crept into her. The drawing room she recognized. Something as normal as a drink she could manage. And she certainly needed a drink.

He nodded to the maid, who retreated to the back of the house, and then he led her not into the drawing room but to the library. He bade her to sit and then, from behind yet another false panel, he poured two tumblers of brandy. She almost asked for whiskey. They sat in silence, a silence that gave her the space to think about her losses, to decipher the dark emotions crowding in on her from the moment she'd seen the shop's front doors ajar. She appreciated that he didn't push her to talk or to think, just paved the way.

"The bookstore has been my safe house for as long as I can remember. Even as the locale went into decline," she said finally. "It was all I had. It was my stronghold and oasis, my den and my escape. Did you see how systematically the shelves were ruined? Everything was laid to waste. And Jupiter and Janus ... I have no idea where they've gone." She couldn't bring herself to give voice to what had happened upstairs. She couldn't even think about it.

He nodded and replied, "It must have taken quite a crew to do so much in such a short time."

She considered that and shuddered at the thought of a gang systematically working its way through her refuge, through her most private things. Somehow the image was even more disturbing than the notion of a single random intruder, even the single disgusting intruder they'd encountered. She pictured a gang exactly like him and wanted to cry.

"Mrs. Duchamp." He interrupted her churning thoughts. "I would in no way question your business dealings, but even honest merchants have enemies. Is there someone who would wish you harm? Is there any reason you can think of for someone to target your shop?"

"No. No one. I've never had any complaints from customers. No rivals to speak of."

"What about the political tracts you print and distribute? Has anyone ever objected or challenged you over them? The printing press, all the print jobs in the back, the destruction of the press implies that someone wanted to stop those activities."

She thought of the broken, unusable press and of the stacks of handbills she'd found, soaked in solvent, an illegible mess of pulp.

"Customers who don't want them simply don't take them. Such things are just as easily found in local churches. I suppose a client or two has frowned upon them, but no reaction so severe as to suggest this. . . ." She trailed off as she remembered her most recent foray in Haymarket.

"Nonetheless, tomorrow, after we talk with the police, you should contact those anonymous authors to warn them of what's happened."

"That will be easy to do."

He looked at her for a long moment, and she realized she may have said too much.

"What?" he asked.

"I—I'm sure it does not signify. A month or so ago, I noticed a child being followed by some shady fellows in Haymarket and made a bit of a fuss with the local police. It came to nothing." She moved on, deflecting his keen attention. "I think perhaps I'm more upset about the devastation of the store than the burglary of my home upstairs, except for my father's ring. A part of me has been destroyed with the devastation of the store. The shop is my life. Some of the books have been my closest friends, my talismans, for years."

"The store can be rebuilt, the building made more secure. Your sense of security has been shaken, but you will feel safe again. And you are completely safe now, here."

"Thank you, my lord." She looked at him for a long moment in return, adding and subtracting values behind her eyes. "You're already so kind to me, coming to my immediate aid with all deftness and surety. I envy your self-possession."

"I think, under the circumstances, we might do away with formalities. Call me Alexander, or Alex if you prefer. You should get rest. Daisy shall show you to your room."

"Alexander," she said slowly, "thank you. You are welcome to do the same." She hesitated, then added quietly, "My father called me Nora." She nodded without purpose and rose to leave. She looked at him, uncertain, and gestured to her attire. "I fear I am . . . I have nothing with me."

"Daisy has been instructed to provide anything you need."

Simple. Authoritative. Everything was taken care of. She had nothing to fear. If anything, she had more available to her at this moment than she ever did in her normal life. Yet her anxiety and alarm and grief remained unabated.

He forced himself to stay in the library, to separate himself from her, as much as every fiber of his being wanted to stay at her side, to watch over her every moment. Her drawn face, her stooped shoulders, everything about her indicated she needed privacy and time to herself. And sleep, definitely sleep. In turn, he needed to work out the events of the day. But she was shaken, as much by the animal's hands on her as by the destruction done to her shop, and he wanted to save her, to erase the awful memory for her.

She knew as well as he did that the break-in was a premeditated act. Whoever stole her keys knew who she was and approximately how long it would take for her to return. With the timing of a military strike, the burglars also knew exactly how to hit her in her most vulnerable spots—the press, the locked cabinets filled with handbills, her father's signet. He hadn't told Withersby about the locked cabinet, and he hadn't even known about the ring. So someone else close to Honoria must be passing information . . . perhaps to Withersby . . . perhaps to some unknown menace.

God, the horror on her face as she'd absorbed the rank and twisted remnants of the printing press, the frenzy with which she'd dug for the ring. At first, he feared she'd go hysterical. But he should have known better. As upset as she was, she never lost control, never lost her quiet air of determination and resolve, not even when she was terrified upstairs. He finished his second brandy in a single gulp. Recalling her anguish, he wanted to run up the stairs and just hold her, hold tight and never let her go. Protect her, erase those terrors from her mind. Cherish her.

He waited through one more glass of brandy, suppressing his own overwrought emotions. He waited until he was certain no one else in the house stirred. When he finally decided he was calm enough to sleep, he slowly made his way upstairs. He walked quietly along the second-floor hallway; guests were always put on the second floor to give them discreet privacy and distance from his usual room on the third floor and his mother's on the fourth. Hearing nothing, he was reassured that Honoria had managed to fall asleep. She would need rest to fortify her for the work ahead.

When he reached the third floor, candlelight spilled out from under the door next to his room. He frowned. Surely, Mother wouldn't have put a guest—wouldn't have put *her*—in the room next to his. The quiet rustling he heard prompted him to knock gently.

"Are the accommodations sufficient? Do you need anything?" he asked when she opened the door a few inches. "You seemed distraught downstairs."

"Do you know that you have a tendency to ask multiple questions at once?" She smiled, a tiny, fragile twist of her lips. "It can be difficult to figure out what to respond to first."

"My apologies." He returned her smile. "Allow me to rephrase. Are you all right, Nora?"

"I am fine," she said, even as her voice shook. When he nodded and turned to go, she moved swiftly. The door opened wider, and she touched his arm. "No, wait!" She shook her head and then the rest of her body started quivering uncontrollably. "I don't know if I can take this. I'm at my wit's end."

He stepped into the room and pushed the door nearly closed.

"It is a shock, but you will survive it. You are a strong woman and will recover quickly. Of that, I have no doubts."

Still, she couldn't stop shaking, and she didn't respond. She covered her face with both hands, her borrowed robe rippling everywhere, continuously, uncontrollably. So he did what his instinct had called for earlier. He wrapped his arms around her and held her tightly. She leaned into him, her hands still covering her face, and she wept.

The candle on the dresser melted lower and lower as they stood there. He held on as long as she needed. Slowly, very slowly, the shuddering ceased, and her breathing became less labored.

"Alex, I have not been completely honest about my printings."

He continued to hold her, but his brain whirred. She'd called him *Alex . . .* and she spoke of *her* printings.

"What about them?"

"Some of them are more controversial than others. And I have been investigating some terribly upsetting situations involving children. I suspect the perpetrators have discovered my inquiries."

"Children? Like the children you mentioned at dinner? What have you found?"

"Oh, it's so much worse. It's horrible. It's evil."

He sat her on the bed and went to pour them both a drink. He brought it to her and then pulled a chair next to the bed.

"Tell me."

She closed her eyes and shook her head, but then she took a sip of wine and began to speak.

"I have reason to believe destitute children are being sold for their bodies, short and long term, and used for lewd photographs, also sold for profit. I believe there's a rather large organization running this horrifying enterprise."

He leaned forward, waiting for her to open her eyes. When she did, she looked at him hesitantly. He took her hand to reassure her and asked, "How do you know this?"

"It's a rather long and winding story. I'm not sure how much I can impart tonight without making a total hash of it and sounding mad."

"Whatever you can tell me might aid in the investigation."

She stood and started pacing. She'd gone back and forth across the room twice before she spoke.

"As I said, I was in Haymarket and a young girl caught my attention. She was unkempt and alone, and yet she had a strange air about her, watchful and too . . . still. With such unsavory characters lurking in that area, I worried for her safety so I watched her for a while."

"How long is a while?"

Her pacing had shifted direction multiple times. At this point, she faced a window, her candlelit reflection wavering slightly against the darkness beyond. Her eyes met his reflected in the glass.

"Five hours."

"Did no one notice you watching a strange child for five hours?"

Again, she paced . . . to the dresser, to the entry, to the closet, to the window, aimlessly.

"Sometime I sat and pretended to write or draw. At one point, I had tea, and oh, how I wished I could call her over and give her a crumpet or some morsel. And she didn't spend all five hours by the peddlers. I ended up following her."

"I begin to think you just might be mad, Nora. What did you see in all that time?"

"I'm sure she went to Haymarket alone. I saw no adults in her company when I first noticed her, nor for the first three hours. But then two men approached her. Two gentlemen, by their attire, although I never saw their faces. They spoke with her for a few moments. I remember she nodded and then curtseyed prettily to each of them. When she walked away, they didn't accompany her, but they followed a few yards behind."

"That is not conclusive of anything."

"I know that. Of course I know that." She leaned her head against a bedpost. "But the girl would occasionally glance back, as if confirming they were still behind her. If they were slowed at a crossing by traffic, she would wait while maintaining a constant distance from them. She drew them. She didn't seem frightened or suspicious. It felt . . . wrong." She stopped pacing. Instead, she sank down to sit on the mattress, appearing deflated.

"Can you tell me more, Nora? If you can't, it can wait until morning, but this may be significant to report to the constable."

"I will tell you this. She arrived at a nondescript corner town house with all the shades drawn. She let herself in through a servant entrance, and the men went to the front door. From what I could tell, a lavishly dressed woman met them, kissed them both, and ushered them in. I overheard them introduce themselves, and one said he was impatient to see more of the merchandise."

"What makes you think anything untoward happened there? What you describe could have a plausible and entirely innocent explanation."

"It was the girl. She didn't have the look of innocence. I feel in my bones she was not safe there. I tried to sneak into the house—"

"You didn't!"

"I had to try! I could hear muffled sounds from the lower windows, but every possible entry was locked tight."

"You almost broke into a mysterious house because of a feeling?"

She pulled herself up, straightened her spine, and looked him full in the face.

"Yes," she said. "And it was the right thing to do."

He could only shake his head slightly. The day's harrowing events, followed by this insight into her activities, would need a clear head to parse out. And she needed rest.

"I have kept you too long. How thoughtless of me. Please, get some rest and we shall talk more in the morning." He made to leave, but, as he reached the door, she whispered. He almost didn't hear her—except that his entire being was keenly attuned to her every breath.

"Alex," she said timidly, "may I request something of you?" She slowly walked toward him, hesitant as a fawn. Yet, when she reached him, she continued full into him, putting her arms around his shoulders. His arms rose to embrace her of their own volition.

"Anything."

She took a deep breath that stretched his arms but didn't loosen his hold.

"I feel adrift. Lost in the wilderness," she explained. He nodded, and she continued. "Could you, that is, would you please stay with me tonight?" She looked at him, beseeching, visibly swallowing her pride. At his look of surprise, she hastened to add, "Not for . . . *that.* God, not for that. Just . . . for companionship. I'm . . . I'm afraid to be alone tonight. I keep going over what happened in my head, and I just need not to be alone with it."

"Of course, my dear. If you wish, I will sit by your bedside and keep the watch all night."

"I do appreciate your thoughtfulness and propriety, but I was hoping for something more concrete, more of an anchor. All right, I'll spell it out—would you lie with me, just lie by my side, just to sleep? Just so I know I'm not alone?"

"Well . . ." He elongated the word. "You have but to command me, Nora, but I must point out some potential pitfalls in your request. As I said, my servants are discreet, but tongues might wag more loosely if we are found abed together, even fully clothed, than if I am chastely seated as your guard." His attempt to lighten her mood was met with another fragile almost-smile.

"We both know the reputation of a widow is tenuous at best. What do I care if false rumors circulate about my private life?"

"If we were caught, the rumors wouldn't really be false, now would they? And, anyway, more to the point, our prior experience suggests to me that my self-control suffers in your presence." At this, he grinned at her broadly, openly. "Frankly, I cannot guarantee we could share a bed without . . . *that*."

She returned his grin with a chuckle and a gentle, genuine smile of her own.

"At least you're honest. I do believe I will take my chances." Despite her lightness, her confidence in his honor made his chest swell ever so slightly. Her smile waned, though, as she added in a tiny halting voice, "I'm . . . afraid."

How could he possibly refuse? Already, he felt deep in his gut that he didn't have the power to refuse her anything.

"Consider yourself fairly warned. I will do my utmost to lie next to you, chaste as a monk." At her sigh of relief, he added, "You are the very devil of a temptress, you know?"

Without a trace of humor, she met his eyes.

"I promise I will ask for nothing. I will do nothing to tempt or inflame you."

As if she needed to do anything other than be within arm's reach to inflame him. But he would never allow himself to take advantage of her under such conditions. It would be unconscionably crude. She needed security and tenderness and companionship. And companionship was exactly what he would provide. He released her with the promise to return momentarily after his evening toilette. When he did, he was still fully clothed in his shirt and trousers. She had tucked herself into bed, covered entirely by the counterpane. He blew out the candle on the dresser and lay down on top of the bedclothes, careful not to touch her.

"Thank you," she whispered.

"Anything for you, Nora. Anything you need."

Chapter Ten

Evans Principle 2: Yes, again! It's that important! Opportunities, girl, opportunities!

She'd never slept in such luxury, not even as the child of a baronet. The linens, the fancy nightdress, the soft mattress, the bed stand itself of thick, carved mahogany, all of it orchestrated to lull its occupant into the embrace of Morpheus.

Except she couldn't sleep.

Perhaps it was the clothing, fine as it was. The rooms above the shop could get devilishly hot during London summers, and so she'd become accustomed years ago to sleeping naked when the weather turned warm. She certainly wasn't accustomed to sleeping fully clothed under heavy blankets. Nearly claustrophobic from all the layers encasing her, she lay still but tense. Pushing aside the edge of the blankets for more air didn't help.

She listened to her breathing, and his. She stared up at the canopy over the bed, trying to count the lines of draping in the dark. But her mind couldn't lull her skin. Her body grew keenly aware of the heat of his body next to hers. And it vividly remembered the feel of him. Her body clamored for attention, even as her mind tried to distance

itself. Every time a wave of nausea washed over her at the thought of
that other offensive touch, she remembered the pleasure, the sensual-
ity of Alex's hands and mouth on her as an antidote. A dull throb
started in her lower belly and made her entire body tense; it grew so
strong that it blanketed her mind, silencing all reason. Some dim part
of her brain recognized that this too was a traumatic reaction, an attempt to block out her troubles. But the tiny voice of reason couldn't
overpower the rest of her.

"What are you thinking about, Nora?" His voice, low and husky,
startled her. She thought he'd fallen asleep long ago. He couldn't read
her thoughts, could he?

"I don't know. I can't sleep."

He leaned closer, without touching her, and whispered in her ear,
"It's all right. Everything will be better tomorrow. I will do everything in my power to help you get the store back in order."

She smiled at his reassurances, amused that he thought she was
preoccupied about the store. So much for reading her mind. She
thought, dimly, she should be more concerned about the shop, but
she wasn't. And, all at once, she realized she didn't want him to think
of her as a delicate flower to protect. She wanted to fascinate him
once more.

She got out of bed. He sat up quickly.

"Nora, where are you going? What's wrong?"

"Nowhere. Nothing."

"Then what on earth are you doing?"

"You'll see soon enough." With that, she pulled the pins out of her
hair and shook it loose around her. Then she gathered the borrowed
nightgown and pulled it over her head. She shifted toward the bed
and stood there, suddenly hesitant.

"What was that?"

She smirked to herself. Of course, he couldn't see her in the dark.
He must be able to discern the rustling to some degree though.

"These clothes are suffocating me," she replied. She slipped onto
the bed against him and heard his sharp intake of breath when her
bare skin slid along his hand.

"You promised you wouldn't tempt me." She heard bewildered
amusement in his voice.

"I know, but it seems my inhibitions have run away from me." She
pulled his mouth to hers firmly. She kissed him, fully, without reser-

vation, opening her mouth to him and tasting his lips. He pulled his head away, but she moved forward to close the distance again. Her body pressed against his, the rough fabric of his clothing sending little jolts along her skin. Here in the darkness, all the heightened emotions of the day concentrated into this whirlwind of sensations. Just for this moment, she wanted to drown out all her cares, silence her mind's accounting and planning, and simply feel.

He gently broke contact with her lips. As he put his hands on her bare shoulders, she felt the groan he tried to suppress. He held her at a distance.

"Nora, we cannot do this. You have been through an extremely taxing experience. You do not know what you are doing."

"On the contrary, Alex." She punctuated her words with kisses wherever her lips could reach. "I know exactly what I'm doing. Anything I need, you said. Right now, this is what I need. I need to be in your arms. I need to feel your lips on me. I need you."

He slid away from her, gently lowering her to the bed before stepping away. The resulting chill was as much emotional as physical. His rejection stabbed at her far more than she ever would have expected. She knew there could be nothing lasting between them, but their previous encounters convinced her that he at least desired her. He'd said as much. Granted, she had so little experience with men, but was it possible she'd read him so wrongly? Was he just cavalierly toying with her affection?

"It would be dastardly of me to take advantage of you in this state, Nora." His low voice carried across the room, likely from the vicinity of the door.

As she squeezed her eyes tightly shut, hot tears flooded them. All the turmoil and horror of the day slammed into her, and it was all she could do to suppress her sobs as tears rolled down her face. Then she heard the muffled sound of furniture sliding along the carpet.

"I promised you I would stay with you this night," he said from close by. She looked up to find he'd moved an armchair from the seating area to just between the dresser and the bed. "And I will do exactly that. I will keep watch over you and keep you safe. Even from our own wicked ways." She couldn't see in the dim light, but she was sure he winked, sure she could hear his eyelashes brush his cheek, even as she ridiculed herself for such an impossible observation.

"Protecting me even from myself," she said idly as exhaustion took her. "A true gentleman." As she drifted to sleep, she thought she heard a soft, low lullaby.

She woke screaming, suffocating, tearing at the hands that imprisoned her and kicking with all her might. Shaking violently, she curled her body up against the headboard and stared around the room. It took her a few moments to realize she was awake and the horror she'd been experiencing was just a dream. The room brightened as Alex—oh, thank God, Alex—lit a candle, dispersing the dark and ominous shadows. She couldn't control the shaking, though.

Standing a few feet away, he eyed her cautiously, as if reluctant to come any closer. It took a long time for her to find her voice. Meanwhile he simply stood guard by her, without touching her, without speaking.

"I was dreaming."

He nodded. She thought she detected pity in his eyes and resolved not to look at him.

"It was . . . that man. I was back in my bedroom, opening the closet door, and he—" Every word made the memory real, made her skin crawl with the feel of the man's hands . . . and his knife. "Only this time," she choked out, "this time you weren't there. He . . . used me. He hurt me. And fighting back as I had in reality only made him crueler. I still see his eyes just before I hit him with my knee. There was limitless cruelty in those eyes. I thought he was . . . no good . . . but when I saw his eyes, the depth of his evil shocked me." Her breaths were still ragged and too quick. "I still feel his hands on me, and it makes me want to flay myself alive. I . . . God help me . . . when he touched me, my body responded. Even in terror, I felt my chest . . . tense. I can't. How could I . . . ?" She looked at him, helpless, still shaking, "What is wrong with me?"

He slowly moved toward the bed, his voice low and steady, as if trying not to startle a cat. "There is nothing wrong with you. The body reacts to extreme danger in unpredictable ways. What you experienced was not pleasure." He gestured as he reached the bed, asking, "May I sit next to you?"

She nodded exaggeratedly, unsure if a nod could otherwise be distinguished from the uncontrollable vibrations of her body. And she reached out a frantic hand to him. To her immense relief, he clasped her hand in his and sat close to her, though not close enough for his body to touch hers. At the feel of his large, warm hand enveloping hers, her shaking eased to less violent tremors. She put her body full against his, and without releasing her hand, his other arm wrapped around her tight to calm her, to secure her. It was heaven. It was torture. But now that he held her, she never wanted him to let go. Nothing mattered but that he was here, filling her senses with his touch, his voice, his scent.

"Alex . . . I want . . . I need . . ." She couldn't seem to speak her mind, this woman who was never at a loss for words.

"What is it you need, darling? Whatever you ask, I would not hesitate to fulfill your wishes." His embracing arm began to rub her back gently.

"I don't know how to ask . . . I don't know what to ask!"

"Try. What are you thinking?"

"That man. The dream. I can't stand it. I want a better memory to replace it with."

He stilled.

"When you and I . . . in the library at dinner . . ." she began haltingly.

"When we kissed?"

She burrowed her face into his shoulder and nodded. Her words became muffled.

"Yes. When we kissed. That was indescribably wonderful. I want that . . . to banish the other sensations. I want . . . pleasure . . . to replace the fear and revulsion."

Still, he didn't move.

"I won't ask you to do anything you don't want to do, Alex," She lifted her head to face him. "Perhaps just a kiss. We don't have to do anything more, if you don't want to. Please, I need you."

He had to laugh. She turned his words neatly against him. Even as the supplicant in this situation, she'd placed him in the role of seduced rather than seducer.

"As you wish." His lips captured hers, his tongue teasing the seam to open for him. And when her mouth responded in kind, he deepened the kiss, delving into her, licking and nibbling and tasting. She couldn't control the tiny whimpers that escaped her, nor could she stop her body from undulating against him. Her need expanded exponentially. It engulfed her, drowning all inhibitions.

His mouth left hers and slowly, so slowly, meandered down her throat and along her collarbone, not assuaging her body's needs in the slightest. One of her hands wove through his hair and nudged him toward her breast, and she moaned and whimpered as his tongue danced along her skin but refused to address the spots clamoring most insistently for his touch. When his lips finally brushed across her peaks—one then the other, just barely touching, she was momentarily embarrassed by her own indecipherable whine.

"God in heaven, please!" Had she really said that aloud?

Only then did he encircle one nipple with his mouth. The exquisite sensations, sharp and electrifying, shot from her scalp to her toes. Back and forth, he lavished attention on her breasts equally, his hands stroking them, shaping them for more effective access. Muscles throughout her body contracted as her back arched toward the source of these unbearably intense jolts of pleasure. The harder he sucked, the more keenly she felt the tension coil and build inside her.

When she cried out at a tiny peak of pleasure, his hands began to roam more freely.

"More," she demanded.

He rolled onto his back, taking her with him, and stroked down her back, down her buttocks, until he slid one of her thighs up against him, leaving her womanly folds open to exploration. And explore he did, first stroking her firmly, knowingly.

"More," she cried as she kissed him hard, trying to mimic the depth of his kisses.

Her body still wanted more. She felt the hot hardness of him through his clothes, glancing against the area made so sensitive by his fingers. She reached down and unerringly grasped him through the fabric. He groaned deep in his throat. Yes, that girth, that firmness was undoubtedly what she needed. When she began to undo his trousers, he quickly finished the job for her, practically ripping his own clothing off and tossing it all on the floor. Surely, that could give her relief from this dizzying spiral of sensations.

He nudged her thighs apart with his knees and raised himself on his arms above her, poised to enter her.

"Are you sure, Nora? Absolutely sure?" he asked, breathing hard. She felt pinned down by him as he looked intensely into her eyes.

"Yes!" she answered. "Please, yes!" She closed her eyes as she felt the energy of his whole body focus into the thrust of his hips.

She was all silken heat. Blinded by the darkness, he was awash with the sound and touch of her. *Please, I need you.* He could not deny her. He felt her, entirely bare and entirely open to him, so consumed and ready. God, but he wanted to fill her to the brim and drive her all the way to ecstasy.

"Are you sure, Nora? Absolutely sure?" he asked, amazed he could even speak. He stared into her eyes, desperate for confirmation that this was a deliberate, conscious decision. That she knew what she was asking of him. And when he heard her cry out, "Yes! Please, yes!" it was all he could do not to explode right then. Instead, he focused all his energy on what she wanted, what she needed. She was hot and wet and more than ready for him. And she needed release.

As he slid home in a single, swift stroke, he met and tore through surprising—shocking—resistance. Her body went rigid, her eyes flew wide open, and she screamed. He immediately withdrew, and her body folded in upon itself, away from him. Befuddled, he stared down at her, unseeing. His hand cupped her cheek, felt the hot tears that streaked the side of her face. *What the bloody hell? How could this be?* Then realization dawned.

"You . . ." he spoke slowly, quietly. "Are you . . . ? Were you . . . ? You had not—?" He took a steadying breath, his hand caressing her cheek. Finally he found the words.

"Your marriage was never consummated?"

She shook her head and then faced away from him.

How was this even possible? How could a man marry this woman and not want to be inside her at the first possible opportunity? Even if it had been a marriage of convenience, consummation was generally an understood requirement for the union to be binding. His mind whirled with questions, while his heart rooted itself to her obvious distress.

"I should have . . ." she stuttered. "I didn't mean to . . . it didn't occur to me . . ." She rolled away from him completely and curled her legs up. "I didn't know what would happen."

Still recovering himself from the shock, he leaned against her and wrapped his arms around her, dismayed by her stiffness, her defenses.

"I'm so sorry," he said. "I would have been . . . gentler. The first time doesn't have to be so painful, so difficult."

"It's my fault. I should have said. It's never been . . ."

He could still hear in her voice an effort to hold back sobs. He stroked her arm, still puzzled.

"I can tell you the pain is fleeting." *Gently, man.* He needed to re-assure her that this wasn't the way lovemaking worked. He felt sure that this moment could scar her irrevocably. "The act of love does get better. And, as you've already seen, that part of it is just one of many pleasurable activities." He continued to stroke her arm and then her back and her hair, without pressure, without intent.

Faced with her sphinxlike silence, he said in a low voice, "Come, now, you can't tell me you've never read the infamous *Fanny Hill*? You, of all people."

She laughed at that, briefly, but with the slightest tinge of bawdy. He liked to make her laugh. He wanted to hear her laugh more.

"No," she replied with a smile in her voice, "a respectable book-seller, much less a woman, couldn't possibly carry such a scandalous rag as that. I'd be run out of town. That's the kind of thing people go to Holywell Street to purchase. . . ." She trailed off, but he couldn't let her slip back into thoughts of the destroyed shop—or of what had just happened between them. "Why *Fanny Hill*?" she asked.

"Ah, well, there's a rather explicit deflowering scene that covers this sort of . . ." He trailed off before deflecting with "So you've never seen a copy?" He had to physically poke her side to get her to re-spond, which she did in a sly whisper.

"Well, I did encounter a small section of it once when I purchased some books from an estate. The deceased must have had unusual tastes because, when I arrived to sort through the library, several tomes were piled in the library fireplace, fully ablaze. At first, it seemed like such an awful desecration, to burn books so haphazardly, but then I spied a few pages on the floor that must have escaped. Turned out they were from that *Fanny Hill*. Outrageous stuff. A few random pages from other smut rags too. If that's what all those books were like, well, per-haps they weren't meant for many eyes."

"Do tell."

"The section I found only had to do with two women . . ." She trailed off, clearly embarrassed, but he would not let her go so easily.

"And?"

"One was, uh, seducing the other."

"And did that shock you?"

"Well, maybe a bit. I found myself more . . . confused."

"Why confused? That women could do such things to each other? That they would want to do such things together?"

"No, no, that seemed, in its own way, natural. I've read Sappho, after all. What I don't understand is why a man would care to write about such an experience that in no way involves him. Sappho wrote in revelry, in celebration, in love. What joy could the writer or his readers possibly get from it, except tawdry titillation?"

He laughed and kissed her shoulder. She stiffened in response, and he rested his head lightly at the crook of her neck. No pressure. No presumption.

"Titillation is mysterious. It can be rather satisfying. There are some commonalities, but there are also widely ranging idiosyncrasies."

"Then, assuming you've read *Fanny Hill*, which category do you think it would fall in among most readers? Common or idiosyncratic titillation?"

"It would depend on the reader, now, wouldn't it? So I suppose that means idiosyncratic." His voice turned firm. He got off the bed long enough to envelop her in the counterpane. "Rest now. You've had quite a day."

She must be completely exhausted, he thought, as she quickly fell into a deep sleep, one so heavy she snored lightly. He laughed softly at the sound of it, as he continued to stroke her hair.

He had never before deflowered a maiden, as people so quaintly put it. In fact, as he recalled some of his wild oats, he belatedly realized how scrupulous he'd been about this one condition. His sexual partners were always experienced, usually rather obviously so as they invited him to their inner chambers and displayed their skills. He'd counted on such worldliness; generally, it meant no expectations, no attachments, no responsibilities. But now, lying here at his side, was an indisputable bundle of responsibilities, soft and vulnerable responsibilities. Her livelihood was in ruins, and, unbeknownst to her, it was ultimately his fault and therefore his responsibility. He couldn't figure, though, how Mr. Withersby had known he'd taken her to the Exhibition. And then, there was her virtue, which he'd so crudely ripped from her. The evidence of her pain withered his desire. He was very much responsible for her traumatic loss of innocence, and he was responsible for rectification.

When he felt low but unmistakable stirrings of desire, he decided touching her, even just stroking her hair, was no longer wise. He rolled away from her and tried very, very hard not to be aware of her supple, voluptuous body next to his. It took him a long time indeed to find sleep.

Chapter Eleven

Evans Principle 11: Intuition and impulse are two very different things. Trust your intuition, but never act on impulse.

Sometime in the night, still dark, Honoria woke, intensely aware of her surroundings. Aware of the fine linen that chafed gently against her bare skin, so much bare skin. Oh. Right. Intensely aware of young Lord Devin's likewise naked and finely muscled body next to her. Oh. Right. Of what had transpired earlier in the darkness. Oh, God. It was almost too much to bear, the absurdity of this moment.

She should be worried for her reputation, she surmised, except that there couldn't possibly be anyone in the world anymore who cared a whit for her respectability. Even in youth, she'd been far from desirable marriage material once she transformed from the daughter of a baronet to the daughter of a merchant. As for her current reputation, one needed fundamentally to be seen in order to be viewed in a negative light. No one saw her. Not really. No one would notice if she became someone's mistress. No one, she realized, would notice if she disappeared or died. There might be the idle "I wonder what ever happened to . . ." And Erich would miss his earnings and need to find work; he might even spare her a moment's recollection as a kind employer. Minnie felt like family, but she and Erich had never been close. A few regular customers might cluck at the misfortune of the store's abrupt and mysterious closure. Her suppliers would note the interruption in transactions. But she doubted anyone would spend time speculating about what happened. And no one would put any effort into looking for her. If she dropped off the face of the earth this night, her absence wouldn't be noticed for weeks, if at all. No one would miss her. No one saw her.

The realization made her deeply, unbearably lonely. Despite herself, she wept into the plush, white pillow beneath her head, trying to be as quiet as dust.

Perhaps he heard a stray sob, or felt the bed shake ever so lightly as she wept, or maybe, just maybe, he subconsciously registered her deep well of sadness. Whatever the cause, she felt his arm tighten around her, which only made her sob harder. Soon she felt him shift and loom over her, propped on one arm.

"Nora, what's wrong?"

She'd embarrassed herself so much in his presence already that she couldn't stand to paint herself as the pitiable lonely old crone. She couldn't trust herself to speak at all.

"Are you still in pain?" he asked as he laid a gentle hand on her shoulder. "From . . . earlier?"

She rolled to her back, careful to hold the blanket tight to her chin, and shook her head. "No. The pain is gone."

"Is it the shop? I know the burglary is quite a shock. It's understandable, but those objects can be replaced. The shop can be renovated. You are safe, and that is the most important thing."

You are safe, and that is the most important thing.

His words shot so directly to the target of her sorrow that fresh tears sprang to her eyes. His hand stroked tears away from the corners of her eyes.

"It's just," she finally said, "been quite a day, as you said. Apparently, I am overwrought, and my mind runs away with me."

"What is it?"

She answered his question with one of her own.

"What do you see when you look at me? Truly?"

"I see a woman. An enchanting, forthright, beautiful woman."

"Such pretty words." She would have scoffed if she had the energy.

"You don't believe me?"

"It's too easy. That's the kind of thing you could say to any girl to make her moon-eyed. What do you see when you look *at me*?"

He left the bed and lit a fresh candle. A warm glow surrounded them, and when he sat on the edge of the bed, he appraised her slowly before speaking again.

"I see lustrous brown hair that you do not have the time or inclination to coiffure. I see deep brown eyes that dance when you laugh, which you do not do nearly often enough. I see that your shoulders are too frequently knotted from stress and work." Somewhere in his catalog, the tone of his voice shifted, as if he'd lost track of his original intent and gotten caught up in his own thoughts, deciphering some code or puzzle. He stroked her hair away from her face. "I see that you are fiercely independent and capable. But I also see that you keep your true self tucked away. You can converse competently with anyone on most subjects, but it takes an exorbitant amount of energy from you. I see that, as much as you want the life of a hermit, you are fundamentally heartsick, lonely for human companionship, even as you prevent others from trying to connect with you in meaningful ways."

She wanted to object, wanted to deny his claims. But the fact that he saw her so clearly took her breath away. He understood her. Whether he would care if she dropped off the face of the earth, she would deal with some other time. For this moment, he saw her. And she wanted to see herself through his eyes.

She reached for him and was confused when he resisted, statue-like.

"Regardless of what happened earlier, my promise to you still stands, Nora. If you say no, I will not touch you. You asked for companionship and comfort tonight, and all apparent evidence to the contrary"—he looked pointedly down at his body and hers—"I will not do anything that you don't expressly wish."

"Kiss me," she whispered, fierce and sure.

He leaned his face toward hers and kissed her lightly, like a butterfly alight. Her hands wrapped around his shoulders as she tried to pull him close.

"Don't tease," she said. "I said kiss me."

"Teasing can be just as enjoyable," he said as his lips trailed lightly down to the hollow in her neck. Still only his lips. His hands were braced on either side of her head, his body hovering above her.

"Damn it, man. I said kiss me." She tried to pull his head toward hers, but he wouldn't budge.

"Oh, but can't you see . . . that's exactly what I'm doing." He suddenly dipped his head to nip gently at her breasts, first one, then the other, back and forth, light as air. She moaned, and possibly squealed, as her body twisted and shook under his mouth.

"Oh, for God's sake!" Her patience at an end, she sat up to meet his mouth, her chest against his, not caring that she might as well try to move a mountain. And he did not disappoint her. With their mouths and bodies pressed hard together, she felt consumed in flames. Their tongues touched and slid and explored. Her fingers wove through his hair as she opened to him.

He pulled away from her slightly.

"You wished me to kiss you, and now I have. What else do you wish?"

"Touch me."

"Why?"

She huffed and said, "Because with you I feel alive, I feel real. Please . . . touch me."

"Tell me where."

She shook her head, shy and self-conscious.

"Shall I give you some options?" He placed his hand on her collarbone. "Here?"

"Lower." Her voice was tentative.

He slid his fingertips down the slope of her breast to the tip and hovered there, barely making contact. "Here?"

She arched toward him, but his hand followed the motion, keeping its distance. She shook her head.

"Are you sure?" His fingers brushed across her nipples again, and she shivered. But that was no longer enough.

"Lower." Her voice grew husky as her body vibrated with tension.

He smiled. His hand traced the underside of her breast and came to rest on her stomach. Her muscles contracted and undulated beneath his palm.

"Here?"

She shook her head vehemently.

"You know where! Please!"

Slowly, he slipped his hand lower, fingers questing, dipping into her dark, downy curls. She gasped. Gently, his fingers stroked her sensitive folds. She sighed and jerked. *Alive*, she said. Yes, every inch of her seemed alive, seemed to quiver at his touch. He found her sweet nub and increased the pressure of his massaging fingers. She writhed and moaned. Then one of his fingers found her, slipped into her hot, wet core to find a spot that made her cry out at the sudden intensity. He immobilized her with his body as his hand worked her. Her body bucked and twisted, yet he leaned into her and would not back down. His mouth covered hers to swallow her cries as he pushed her over the brink.

His hand gentled, and his mouth moved lower to lavish attention on a nipple, while her shudders subsided.

"Have I touched you to your satisfaction?" he asked eventually.

She pulled his mouth to hers again, whispering a quick "Yes" before she entangled her tongue with his. He lay his head down next to hers.

"Do you think perhaps you can sleep now, darling?"

"But—" She still clung to him, and then she used actions to replace words. Her hand slid down his arm to his hip. He sucked in his breath involuntarily. When her questing hand finally made its way to wrap around his throbbing member, it was his turn to tremble.

"Are there any other services I can provide for you, my darling?" His attempt at an offhand tone proved wobbly and unstable, at best. She laughed low in her throat.

"Yes," she said emphatically. "Love me."

She didn't care anymore that her voice broke, that it dripped with desperation, that she begged. "Love me," she said. Right then, it was all she wanted.

Despite the repeated waves of pleasure, her body still craved more, knew there had to be more, even if it involved pain. It wanted with a greed she didn't recognize and couldn't control. He paused above her, and she looked in his eyes, those soft green eyes, glittering at her like cut emeralds.

"I promise—I promise you," he said, "this will not hurt like last time. There is so much pleasure to be had beyond the pain."

She nodded solemnly, not trusting herself to speak.

"Do you trust me?" he asked

Tell him! He already knows the marriage wasn't complete. She shut her eyes to silence the voices in her head. Of course she trusted him. It was she who shouldn't be trusted. *Be honest with him!*

"Nora?"

She opened her eyes at the pleading tone in his voice and stared at his mouth. *I want this so much. More than I've ever wanted anything. Just this once. I'll let him go, but let me have this moment.*

"Nora, please say you believe me."

Without speaking, she lifted her lips to his and wrapped her arms around his shoulders to pull him down to her.

Slowly, so slowly, he came into her, filling her incrementally, inch by inch. He breathed heavily with the exertion and focus. The sensations were indescribably strange to her. He was right—there was no pain at all. Instead, she felt such exceedingly unique friction—soft and hard, smooth and ridged, sensitive skin sliding against sensitive skin. Then he fully impaled her and hit a spot that made her cry out, this time in stark, overwhelming pleasure. He groaned as he withdrew almost completely and slid firmly into her again. Whatever his hands and mouth had done to her before were ripples on a pond, compared with these tsunami waves of ecstasy that made her practically jump out of her skin. She couldn't catch her breath as he thrust into her again, again, even deeper, even harder. Her hands dug into him, one on his back, the other on his buttock, her legs wrapped around his, all to pull him ever closer. Her back arched, all her muscles tensed, her body shook—until now, and now, and now again, the pleasure exploded through her and she cried out insensibly. Even as the waves subsided, she felt him continue his onslaught, still fully erect within her, driving faster and harder. He seemed to fill her even more, impossible as that seemed. Without warning, yet another explosion of ecstasy, even more massive than the first, left her flailing, screaming "Oh, Alex! Alex! Oh, God!!!" with him putting his hand over her mouth to quiet her while he thrust into her one last time, releasing himself into her fully.

Long moments later, when their breathing and heartbeats returned to normal, she risked a glance at him. He looked bloody well pleased with himself.

"That was . . ." His voice trailed off as he searched for just the right word, stroking her shoulder.

"Indeed," she replied. They breathed in unison as they drifted off to sleep together.

Chapter Twelve

Evans Principle?: Oh, I've lost count, my girl. Anyway, don't waste time on regret. Ever forward!

Night serves as an excellent cover. Wrapped in dark silence, one feels a modicum of anonymity and one's inhibitions may fall away. But day inevitably follows. The sun sanitizes, and daylight leaves few hiding places.

Nora woke suddenly to bright sunlight in her eyes and two maids bustling about the room. One of the two maids was tying back the drapes she'd just opened wide. The other, surreptitiously eyeing her with a frown, was laying out clothing.

"Oh, you needn't trouble yourself, miss," Honoria said quickly. "I'll just wear my clothes from yesterday."

"Lady Devin instructed us to clean them for you and bring you these for now," the girl said quietly, "and there's a bath drawn for you, ma'am." No sign of Alex. Only right, she told herself, that he would prevent the servants from a scene, that he would need to prepare for the day. He didn't leave *me*, she told herself. He just needed to leave; it was the proper thing for him to do.

As she left the bed, she saw traces of last night's events and wondered briefly what the servants would make of that. Monthly courses, most likely. Perhaps. And what did it matter? Few people would expect or believe what had transpired; she barely believed it herself. And yet . . . as she bathed, her body announced its many complaints: joints popped, her thigh muscles ached, sore sensitive parts would not be ignored. When she returned to the bedroom, wrapping a thick dressing gown around her, she looked at the serviceable clothes laid out for her, along with cloths that reassured her the maids interpreted the soiled sheets acceptably. She also found the young maid standing by the door, staring at her balefully.

The girl curtsied and said, "I was instructed to help you dress, ma'am."

"There is no need. You are free to go," she said. She expected the maid to be relieved and eager to leave, but the girl's expression hardened. She couldn't resist asking, "Is there something wrong?"

The girl shook her head slowly.

"I assure you that you are welcome to speak freely with me. I am not one to put on airs or expect people to hold their tongues around me."

"My employers are all that is kind. I would not wish to displease them in any way."

Honoria looked at her more keenly and finally discerned her anger.

"Please, you may be completely frank. Whatever you have to say to me will not be repeated. This is between the two of us. I give my word."

Still, the girl stood, as unyielding and unmoving as granite.

"I swear on the lives of my beloved parents, I will not tell another soul. You are so clearly dying to say something to me. Speak your mind, child."

The appellation must have been the flint required because the young maid instantly blazed.

"Who are you to sneak your way into this family? You don't deserve to be here, getting the treatment of a queen!"

She was horrified by the accusation. The girl's intense response suggested more than the usual employee loyalty. She strove to respond calmly.

"I assure you I am not sneaking my way into the Devin family. It is no business of yours, but I was in dire circumstances last evening and the Devins were kind enough to assist me. You must be familiar with their generosity and kindness. I have no intention of being a nuisance to them or of imposing on their hospitality any more than is absolutely necessary."

"Oh, I know full well what you did. The master will tire of you and toss you aside like the gutter trash you are."

"You don't even know me. Why would you assume that I am, as you say, 'gutter trash'?"

"He deserves someone finer than you, younger, prettier. He deserves a real lady for a wife."

"As I thought I made clear, I have no designs regarding the Devin family. Lord Devin is free to marry whomever he wishes, and like you, I hope he finds a lovely wife suited to his needs. I am not on the marriage market."

She couldn't comprehend the previous night's events, much less face accusations from a little chit who knew nothing about her. Her mind whirled with unfamiliar—and extreme—emotions. Even as she dressed, every motion seemed strange, as if she didn't belong in her skin. The shop needed her attention, but she could not focus. Her body and her heart were already too much at war to give her head any opportunity to chime in. She'd been distraught, she told herself. That was why she'd turned to him—for comfort and escape. But she couldn't absolve herself from responsibility. She'd wanted to be with him; in all honesty, she wanted him still. Right now. But there was no future for them together, just as the brazen maid has said. Eventually, he needed to marry a perfectly respectable daughter of the peerage and produce little perfectly respectable heirs. The only way she could be with him was as his paramour, which meant there was no way.

"I will not be his mistress," she said aloud, as if to convince herself. "I have my business to consider. And I have my self-respect." She repeated the little speech over and over until she almost believed it. Then she went to find Lord Devin. *Drawn like a moth to flame*, she thought, *and we know what happens to the moth.*

In his office, seated behind a large, walnut desk with an ornately carved front panel, Lord Devin was so much more formal, distant. The butler's presence could also be a mitigating factor, she acknowledged. She wasn't sure what she expected—certainly not that he would rush to her and sweep her into his arms with a declaration of undying love—but she hadn't expected the generic cordiality he might use to greet any acquaintance.

"Good morning, Mrs. Duchamp." He said, lifting his eyes from the sheet on which he was writing. His expression seemed warm, if professional. She wasn't sure how to deal with him.

"Good morning, Lord Devin. I came to thank you for your hospitality. I will be returning to my shop now to assess the damages."

"Wait a few moments. After I finish here, I will accompany you."

"There's no need. You obviously have much to do. Please don't trouble yourself on my account."

At that, he looked at her sharply and slowly shook his head.

"Johnson, take care of these. I will review the rest later." His butler agreed and took his leave quietly, pulling the door almost closed behind him.

Devin walked around the desk toward her but stilled as she retreated, maintaining the distance between them. He frowned.

"I insist that I escort you, Honoria. The shop may yet be unsecured; you should not go alone. It is no trouble. And," he added more gently, "it will give us some time to talk."

Time to talk. That was exactly what she wanted to avoid.

He'd left her bed at the first streaks of dawn and slunk back to his room, confused and weighed down by heavy guilt. He didn't want to want her. He didn't want to like her. But he did. He'd thought foolishly that his irrational pining after her would subside once he had her, but it didn't. This morning, he'd wanted more than anything to stay wrapped in her arms, to watch consciousness slip into her skin, to protect her, to plan a future with her. To be her anchor in the storm that began for her yesterday and would undoubtedly get much worse before it broke. But he could do none of these things. So he'd left her bed while she slept—like the underhanded sneak he was.

He desperately wanted to protect her, but how could he do so if he didn't know everything about her? She'd been so strong at the shop, so self-possessed, and yet last night she'd allowed him to glimpse her vulnerability, allowed him to care for her. It was an awesome responsibility. One thing he knew: the decision was already made; he would protect her just as he would everyone he . . .

His thoughts caught him by surprise.

Love? Could that really be what he felt for her?

The swell of emotion in his chest surely went beyond altruism. But it wasn't love. The overwhelming pleasure and desire to please that he'd experienced with her again and again in the night went beyond physical need. But that signaled affection, not love. He'd guarded his heart so carefully, so completely. Yet she'd stumbled past his defenses, as if by accident. Whatever he felt for her, he must fold her into the same absolute haven he ensured for his mother and his siblings. His life had been lived for them, and now he had to adjust the equation.

But what if she finds out about Withersby?

It wasn't a long coach ride to the shop, but it began as an oppressively silent one. He wasn't sure what was going on in Honoria's mind, but his disordered mind couldn't focus.

"Nora, I don't want to pry," he began.

"That kind of prelude is never good."

"I have some questions . . . about your husband."

"That's not a subject I wish to discuss."

"Perhaps after last night, you owe me a little leeway on this matter."

A chill suffused her. She did owe him a great deal. At least she could afford some modicum of honesty.

"All right. I will try."

"There is, I think, the obvious question."

"Right, why my marriage was never . . ."

"Yes, why your marriage was never. So?"

"As I told you, my father died when I was eighteen. A month after his burial, I went on a trip to the north. To call it a holiday would be inappropriate; still in mourning, I wasn't going for enjoyment. The doctor said it would be good for my nerves." Speaking haltingly and feeling suffocated, she took off her gloves. "I met Mr. Duchamp. Then things happened so fast. He wooed me. Within a week, we eloped to Gretna Green in Scotland." As she wove the tale, her insides twisted and heart revolted. She felt she might be sick.

"Then, practically before the ink of our signatures was dry, he died in a freak horse-riding accident. As if to add to the horrible absurdity, our wedding certificate with the witnesses' signatures caught fire. It was an absurd travesty. And there you have it."

When she first returned from Scotland, she'd had to repeat her story so many times it became rote. She wished for that mechanical repetition again but couldn't achieve it. Every word stabbed at her. Years ago, people had accepted her story mainly because she was able to show the news article announcing Mr. Duchamp's death and naming her as his wife. Even the banker and solicitor disposing of her uncle's will had been kind and surprisingly unquestioning.

"You haven't answered my question. How is it that the marriage was never consummated? One night, nay, a few minutes would have sufficed."

"Don't be crude. There wasn't really an opportunity." She floundered. "We knew each other so little. The accident was the morning after the ceremony."

"I am truly sorry for your loss. And I know I am the worst sort of cad to push this question . . . but I would think the wedding night offered ample opportunity for consummation."

Her mouth dried up and her throat tightened. She stared out the window to avoid his gaze.

"As I said, we didn't really know each other. We'd agreed that we should delay the physical aspects of the marriage until a time mutually agreed upon."

"Fair enough. I am truly sorry for prying."

She nodded acceptance.

For several moments, the only sounds came from the street. The tones outside shifted markedly from Grosvenor Square to Portland. The mostly silent and genteel gave way to the boisterous calls of vendors to one another as they began the task of opening up shop.

"I don't think you've ever had proper time to grieve for all these loved ones you've lost." His voice cutting through the growing din outside was low but unmistakable. His sweet sincerity was her undoing. He trusted her completely. She couldn't let him.

"I'm sorry," she blurted as she faced him. "There is more to this story, and I know you will be furious and horrified and want nothing to do with me. So it's best I tell you before we get to the shop. Then you can simply drop me off and go on your way."

She straightened in her seat, tucking her skirt against her legs and wrapping her shawl tightly around her shoulders.

"My uncle was the head of the family. He died in 1829, and I was his only heir . . . well, heir to what was left after he lost everything that was entailed. He hated me. He always said it was a shame I'd been born. Really, I think he hated, or at least disdained, all women. I know he abhorred my mother." She could only ever picture her uncle scowling. "So it was no surprise that he bequeathed the bulk of his estate to the church, and it was likewise no surprise that what little he bequeathed to me came with stipulations. To receive the meager inheritance, I had to marry, and I had to do it by my twenty-first birthday. Do you understand why he would set those rules?"

"I can only assume that it would be because, upon marrying, a woman's property becomes her husband's."

"Exactly. I was never supposed to have control over any of his estate, a condition not out of the ordinary. Yet my father was so indulgent and so blind. He disregarded my uncle's will, assuming that he would pass the store on to me as my livelihood. But when he died so abruptly, the medical bills and burial arrangements were exorbitant. He left me the store, but it was running in the red and in need of renovation. And the costs of his death took the bulk of the existing funds. Under those circumstances, I would have lost the store within a year. I needed to claim the inheritance from my uncle. So I closed the store temporarily, took what little I had saved, and went on a quest to find a satisfactory husband. I made my way toward Scotland, since I knew marriages could be done quickly and easily. I wasn't thinking clearly, I know. It's ridiculous. But my uncle hadn't specified what type of man I should marry so I was confident that I could convince someone—pay someone for a marriage of convenience."

She paused for breath, struggling to hold at bay the memory of her suffocating anxiety. She'd pored over the accounts, looking for ways to keep the shop running. It was all so unfair. *If only I'd been born a man!* And then she'd hated that thought as well.

"All common sense fled. I was in a dead panic and knew only that I had to acquire a husband. I did meet a Mr. Duchamp at some coaching inn along the way to Gretna. And he did die in a freak horse-riding accident. That is sadly true. But he never courted me, not even for a moment. We had dinner together twice, with a table of other tourists, in the public dining room of the inn. What I could surmise was that he had no connections, no wife, no family. He was a wanderer, who prefers the life of a nomad. We, in fact, did broach the subject of a marriage of convenience, but it was only in jest—a joke that, in exchange for marrying me and securing my inheritance, I would fund his travels."

If she hadn't been so keenly aware of Devin during her confession, even without looking at him directly, she would have missed the moment when he infinitesimally moved away from her. The smallest shift, really, one that could simply be accounted for by the nature of coach travel. Yet she knew better. And he hadn't even heard the worst yet.

"I could have convinced him to make the joke real. I know I could have. We were headed in the same direction anyway. The problem," she continued, "is that the fool died within sight of Gretna Green." She caught herself and changed her tone. "It is sinful for me to speak so of the dead. A misstep by his horse ruined it all. He fell off his mount, down a small rocky hill. By the time he reached the bottom, the poor man's neck was broken. Locals rushed to his side and called the doctor, but he was dead within a matter of minutes."

She'd truly felt beyond salvation then, not so much because there would be no marriage but because of her uncharitable anger toward Mr. Duchamp for dying when she'd been so close to safety. She couldn't say that aloud now.

"So how did you become Mrs. Duchamp?"

"Everyone could see that I was distraught. A couple kindly took me to their home to comfort me, and they quickly assumed our purpose in coming. I—" She broke off, unable to face her own immorality. It was so much worse to put what she'd done in words. "I told them that part of our impetus for marrying so quickly, without bothering for banns at home, was that I was with child, and we wanted to legitimize the babe sooner rather than later. With no one to mourn his death, no one would care to contest an imaginary marriage. I had everything to gain, and nothing to risk. And suddenly it seemed so easy. I could still get my uncle's inheritance, and I could do it on my terms."

"You mean to tell me . . ."

She couldn't look at him but nodded, blinking back tears of humiliation and guilt.

"I lied. We were never married. I have never actually been Mrs. Duchamp. I didn't even know him. There was a marriage certificate but no actual marriage and therefore no consummation. Considering my modest position and my meager inheritance, no one saw any need to contest the certificate or investigate my claims."

Silence.

The carriage hit a bump, jostling them. She couldn't help but notice that, when her foot was jolted toward his, he jerked away as if scalded.

"Why did you not tell me before?"

"When exactly would have been a good time to say, 'Oh, by the by, I'm a virgin and a liar pretending to be a widow for the past twenty years'? During dinner with thirty guests? In front of the mob at the Crystal Palace?"

"You had plenty of opportunities. For truths like that, you make the time."

"Said by someone who presumably never, ever lies? Someone who has no secrets of his own?"

"We are not talking about me right now," he snapped. "You have been living a lie and, in the middle of the most intimate thing two people can do together, you did not think I deserved to know?"

"No, I didn't think you needed to know."

That shut him up. He knew now how she regarded him. And now, he thought bitterly, he had exactly the kind of information Mr. Withersby and his client could easily use to destroy her livelihood. It didn't take much for a woman's respectability to be tainted irrevocably. She might not be seen as a "fallen" woman, but such lies would cast the shadow of immorality on her entire person and on Evans Books. No one would believe a woman of low character wouldn't end up a "fallen" woman.

Chapter Thirteen

Evans Principle—Umpteen: Trust your instincts, especially when they tell you to run. There is no shame in logically calculated retreat.

Icy silence reigned during the remainder of the trip.

As she approached the shop from the street, she saw that Minnie, ever dutiful, was already inside, picking books up off the floor. It was a tremendous relief to see her earnest, reliable figure; her presence gave Nora a much-needed sense of routine and discipline.

When she walked through the door, Minnie dropped the books in her arms and rushed over. Already covered in grime, the girl seemed hesitant to touch her.

"Oh, Mrs. Duchamp, thank heavens you're safe. This is terrible. When I couldn't find you upstairs, I feared the worst. Where were you?"

"I'm touched by your concern, Minnie. When I found the shop burglarized yesterday, it was determined that I should spend the night in safer quarters." Safer quarters—a lie if ever there was one. "It was so good of you to come, Minnie. But perhaps you should take the day off. I can handle all this."

"Neither of you should have to muddle through this filth," Devin interjected. "I have made arrangements for cleaners to handle every-thing." As usual, he spoke as if his word was law. Even after her hor-rible revelation in the coach, he intended to salvage the store for her.

"That is too kind of you, my lord." She stumbled on the "my lord," and they both flinched. He wasn't hers, and they both knew it, espe-cially now that she'd revealed the truth. "I cannot accept such extrav-agant help. It is my shop, my responsibility. I will attend to it. Minnie and Erich will help." Minnie nodded vigorously.

"Mrs. Duchamp, the damage and refuse are too much for the three of you to repair. I have people on staff to handle this and do it well. You can repay me in books, if that assuages your conscience."

She felt as if he'd struck her. *Assuages your conscience.* The past twenty-four hours were too much to face all at once. The door chime saved her from having to think further.

"Honoria! Minnie sent word, but I never dreamed it would be this terrible!" Marissa rushed in like a whirlwind and embraced her. "Are you well? You look awful!"

She mustered a weak smile and said, "I will be fine, Marissa. I'm sure the damage looks worse than it is."

"That's you all over, making molehills out of your mountains! Well, sweetie, you can count on us for whatever you need. If you want us to don our aprons and dig in, just say the word."

Keenly aware of their audience, she replied, "You are always so kind, Marissa. I may have mentioned making the acquaintance of the Devin family." Throughout the perfunctory introductions, which she tried to complete as succinctly as she could, Marissa gave her unmis-takable inquiries with her eyes.

"Why, yes, you'd mentioned that you attended a lovely dinner with Lady Devin. How nice of Lord Devin to come to your assis-tance."

Not now, Marissa! She tried to deter Marissa's questions with her own facial expressions and finally with a distinct single shake of her head. Her efforts only encouraged Marissa's interference. Could this moment get any more awkward?

"It's so convenient that you are here to come to our Honoria's res-cue. What perfect timing."

"Marissa, dear, I don't want you to suffer this mess. It's more dis-gusting than you can possibly dream."

"I'm sure it defies description. The smell alone is overwhelming, I'm sorry to say. I'll come back tomorrow in Mr. Clarke's galoshes." Marissa was making her way slowly toward the door but then stopped abruptly. "Oh, no! The printing press! Was it damaged?"

"Likely beyond repair, unfortunately." She looked pointedly at Marissa. *Not now!* "And I can't afford to replace it yet. I shall have to review unfinished orders and contact those clients immediately."

"Would you like the girls to come over on Thursday as planned? I'm sure they would like to help you as much as I do. We have much to discuss."

"You are all too kind, and I do know I can call upon you for anything. But I have no idea what to do about this week."

"If I may," Lord Devin interjected, "I still believe this building is unsecured. Mrs. Duchamp, my mother bade me to remind you that you are welcome to stay at Devin House as long as you feel is necessary. You are likewise welcome to receive your friends there."

Devin House? Marissa's raised brows asked. Her stomach dropped as her friend said aloud, "I had no idea you had such powerful friends, Honoria. What a blessing." Enveloping her in an extravagant hug, Marissa spoke low so only she could hear. "You have much to explain. Do what you must to minimize delay."

She pulled away, but before she could respond, her friend added with an obvious wink, "Don't do anything I wouldn't do, dearie! Send us word about when and where you wish us to visit you."

"Wait, Marissa!" But it was too late. If Marissa heard, there was no indication as her friend simply strolled away. This was unbearable. "I cannot continue to stay at Devin House. I'll have all the locks reinforced today. You can check them yourself. But I am staying here."

"Do not behave like a petulant child, Honoria—"

"Please, Lord Devin, do me the courtesy of addressing me properly in public . . . in my place of business." She knew she was being overly sensitive, overly dramatic, yet she couldn't stop herself. She needed to reestablish her authority. Evans Books was her domain.

He bowed and continued. "Mrs. Duchamp. The damages here seem to go beyond simple burglary. They suggest malice, meaning whoever did this is not merely concerned with stealing from the shop. They wish to do you harm. In good conscience, I cannot allow you to stay here unprotected."

Throughout Mrs. Clarke's whirlwind visit, Minnie had drifted into the shadows. Not particularly talkative by nature, she seemed even more withdrawn than usual, and Honoria couldn't help but worry. While Lord Devin explored the building, checking windows and other modes of entry, she drew her assistant into the back office. The girl's immediate verbosity indicated just how distraught she was.

"Oh, Miss Honoria, I'm so very sorry about all this! It's so terrible. I should have been here to prevent it. I should have been more vigilant about the locks." Minnie looked around the back room wildly. "How will we ever get this back in order again?" She started scooping piles of torn paper off the floor but stopped abruptly, jerking back up and dropping everything. Her face a twisted mask of disgust, she said, "That's the devil's own stench. The bottom layers are soaked in filth. Oh, miss, it's all my fault!" Minnie rubbed her hands against her apron over and over.

She rushed to console the poor girl who was so much more than a servant to the Evans family. "Why, Minnie, none of this was your fault! I explicitly gave you and Erich the afternoon free while I was out on a social call. You couldn't have predicted this would happen. Frankly, it's best you weren't here when those ruffians broke in. Heaven knows what might have happened."

Minnie just shook her head, looking at the floor.

"Are you well, Minnie?"

When the girl's eyes met hers, they were troubled, but all she would say was "Yes, miss. I'm just terribly sorry about the shop."

"It's not your fault, dear. We'll fix it together. You'll see."

After Minnie's departure a little while later with a promise to return early the next day, Devin spoke frankly and surprisingly. "I do not condone your lies. But who has not lied to protect what they value? You did what you had to do in order to survive. You harmed no one. Who am I to fault you for that?"

"You'll forgive me if I find your reaction surprising and possibly disingenuous."

That earned her a supercilious raised brow.

"You doubt my sincerity?"

"I'm sure you think you mean what you say."

"So you doubt my rationality? That is so much the better. Rather than a liar, I am incapable of knowing my own mind." His arms fisted at his sides, and his jaw clenched—the only outward signs of his fury.

Yet she could feel hot waves of anger radiating from him. She longed for the frigid silence of the carriage ride, rather than this incendiary—well, she couldn't even pin a word to it. Their stances put her in mind of Jupiter and Janus, one cat chasing the other to play, pawing and swiping and pouncing to incite a reaction from the other. But she didn't want to play this game any longer. After the night they'd shared, she couldn't afford to be drawn in any further.

"You know, I'm sure that I cannot stay at Devin House. It would be entirely inappropriate, especially under the circumstances. Today's priority will be to have the locks and windows at least temporarily fixed." She would remain here, in her own home, under her own roof. "You and your mother have been all kindness and generosity, but I believe this must be the end of our association."

Early the next morning, Minnie handed her a note with the now-familiar D seal.

Dear Mrs. Duchamp,

My dearest friend (for even in our brief acquaintance, I already feel you are very dear to me), I am beside myself wondering how your cleaning and repair of the shop must be progressing by inches. It is surely too much of a burden for you alone. What are friends for, if not to aid one another in times like these? I do wish you would let the Devin family assist you; I feel it is reasonable and not at all boastful for me to say that we have abundant resources to put at your disposal. Without doubt, my son Alexander can handle the repairs and renovations quite efficiently.

I do not, however, wish to oppress you with well-meant charity. Instead, I have a proposition for you, one which would be a mutual act of kindness. I have decided to retire to Sharling Worth, a Devin property in the north country, because I find the city too hot and the crowds too pressing. It is a wonderful place—with a serene lake, lots of open space for walking and riding, and breathtaking gardens (which I can say because I have absolutely no hand in them—our gardeners are magicians!).

It would be a great honor if you could accompany me on holiday for a couple of weeks. As lovely as Sharling is, it can

be rather . . . quiet . . . especially since none of my children will
be accompanying me. You would love it there, I'm sure of it.
    Please do consider joining me; I would be in your debt and
I'm sure we would get along swimmingly.

Affectionately,
Lady Rose Devin

P.S. Honestly, my friend, when was the last time you had a hol-
iday? You deserve one now more than ever.

As much as she genuinely liked Lady Devin—and she could easily see Rose quickly becoming her closest and dearest confidante—
she could not afford to continue this acquaintance. Her involvement
with the Devin family had already distracted her in so many terrible
ways. If she hadn't gone with them to the Exhibition, she wouldn't be
in the middle of this very literal mess. She could not quite bring herself to regret spending the night with Alex—Lord Devin, she cor-
rected herself—but she had to close that short and chaotic chapter of
her life and get back to business. She didn't belong in their world,
and she couldn't ignore how her own was quickly crumbling.

Dear Lady Devin,
Your kind invitation touched me deeply. I regret to inform you
that, given the needs of the shop, I cannot possibly travel with
you. I have determined there is simply too much I need to do
here. You must know, however, that I hold you in the highest re-
gard and would certainly accompany you if circumstances
were otherwise. You have been a true friend to me, and I will
treasure your kindness always.

Cordially,
Mrs. Honoria Duchamp

She should have known her response would bring Lord Devin to
her door yet again. She'd waited a few days to send her response. It
took less than twenty-four hours from the time Minnie left to deliver
her reply to Lady Devin for the news to travel to him and for him to
appear.

"You need a holiday," he said simply.

"You're rabid. I can't possibly go on holiday. I have far too much to do here. A holiday would delay the shop's reopening. It requires far too much time and attention for me to up and abscond with the likes of you." *Not to mention more money—and more of my heart—than I can spare.*

"One point of fact—I have the resources at my disposal, and at your command, to continue the shop's repairs without disruption." When she opened her mouth to object, she was silenced by the devilish glint in his eye. "A second point of fact—I never said I would take you."

"Oh. Why does this matter to you?"

"As my mother's invitation surely made clear, she is planning a sojourn in our country home and wishes for your companionship."

"Companionship, yes."

"Yes, this was entirely her invitation. I have nothing to do with it. It would truly be an independent holiday. No dinner parties or social calls. You could go walking, or riding, or boating, or swimming, tasting a life of leisure. If you please, you could spend the entire time in the library reading."

"Swimming?"

"Yes. That appeals to you? Our house is by a lake. My family has spent many a summer day boating, swimming, and fishing. Great fun. Just you and my mother. You would love it."

"Your mother is quite lovely, but I simply cannot." She paused as she shuffled some paperwork for no good reason. Then she forced herself to ask, "Does she know of what's happened between us? I don't think I could . . ." She trailed off, unable to voice how embarrassing it would be if Lady Devin knew of their transgression.

"I certainly have not told her. She is quite perceptive, though. She likely knows or at least suspects what is between us. After all, she has known me all my life. I think you will find she has rather progressive views, although she keeps her own counsel publicly. And she likes you."

She considered it. She actually considered the indulgence of a holiday, the likes of which she only vaguely recalled from early childhood. But she had the Needlework for the Needy Association to consider. She was supposed to be the next host in just a few days' time. And she'd already been derelict in her duties once because of Lord Devin. She kept trying to think of reasons to reject his offer, even as the child in her begged to go on holiday and the adult in her begged to return to Lord Devin's arms. That he wouldn't be there certainly helped alleviate her concerns about her own lack of control. And part of her desperately wanted to escape the world she was in.

Chapter Fourteen

Evans Principle XX: Everyone needs a holiday now and then, even you. Rejuvenation is good for business.

And so, Honoria found herself floating in a lake, staring up at a robin's egg sky, and occasionally wiggling her toes when tiny fish came near. She was still a bit confused as to how she ended up here at the Devin country home, Sharling Worth, enjoying an actual holiday, swimming in a large, clear lake.

Impressive as Devin House in London was, it was dwarfed by the grandeur and gravitas of Sharling Worth. Not only twice the size of the city dwelling, but generations older, Sharling Worth dominated its environment. Softly rolling hills fell away from it and a dense forest framed it from behind.

Like any good castle, it was guarded by what might as well be a dragon or at least the hound of hell. She hadn't been in the front hall for more than a minute before she was bowled over by a massive wall of black fur with a whipping tail that could no doubt chop wood.

"Juno! Down! Out with you, girl!" A reedy woman dressed in serviceable gray serge was brushing her hands on her apron as she rushed in to grab the dog's collar. The great she-beast managed a few sloppy licks of her face before being pulled away. Juno. The coincidence unnerved her. That was how Lord Devin had easily guessed Jupiter had a sibling Janus. Just as the thought occurred to her, she gave instructions to the butler to have the carrier containing the two felines taken directly to her room. When the pair returned home a few days after the break-in, they'd been filthy, thin, and skittish. No need to tempt the Fates by allowing these four-legged gods and goddesses to clash just yet.

She needn't have bothered with such caution. At the earliest opportunity, the next morning, Juno snuck into her room—actually rooms. Such a luxurious surprise, not only a bedroom but a sunny and spacious sitting room with a view of the gardens behind the house and the forest in the distance. Jupiter, true to his name, had sprung out from behind the bed at first light. Janus stationed himself regally on one of the bed pillows. Juno had followed a maid delivering breakfast into the sitting room—and bolted into the bedroom when Nora emerged.

Immediately, the cats closed ranks on the bed, coming to its foot with their backs arched and tails high. Juno came right up and laid her head on the bed in front of them. Without moving, she sniffed at them curiously. Considering the large dog's exuberance when she first arrived, she was stunned at such submissiveness. While Janus, ever suspicious of strangers, backed away watchfully, Jupiter simply touched Juno's snout with her paw and then laid down close enough for Juno to nudge. Within a few moments, both felines were moving in step with their new canine friend. It was a miracle to behold. She couldn't help but wonder what insight was there to be gleaned from such easy camaraderie among presumably natural enemies.

She hadn't gone swimming since she was a child, but her body quickly recalled the movements, the sensation of propelling herself through the water like a snake. Only now, in a billowy bathing dress, she felt more like a floating mushroom than a snake. It was an uncharacteristic extravagance, this bathing dress she'd purchased only days before this holiday. But she was so taken with the promise of swimming that she probably would have paid twice the price for this ridiculously ugly and uncomfortable thing.

She'd been looking forward to the freedom of the water. But this monstrosity of fabric hindered every movement. No one was near. No one would see her. It took less than a minute for her to convince herself and start undoing the buttons on the front of the dress.

Well, this wouldn't do. She now had the dress at least half off, but the buoyancy made it difficult for her to get the dress the rest of the way. It bunched and twisted at her waist and thighs. *Well, in for a penny*, she thought, and then she took a few deep breaths and dropped her head underwater, twisting and pushing and pulling to free herself. Just a little more. At some point, through the muffling water that filled her ears, she thought she heard a screech owl.

He saw her head go under, her arms and legs thrashing. *Oh, dear God, no.* He called her name as he ran, full speed, to the edge of the dock and dove in, fully clothed, Juno leaping in with him. He swam as quickly as he could toward her, but just before he could get to her, her head stabilized and she looked at him, shocked but clearly conscious. In fact, she looked disturbingly, furiously lucid.

"What on earth are you doing?" she nearly shouted, trying to avoid Juno's splashing.

"I thought you were drowning! I thought to rescue you!" His emotions heightened, he realized his voice was probably a bit louder than it needed to be too.

"That's ridiculous. Certainly not. I'm an excellent swimmer."

He arched an eyebrow. She did seem to be keeping her head above water without any trouble, even with Juno circling her.

"Then what the hell were you doing?"

"I, uh, wanted more freedom of movement." Her tone calmed, although her meaning was unclear.

"I see," he replied noncommittally. And then suddenly he did see. Her bathing dress floated a few feet behind her. He wasn't the only one who noticed. Juno made a beeline for what she surely thought was a new chew toy. And then Alex's eyes caught sight of the curves of Nora's body visible near the lake's surface, bare and pale and lush. His throat seized.

"What are you doing here, anyway? You said you were to stay in the city," she said accusingly.

Still distracted by the sight before him, he only managed, "I could not stay away."

"I can understand why," she said, unaware of the direction of his thoughts. "It's been quite a long time since I've known the pleasures of the country. I used to love swimming as a child, but back then my father let me wear an undershirt and short pants. So I'm not used to being encumbered by so much ridiculous fabric. It was weighing me down severely."

"I see." It was all he could think to say. No other words came to mind. He hadn't actually seen her in the dark. And he still couldn't see much of her now, but, oh, how he wanted to.

"And so I took it off."

He swallowed. "Yes, I can clearly see that." Her face froze and he saw the dawning realization in her eyes—realization of what he was already achingly aware of. She was here treading water—clear, calm water—in the middle of the lake in nothing but her own skin. He decided her expression right then was priceless, and all too fleeting.

"Have you seen your mother?" Her arms slicing gracefully through the water as she increased the distance between them. "I hear your sister and her family are due to arrive any day now. You should help your mother prepare."

"It had been quite some time since I had the pleasure of a swim myself," he replied. "There is plenty of time for me to engage in familial obligations later."

"Now what do you think you're doing?" She eyed him skeptically as she kept trying to move farther away. He was the stronger swimmer by far. No matter how much she tried to put distance between them, he continued to close the gap.

"Making the most of the situation," he replied.

"How do you figure we can manage to do anything and still stay afloat?"

That made him pause and tread water momentarily. She smiled. She couldn't articulate what she felt, but some stronghold inside her had been opened, and she would not deny herself. Perhaps it was the setting—just the two of them alone in a primordial lake, as if no one else existed, as if time were inconsequential, as if they could do anything they wanted. It didn't take him long to read her smile accurately if the hunger on his face were any indication, but it took him a bit longer to recover his voice.

"True," he said, finally. "We should get to shore or at least to the dock, as quickly as possible."

"No! Not like this! And certainly not the dock! No splinters for me, thank you." She immediately felt out of her depth. She wasn't prepared to deal with the consequences of her own desire.

"You shall have to get out sometime, Nora," he said as he made his way purposefully across the lake toward shore. Damn, Juno had her bathing dress.

"I propose a simple trade," he said, turning back toward her, his eyes glinting mischievously.

"Well, don't keep me in suspense. My arms are getting tired."

"Perfect. I propose we get back to shore where you can . . . rest your arms. And once we are done, I shall give you your dress."

"Once we're done?"

"Yes."

"Out here in the open?!"

"Yes."

"You're mad." And yet she couldn't quell the swift beat of her heart or the echoing throb lower down her body.

"Probably. Still, you have heard my offer. Do you agree to my terms?"

How could she not? Without a word, she turned and swam toward shore.

As he watched her swim, he grinned. She moved so gracefully in the water. He knew he could outswim her, overtake her even fully clothed, but he couldn't resist watching her. Glimpses of her calves, her buttocks, her back, as she sliced efficiently through the water, tantalized him. He followed leisurely in her wake, enjoying the view.

As soon as he found his footing, he reached for her. Soaked and clinging, his clothing was an unwelcome impediment to both of them. He couldn't help but notice that she clawed at his buttons as eagerly as he did, and his desire spiked sharply. They were both still waist-deep in the water when he finally tossed his smalls toward shore.

The water made it easy to slide her body against his, but that didn't account for the ease with which she slid her legs around him. Her willingness shocked and thrilled him. His want was overwhelming. On impulse, he thrust his cock unerringly into her sheath, hot and tight and welcoming. Her eyes widened as she gasped and clung tightly to his shoulders.

"I am sorry," he said, instantly contrite at his selfishness but unable to stop himself. "I should have waited. I should have gone slower, should have done more to please you first."

She laughed. A wild, unbridled sound. Unbelievable. Her laugh rang around the lake. Then she flattened herself against him and kissed his neck. A light drizzle had begun, misting her already wet hair and giving it an ethereal glow.

"As you've already observed, I appreciate the direct approach. Don't worry about me." She rubbed against him. "I can take care of myself." She pulled his head toward hers and kissed him deeply.

He groaned at her enthusiasm, and his hips began to move against her, thrusting slow and methodical. But he hadn't anticipated the effect of buoyancy. Even with them both struggling to get closer, to practically consume each other, the force of their movements was blunted and ineffectual.

"I did not think this through," he said as he stilled. "I just needed to be inside you." She panted against his chest, and he felt her shiver not just in his arms but through their joining. The sensation shot through his groin and up his spine, fanning the flames higher. He could not let her go right now, even if the world depended on it. "Just hold on."

He felt her nod, felt her lightly clamp down on his shoulder with her teeth. He groaned again and, without disengaging, carried her onto shore. He grinned as he identified a convenient boulder, a natural table at the perfect height. For a few moments, they just held each other, her head buried in his shoulder. The feel of her in his arms was beyond words.

"I love you," he blurted out, shocking even himself, as he braced her against the rock and thrust home. She gripped his shoulders as he began to move in an ancient rhythm, but she didn't show any sign she'd heard him. The rain grew stronger, drops pelting them both. The only sounds from her were whimpers and pants as her hands slid lower, pulling him to her harder. After she cried out, he lowered her down onto the rock, still hard within her and gave her just a moment's respite before beginning their dance anew, their bodies slick and needy.

He leaned over her, his head against her neck, and whispered again, "I love you."

Her arms came up between them and pushed lightly but firmly against his chest.

"Don't," she said. "Don't use your pretty pillow talk on me. I know what we have here, and we don't need to pretend it's anything more than it is."

He wanted to protest, wanted to tell her how true his words were, but the realization was still so fresh that he feared it. He didn't trust himself to speak again and so he let his body, already so close to exploding, speak for him. Their moans mingled and echoed across the lake, and when she cried out in ecstasy again, he tried to cover her mouth with his, not to muffle her but to taste the intensity of her pleasure. And when his own peak overcame him, he groaned his love into her damp hair and emptied himself into her.

As their breathing slowed, he lay next to her with his arm draped possessively over her breasts. The downpour eased to a gentle but steady shower. Suddenly, she leapt up and began spinning in slow circles, her head thrown back and her arms spread wide. He loved the sound, and the sight of her—unrestrained, unburdened, celebrating the moment with abandon. He suspected she was a pagan in a previous life. When he said as much, she raised her head and laughed.

"I can't help myself. This all feels so unreal. I've never dreamed, never imagined how wonderful it could be to dance naked in summer rain. It's as if we're Adam and Eve in our own private Eden." Her spins grew faster and more erratic until, midway across the shore, she stopped and swayed dizzily. Her arms began to undulate, in imitation of the Eastern dancers they'd seen at the Exhibition. Some music in her head made her hips to sashay back and forth, a vision that mesmerized him. Eyes closed, she continued to move in a private rhythm until he simply had to swoop her into his arms. And dance with her, slow and close.

"You are so enamored of the weather that I can only deduce our interlude must have been rather unsatisfactory." He hoped his tone was suitably light, masking his uncertainty. But she looked up at him shrewdly.

"You can't seriously doubt how very satisfactory that was, exquisite even. It would be clear to anyone within a mile's radius, anyone who had the capacity of hearing. Could you possibly be insecure about your prowess? Impossible. You are man at his most elemental. You are Adam before the fall."

"Then why will you not say you love me?"

She stilled, immediately sober. Her hands pulled out of his.

"This is a fantasy, a momentary respite from the real world. You do not love me. You cannot. And I cannot love you."

He reached for her again. "How else can you explain this? You feel it too."

"Just accept what we have. Nothing like this can last. You will need to marry one of those lovely girls who attends balls in bell-shaped white dresses, who can manage your household proficiently, and bear you children to carry on the noble Devin line. You most definitely don't need a—" She couldn't bring herself to continue. She shivered.

"We shall discuss this later. It is getting cold, Nora. I should get you back to the house and in dry clothes."

As they walked back, weighed down by their sopping garments, the grounds brought back memories of her childhood: the mist, the scent of damp earth and crushed weeds, even the slight suction of mud on her feet.

"My father taught me how to swim. During the week, while he worked at the shop, my mother and I resided at Poppyfield Manor. Don't laugh, it really was called Poppyfield. He would spend his days off at home with us. Whenever we had the chance, he took me to the pond to swim. Such a long time ago . . . I took those golden days for granted."

"I think all happy children do." His tone disturbed her.

"Were you not a happy child, then?"

"My childhood was what can be expected for a viscount. I was raised to be a man. What made you so happy?"

"My parents doted on me. We didn't have much money, and my father didn't have much free time. But I realized in adulthood that whatever they had was devoted to me. My father taught me to read, to swim, to ride. It didn't matter to him that I was a girl. He taught me everything he knew. Minnie's parents were our only servants, so loyal and dependable. I've known Minnie all her life. They were like family. She and Erich are all I have left. It's been a long time. I'm sure my memories reflect brighter because of the distance, because of their loss. I only remember the good."

"The last time I spoke with my father," he said haltingly, "the day before he left for his fatal trip, we argued. Our relationship was generally cordial and polite. But that day it was as if he felt some push to bare his soul. He talked about how much he loved my mother, how deeply he loved each of us, and I laughed in his face. He talked of how he wished he could share the magic of his voyages and excursions with us, the joy of discovery, the wonder of unexpected beauty. He told me he wished I would—how did he put it?—that I would let my soul take wing and seek out my own adventures. It was infuriatingly self-centered. And I told him so."

"You loved him."

He shook his head.

"The last time we spoke, I told my father that he was a miserable example of fatherhood—that, with all his talk of wonder and beauty, he sacrificed his family's happiness for his own selfish desires. I told him he was not truly a father, just another occasional guest regaling us with entertaining stories and pretty artifacts. I told him he should be ashamed of himself."

"Oh, Alex. You were young."

"I was all of eighteen, old enough not to be so petulant and emotional."

"You were young," she said firmly, "and you'd obviously been concealing your pain for a long time."

"It was not pain. It was fury. How dare he abandon my mother time after time? How dare he abandon us? Andrew and Amelia needed a father; they needed guidance and direction only a father can give. My mother needed a true spouse, an active partner. Instead, he gallivanted and played, focusing only on his own whims."

"You loved him, and he loved you as well as he knew how."

"If he had not gone, he would not have died."

"You don't know that. Any of us could die as a random fluke at any time. My father died crossing a city street; he didn't need to travel hundreds of miles."

"I was not the son he wanted. If I had been, he would not have felt the need to leave."

She wrapped her arms around him, wishing she could offer him absolution.

"I know it to be an irrational thought, but there it is. I was a disappointment to him. I was not manly enough, not brave enough, not worldly enough. I live a small life, and this life was a disappointment to him."

His words echoed her own self-doubts so astutely, her eyes watered. *A small life.*

"You're a good man, a fine man. You are the most sober, responsible man I know. You could never be a disappointment."

"He wanted me to be like him, to take risks, to embrace danger and adventure. He saw me as a bore and a coward."

For a moment, she saw the child in him, desperate for approval, and she longed to comfort him. But she knew such reassurance would be meaningless to him, coming from anyone but the one person whose validation he most needed but could never have. She knew the feeling of not living up to the expectations and values of a parent long deceased. No one else could assuage the guilt; one only learned to live with it.

Chapter Fifteen

Evans Principle... well, not so much a principle as good advice, dear: Expect the unexpected, especially in a room filled with books!

In the light of a new morning, Honoria berated herself for being old enough to know better than to succumb to purely physical pleasures. The guest room wasn't large enough for her to escape her thoughts so she practically ran to the one room she could trust as a refuge in any building: the library. She breathed a sigh of relief to find it unoccupied. Even though she'd only been in this particular library once since her arrival, there was always something soothing and familiar about being surrounded by so many paper and leather volumes. She decided to start at one end of the room and work her way around to see how the books were organized. Every house had a system; the most practical and literal would alphabetize while the more creative and fanciful might group books by topic or theme or personal whim. She'd sorted through many an estate that had a wall for practical matters like agriculture, another for philosophical texts throughout the ages, and yet another for literary value. Activities like this were exactly what she needed to distract her from the emotional chaos of what had happened the day before at the lake.

As she made her way carefully through the shelves of this room, however, no particular system announced itself to her. With Dante between Mary Wollstonecraft and Olaudah Equiano, there didn't appear to be any rhyme or reason to the arrangement of books in this room. She started at one corner, making her way methodically along a wall. Broad mahogany columns interrupted the shelves on each wall, separating them by quarters. Eventually, each quarter seemed to resolve into a different personality. On each wall, the right-most quarter she examined seemed without logical organization whatsoever, the second followed a very mundane alphabetical order, and the third (usually made up of political treatises) was organized by political party. It took her until halfway around the room to realize the sections must belong to different members of the Devin family. She guessed that Amelia was the right-most quarter, in part because it held more novels and light, happy pieces. She sensed that Alexander's sections were not the alphabetized ones, which would be rather too obvious for him. Instead, she surmised that his was the left-most section on each wall, with books grouped by purpose and then alphabetized within each group. When she reached the last wall, she noticed a small, worn volume with an open back on a shelf above her head; a dun-colored item, little more than a stack of rough pages sewn together, shouldn't have drawn anyone's eye amid so many elegant stacks of books, but she couldn't resist a closer look at the unusual binding and yellowing parchment. She had to stretch on her toes and lean against a mahogany dividing column to be able to reach said volume, and was so intent on the prize that she was startled when the wood beneath her fingers slid sideways.

A secret panel! She felt a bit foolish when she looked inside and discovered it was simply a storage space. This area held writing paper, fresh quills, and ink bottles. Unable to contain her curiosity, she peeked into each storage panel set into the dividers.

When she arrived at the far end of the room and slid the last panel aside, she was astounded to see a beautiful—truly lovely—cello. The burnished wood of the instrument glowed.

"What are you doing?"

She jumped a million miles, not just because of the surprise of being discovered . . . that voice was imprinted on her brain and her heart.

"I didn't mean to snoop," she said hurriedly. "I was merely curious about the way your library is organized. Your mother did say I should make myself at home."

"By all means, pick any book you like to occupy your time." He strolled directly toward her, past her really, to close the panel next to her gently. "I do not think, though, that my mother's invitation grants you the right to go through the family's drawers and cabinets."

Her face went hot. She nodded.

"No, of course! I overstepped my boundaries. I do apologize."

He said nothing in response, focusing his gaze on the panel he had just slid shut. Her curiosity got the better of her, as usual.

"It's a magnificent piece of work, that cello."

"It is a Stradivarius."

"Really?" she whispered. "Are they as impressive as their reputation attests?"

He looked at her long enough for her to feel uncomfortable before he replied, "They are, beyond belief, more impressive than purported. This one elevates music from mere pleasure to sublimity."

She finally deciphered the signs of his demeanor.

"That's your cello! You used to play?"

He nodded, almost sheepish.

"Would you play something for me?"

"I have not played in quite a long time. I am unaccustomed to playing for an audience."

"I hardly constitute an audience. It's just me. Furthermore, I probably couldn't tell the difference between the scales and a sonata. I've just never heard an actual Strad."

She was delightfully surprised by his acquiescence and waited patiently while he set up the music stand and tuned the cello. She was actually content to witness his tuning session. When he began a concerto, however, she was struck dumb. Soon, completely taken over by the music, his eyes closed and his body swayed. Taken over by the music, he was mesmerizing. This was passion.

The piece he'd selected was nearly violent in its range. The deep bass notes vibrated through her; she could only imagine how much more visceral an experience it was to be playing, to feel the notes transmitted through his own body. A strange thing began to happen; she wasn't sure when it started. But each stroke of the bow seemed to echo in her flesh. The swift back and forth movement of his arm tingled across her breasts; the gradual dip into lower octaves spread lower through her, vibrating through her core. She stared at his hands, working the instrument masterfully, drawing out exquisitely vibrant and moving tones. Her body nearly shook as she felt the piece build, deeper and more intense.

He opened his eyes, and the intensity of his dark gaze speared her. Could he know the tumult rushing through her body? She panted, unable to control the feelings coursing through her. His fingers, so masterfully controlling the strings, so powerfully drawing the bow, might as well be playing along her sensitive skin, so extreme was her physical response to his music. She half feared she might come to an internal crisis sitting there before him. And he might see it all.

As the piece came to an end, she whispered, "Bach was my mother's favorite."

"Mine as well," said a soft voice from the doorway.

"Lady Devin—" "Mother—" They spoke simultaneously as Lord Devin rose from his seat.

"Please do not let me disturb you, Alex. It has just been so long since I have heard you play. You have such a gift." His mother looked wistful, almost sad.

"How long has it been?" Honoria could not resist asking.

"Eight years," he said tightly.

Since his father's death, then. She wasn't the only one struggling with unruly emotions. Lady Devin blinked back tears, while he put away the cello carefully. "That was lovely, son." And she quietly left the room.

"We should do something . . . else." His eyes burned into her.

"We're not doing that!"

"Then we should get out of this room, perhaps even find solitary activities . . . because, at this moment, I very much want to do . . . *that*."

"A game of croquet?" she offered.

No.

"A swim?"

His look spoke volumes. No, a swim would not prevent *that*.

"I know! Let us go riding. I would love to see more of the grounds."

His expression darkened, and he blustered. This man who never misspoke suddenly stumbled over syllables. "Oh, I forgot—that is, I must—you are welcome to take one of the horses but—oh, ahem, I am sure a groom can accompany you—"

She was having none of that.

"A moment ago, you would have done anything to stay in my company. What happened?"

"It is . . . the horses. I know we have beautiful horses; I visit them whenever I am here, give them treats, admire their . . . size."

Given his sharp discomfort, she appreciated his attempt at candor. "Can you not ride?"

"Of course I can ride!" His voice turned shrill. "Every man of my stature knows how to ride a bloody horse. It is supposed to be as bred into them as tying a cravat, reading bloody Aristotle, and firing a damned pistol." He was breathing heavily now, frustration lacing his words in a way she couldn't interpret.

"I can ride," he repeated unnecessarily.

"But you dislike it?"

He flipped his hand in front of his face as if to swat away her question.

"Why do you dislike it so much?"

He didn't want to remember, didn't want to dredge up the embarrassment and resentment. But it was already there.

"It was my father. He said learning to ride was essential. No surprise, but his reasoning was that sometimes you had to travel on a pack animal . . . a horse, a mule, a camel, maybe even an ostrich. He had quite a way with horses. He could calm a feisty stallion within five minutes and then make it dance his attendance within ten. I'd seen him do so. And I wanted more than anything to be like him. I did not want him to leave me behind. So I made a concerted effort to become an expert horseman."

He sat back in his chair, remembering.

"I always picked the most spirited horse in the stable. If Father's headstrong Medusa was away with him, I mounted Balthazar, a true beast from hell. I was thrown almost every day, sometimes multiple times a day. Bruised and aching, I refused to give up, even when I came to realize it was too much horse for me. Looking back, I would have learned more effectively if I had started with more amenable horses. One day, Balthazar nearly broke my neck and trampled me. I was in bed for a month. Perhaps even worse, one of his legs was broken in his frenzy. We had to put him down."

He stared at nothing. She wanted to go to him, comfort the child who'd been so desperate to please and so badly hurt. Yet she could not.

"When my father returned from wherever he was," he continued, "his disappointment hurt far worse than the physical pain. Rather than forbid me to ride, he sold our more spirited mounts, except for his own. He need not have bothered. I have not ridden anything more lively than a pack mule since then."

"Many horses have more amenable dispositions, you know," she said lightly. "By the sound of it, virtually all others would be more pleasant than Balthazar."

"Of course, I know that. In my mind, I know it. And I have ridden some tame beasts. But when I get near any of them, my mind slips. Rationality is lost. Instead, I taste fear and have to force myself to mount. I cannot describe it sufficiently. A kind of blind panic takes over until I have alighted at my destination."

"What a difficult burden, considering the lands you are responsible for."

"That is what I have a manager for." It was all he was willing to say to her about the subject. "Speaking of my manager, I recall that there are some pieces of business I must attend to, if you will excuse me."

She nodded and watched him escape swiftly.

When she returned from her evening walk, she was not at all surprised to find him sitting in her room. But she was surprised that he was sitting in the dark and that he didn't speak when she entered. It was improper for him to be here, of course, but they'd already broken so many bounds of propriety. His mother's room was on the other side of the house. The servants had no purpose for being in this wing. No one would find him here. Even if they did, at this precise moment, she didn't have the energy to care.

"You were quiet at dinner," she said, casting about for something to say. It was true. His mother made several attempts to engage him in conversation at the table, but he participated as little as common courtesy allowed. At one point, his mother gave Honoria a questioning look, but she could only raise her shoulders and shake her head. Something clearly wasn't right, but she couldn't fathom the problem.

"I have a lot on my mind this evening."

Once she lit the lamp on the writing desk, she noticed his unusually serious expression. She suspected its cause and knew the decision she'd made at dinner was the right one.

"You should know," she began, "I've decided to go home to the shop tomorrow morning. There is so much to do. I've enjoyed this trip immensely, but now it is time for me to return to reality. Your mother has arranged for her coach to take me while she stays another week."

He remained silent, his expression unreadable, so she continued.

"Your mother has been so gracious, so very kind. In such a short time, she's become the closest thing I've ever had to a friend. But I'm sure that's just her way with everyone."

"She likes you. She enjoys your company. You should stay."

"She doesn't really know me."

"My mother is a perceptive judge of character. She knows you well enough."

"Does she know about my sham of a marriage? Does she know about us?"

He shrugged. "Your . . . marriage . . . is not her concern. As for us, she probably suspects, as she is not blind."

"Do you always parade your mistresses in front of your mother?" she asked, indignant on his mother's behalf. But he sidestepped the question.

"So you are my mistress now?" He looked at her intently.

"Experiential evidence points to that conclusion, doesn't it? That's why you're here right now, isn't it?"

He shook his head slowly, looking down at his hands as he turned them over and over in front of him.

"I do want you," he admitted. "It seems I cannot stop wanting you." At this, her belly fluttered in sympathetic response. "But that is not why I am here. I am, after all, fully capable of controlling my rapacious lust when needed." He quirked his mouth and stood and, as if to prove his words to both of them, moved toward the windows, away from her and away from the bed.

"I've never been good at reading minds," she said, impatiently. "If you're not here for that, why are you here?"

"I am here because I . . . because I love you."

"Stop." She couldn't bear to hear. She couldn't bear the hope stirred by his words.

"As if I could."

"No, really, stop talking to me like this. Right now." She was suddenly furious. "I told you already it's unnecessary. And you can't love me. You cannot. Infatuation it may be, and it will pass. It always does. But don't speak to me of love."

He strode up to her, fast and fierce. His eyes hardened like jade.

"Why not? Why do you censor me? I love you. This is not some fleeting and immature infatuation. I love you. And I have every right to say so."

"It's not real," she whispered. "I am a nobody, and you are . . . you. This is an airy fiction built on paper and dust. It will end, and it will shatter us both. And we both have too many serious responsibilities to let this distract us."

"You are not a nobody. You were born to nobility. What do I need to do to convince you?"

"There is nothing you can do to convince me. I am not nobility now. I am a shopkeeper. I earn a living, and there can be nothing between us."

"Marry me."

"No! Don't be ridiculous."

"What do you mean no?"

"No. You aren't sincerely asking, and I couldn't accept, even if you were. This isn't real. It's impossible."

"So what do we do now?"

"I don't know." After a moment, she added, "We should say our good-byes then and be done with it."

He walked up to her and put a finger under her chin to tilt her face up to his.

"I will never be done with you," he said, low and fierce. He touched his lips to hers gently. "Do you hear me? Do I have to print it in the *Times*?" His movements were so slow, but his intent could not be misinterpreted. He drew her into him as he worshipped her skin with his mouth.

One last time, she promised herself. *Just this once.* There was no point in denying she wanted this as much as he did. Her desire for him, keen and intense and bitter, tore at her heart and tightened every nerve in her body. Just this one last time she would revel in his touch, take whatever pleasure he offered, and give herself up to this tide of bittersweet ecstasy.

This time was different. Their previous encounters had been moments frozen in time, frenzied and near-senseless interludes where reason and logic had no place. Their first night together had been frantic and emotional, fueled by the intensity of the shop's destruction and her overwrought nerves. Even their afternoon at the lake seemed to stand apart from her real life; they'd been transported to a temporary Eden. But this time . . . when their lips touched, when she slid her arms around his shoulders . . . this was a conscious, rational choice. What had happened between them before was like a hazy dream. This night was the one she would remember with absolute clarity. She wasn't swept away. She wasn't seduced. She would deliberately take what she could get and give what she could spare.

She stretched up to meet him fully, gripping his arms. As his arms tightened around her, she slid her hands into his hair and sighed against his mouth at the intensity of openly acknowledging her desire for him and her pleasure at his touch. How had she come to this point? If someone had told her mere weeks ago she would be here, now, in this moment, she would have called a physician to have the speaker examined. How had this impossibility come to be? She was Medusa to his Perseus. How had she not consigned him to stone? And, she could not help but wonder in the deepest recesses of her heart how long it would be before he would slay her, carrying her heart instead of her head away as a trophy.

So quickly he'd learned what pleased her. And yet, she needed just a little . . . more. As he lavished extravagant attention on her left breast, her own hand stole up to the right one. She wasn't sure when or how her body had become so greedy. While he laved her nipple, she stroked and tweaked and rolled the other nipple between her fingers to sharpen the exquisite sensations. When he caught sight of her hand, his low laughter rumbled through her.

"In dereliction of duty, am I?" He bit lightly on the first nipple, causing her to convulse, before shifting to the second, dislodging her hand. "Allow me."

He molded the now-abandoned breast with his palm while lashing the new one with his tongue. His hands gently pushed her abundant breasts closer together. He glanced at her devilishly. Surely not! Then he took both nipples into his mouth at the same time! *Dear God in heaven!* Such intense sensations rocketed through her that she bucked and shook. The keen sensation of his hot mouth, working in tandem on both breasts, made her gasp and thrash and moan. Words couldn't describe the steep dual crescendo of pleasure shooting through her. She needed a new word for pleasure.

"I knew there had to be a solution," he said, when he finally released her breasts and laid his head on one.

"Clever lad." She breathed heavily.

He raised himself up on one elbow and drawled, "Now show me what else you like."

"Well, I do like this." She smiled and slid her hand down to stroke his hot, hard length.

He moaned but took her hand and raised it to his mouth. He slipped two of her fingers between his lips, sliding his tongue between them ever so gently, and then said, "No, not yet. *Show* me what *you* like." His inflections made his meaning clear, and his eyes held a challenge.

Not one to back down, she answered by shifting her position for more freedom of movement and hooking one leg over his. She was well practiced in taking care of her own needs. So she put her hand in that secret place, parting her own folds, and began to rub firmly but gently. She found the sensitive nub and tried to concentrate. She closed her eyes to focus on the task at hand and was soon breathing heavily while a mild tension built in her lower abdomen. He sat up for a better view, and she bent both knees, legs spread, as much for her benefit as for his. But for all her rubbing and stroking, this time she could not bring herself to finish. She made tiny adjustments to her positions but could not come to the end. Soon, her hand tired, and she gave up, irritated. "It's not working!"

"Shh." He put his hand where hers had been and slowly stroked. "Does it usually work?"

"It *always* works. Every time. I just don't think I can concentrate with an audience."

He chuckled wickedly. She even thought she detected smugness.

"Since I am at fault for your bind, I must do what I can to assist you. Teach me what pleases you." His intent disarmed her. He stoked her flames and then slid a thumb into her soft, wet folds. She hadn't noticed before how large his thumbs were.

"Oh!" she said, when he swirled over a particularly sensitive area.

"Is that a good spot, then?" he asked, unnecessarily. He swirled over it a few more times for confirmation, smiling more broadly each time she bucked.

"Hmm," he said. "Let's try another." He swirled his thumb in a different direction, with milder but still positive effects. She couldn't speak.

"And one more test for good measure." His thumb pushed in a little deeper and swirled against a new spot. This time, sensations radiated through her. Her back arched, hips lifting off the bed, and she cried out.

"It would seem we have a new winner." He set himself to targeting that spot, teasing and thrusting with his hand. He stuffed a corner of the counterpane in her mouth to stifle her and captured a nipple in his mouth as his hand continued to drive her higher and higher. She came hard, screaming into the bedclothes and shuddering endlessly.

When she could finally breathe again, she said, "God above, what have you done to me?"

With a devilish gleam in his eye, he covered her body with his. As the tip of his manhood nudged her warm, still-throbbing entrance, he whispered, "Oh, my dear, we are just getting started."

"Wait!"

He groaned as he struggled to master his body. "Wait? I do not believe I can. For how long? What's wrong?"

"Nothing is wrong, Alex," she whispered as she pushed him away and wriggled from underneath him. "But I want an active role in this too." She pushed him onto his back and began her own expedition down his body, prompting guttural moans from him with her hands and then her mouth. The more she heard, the more she wanted to push his pleasure further. When they were both panting with intense need, he leaned his head toward her and wrenched her mouth up to his.

"I love you! I need you now!" he exclaimed against her lips. "Take me, damn it. Take me into you now!"

She took the reins without hesitation, guiding him into her entrance. The novel sensation of control made her giddy, and she took him in ever so slowly, smiling at the way his breath hitched, the way his hands gripped her hips, as their bodies inched together. Not too fast. Not too soon.

When they were fully joined—finally—she arched above him and began to rock slowly, sliding up his cock almost entirely and then inching back down, reveling in the feel of him filling her bit by bit. The sight of him, eyes closed and head thrown back, spurred her to move more forcefully, making them both pant and moan. He sat up to meet her, whispering words of love, as she rode him harder, faster, her fingers digging into his back to bring them ever closer, never close enough. As her crisis neared, she felt him grow impossibly firmer, thrust impossibly deeper, and suddenly they both exploded together—she buried her cries in his shoulder as he shouted, maybe her name.

She would tuck this memory away, perhaps let it warm her on cold winter nights, alone in her room above the bookshop. But she would let him go.

Chapter Sixteen

Evans Principle 4,012: Self-preservation is sometimes indistinguishable from cowardice. Do what you must to thrive or at least to survive.

The coach was ready. There was nothing to do but leave. She'd already said her good-byes to Lady Devin. And she didn't want to see the face of that snake, that Judas, that devil ever again. *I love you*, he'd said. *Marry me*, he'd said. She'd known it was a fiction; she just didn't realize it was blatant, self-serving, despicable manipulation. He hadn't just built a fairy tale; he'd built a trap. If she saw him, she couldn't account for her actions or for any appendages he might lose. She needed to get back to her home, back to her shop, and get her things in order. And now she needed a long, scalding bath to wash away the tainted memory of his skin against hers. She'd tried so hard to be cautious, suspicious, but he'd broken her anyway.

Once safely inside the coach, ensconced in its dark, close interior, she allowed herself to reflect on the conversation she'd overheard. She hadn't meant to eavesdrop. On her way to tea, she'd intended to see if Lord Devin—Lord Pisspot!—was available to escort her. She just wanted to see him. Oh, how girlishly foolish she'd been. The door had been slightly ajar, and she'd been taken aback by the voices within, sharp and unfriendly. Unwilling to impose or interrupt, she'd been just about to continue downstairs when she heard her name.

"Mr. Withersby insists that you terminate the threat Mrs. Duchamp poses and that you do it immediately. We now know she is responsible for these publications, and we are prepared to take more serious steps if you do not. But these delaying tactics are insufficient. She must not be allowed to continue her investigation, and she must be immediately discredited."

Honoria thought the visitor's voice sounded familiar but couldn't place it. She couldn't hear the content of Alex's response, either, only the timbre of his voice. It was angry but not affronted or indignant. It was damning.

She slouched back into the coach cushions and thought about her first few meetings with him. His inquisitiveness, both in her and in the shop, made so much more sense now. She'd known all along he couldn't genuinely be interested in either, but it hurt viscerally to know how thoroughly he'd deceived her, how completely he'd seduced her.

Her stomach clenched as her memory of their encounters unfolded behind her eyelids. Even last night, his declaration of love was all part of an elaborate falsehood. Her skin crawled as she thought of his caresses, of every kiss, of every stroke, of every damned thrust that now made her want to turn herself inside out. She'd guarded herself so carefully for so long. To be so easily fooled and so thoroughly debased made her want to skin herself alive. He'd made her feel valued, made her feel desirable, made her believe he just might . . . possibly . . . love her. She gripped at the leather of the seat, wanting to tear it apart, wanting to destroy something.

As the carriage put more miles between her and Sharling Worth, she forced herself to focus on what to do next. She would have to dismiss the Devin workers and complete the repairs herself. The Needlework ladies could perhaps be of some assistance, but she hated to ask. Perhaps most importantly, she would have to figure out how to replace the press.

All she could think of were problems upon problems needing attention. He'd made her believe he could help solve them. Little did she know he was the problem, incarnate. Resting her head back against the squabs, she fought back tears. Weakness would not do. She needed to be strong, needed to find the Mrs. Duchamp that she once was and reestablish her position of safety and reliability. That was a life she knew and trusted.

Chapter Seventeen

Evans Principle Theta: Kindness is not the same as weakness, even though others may try to interpret it as such. Be as kind to yourself as you are to everyone else.

After the visit from Withersby's henchman, Alex furiously tried to figure out how to get Honoria out of this situation. He closed himself up in his study for over an hour trying to puzzle through scenarios: convince Honoria to stop investigating the company and publishing her findings, convince Withersby it wasn't Honoria's doing and have him call off his dogs, or perhaps simply guard Honoria around the clock and fend off whatever attackers were sent her way.

He was so preoccupied with these thoughts that he didn't find out about her departure until lunchtime, when he went to find her.

The note she'd left for his mother simply said she felt she was needed back at the shop. But he couldn't help doubting the coincidence that she left so soon after his unpleasant meeting with Withersby's man. She'd left no note for him. Not a good sign. By now, she was miles away. He could only imagine what must be running through her mind. How much had she heard? He must look like the worst kind of villain. He needed to go after her, and he sped out the door unthinking.

Only the sight of the road managed to jolt him out of his tunnel vision. Their coach was taking her to London at that very moment. His best chance of catching her was . . . on horseback. A hollow pit formed in his gut as he looked in the direction of the stables, his mind doing calculations on speed and power. There was nothing for it. His mild Proserpine didn't have the strength and stamina for this purpose. Even as he felt chills run down his spine and out to his extremities, he knew he not only had to ride like the devil but on the animal he now thought of as the devil incarnate: Andrew's enormous stallion. Black as hell and just as fiery. Zeus. On Zeus, there was a chance he could catch up to the coach before it reached London. There was just as much chance he'd break his fool neck. But it was worth the risk. He had to get to Nora, had to face her wrath, and maybe, with God's grace, convince her of the truth.

The stable master called undecipherable warnings to him as he rode away. Control was an illusion. He hadn't been able to control Withersby . . . or the way the truth shot out in unruly directions. He couldn't control what would come out about Andrew's romantic relationships. Zeus wasn't in his control; he felt it clearly in the horse's muscles, in his own panicky but ineffectual grip on the reins. None of that mattered. All that mattered was getting to Nora.

She didn't hear the swift hoofbeats until they sped right past the carriage. Alarm gripped her as the coach pulled up suddenly. She'd been told that highway bandits were rare on this stretch but not impossible. Then she heard *his* voice shouting for the carriage to halt. Heard a heavy thud, followed by the sound of something landing heavily on the ground. Followed by an awful groan. *His.*

She couldn't get the door open fast enough. The driver was already on the ground by him. She gripped the doorjamb as she gingerly lowered herself to the ground and then ran to his side as fast as her skirts allowed. She grabbed his hand, finding it warm but slack.

"My God, Alex, what happened?! Alex!"

"I saw it all, miss," said the driver. "'Twas Zeus, miss. Caught his foot in a hole and slammed into yonder tree. They were flying when they wheeled so it was a right brutal hit."

She could see the beast, huge and intimidating as night itself, stomping nearby. Clearly, Zeus was still shaken by the accident himself. Fortunately, he didn't appear to be limping. Such a stumble could easily lame the animal, which equaled a death sentence. The wild look in his eye suggested he might bolt at any second, but the rest of him showed remarkable restraint, as if he knew his place was here.

Focusing on the horse gave her a moment to brace herself before looking down at the rider, at Alex. During the carriage ride, she'd resolved never to see him again, damn his bloody hide. She'd never been more certain of anything in her life. He'd nearly destroyed her. Everything from him—every word, every moment, every sensation—everything had been a lie. And she would never let him near her again.

But when she heard those sickening thuds just as she realized it was him, all her rationality and anger and resolve disappeared. Her heart seized. Fear for him . . . and love for him . . . gripped her so hard she thought she might go mad. It was a long moment before she could bring herself to look at his face. Her hands shook as she ran them over his throat lightly, looking for a pulse. She found one, fast but steady, yet his eyes remained closed.

The driver came up and handed her some salts he'd found in a traveling case. When she held them to his nose, he shook his head briefly and lethargically.

"Alex! Alex, can you hear me?" Desperately, she patted his cheek and brushed hair from his forehead. She wanted to shake him awake—rather violently, given her anxiety—but couldn't risk causing him further injury.

He moaned as his hands reached for the one touching his face.

"It's me, Alex, it's Nora. Please, open your eyes."

He mumbled something she couldn't hear. She bent to his lips and whispered, "Say again, please. I'm here with you. What can I do?"

Then she heard it. No more than a breath.

"I'm sorry, my love," he said.

She sank back on her heels and burst into tears. Between her sobs, she said haltingly, "You—you have to be all right. I—I can't—I cannot bear to—lose you."

He opened his eyes and smiled, actually smiled, at her.

"You cannot get rid of me that easily, love."

She could not bring herself to smile in response, but the sight of him conscious eased her nerves tremendously.

After perhaps as much as an hour, she and the driver helped him to stand, and he seemed to suffer no serious injury. The driver assisted him matter-of-factly into the carriage and went to hitch Zeus to the back. Only after they were safely ensconced did she realize how much they must have revealed—she'd used his given name, for heaven's sake. Her face burned with shame.

He rested his head back with a groan, wiping away all thoughts of external scrutiny.

"If it would make you feel better to lie down, don't mind me."

"No, being vertical is definitely better." He shifted, though, and closed his eyes only to reopen them almost immediately. "Oh, mustn't do that."

"What happened?"

"When I close my eyes, I feel nausea. Not a good sign. A tutor at Eton always warned us during cricket that we should watch for nausea, dizziness, and blurred vision if we ever caught a good hard knock on the head. And we should avoid falling asleep if we do have those symptoms." He groaned again, also not a good sign, considering the general British male's "stiff upper lip."

"I hate to sound uninformed, but what would that mean exactly?"

"It would mean I have a concussion, a brain injury." He spoke flatly and stared at the ceiling of the compartment.

She gasped and made to move toward him. "That sounds serious. We must get you to a physician!"

"Not much a physician can do at the moment. There is no definitive treatment for it, except to immobilize the skull and give the brain time to heal. Some surgeons might even suggest drilling a hole in the skull, but I would prefer to avoid such a course. I am reassured by the fact that I have not lost consciousness."

"But you did! When you first fell off Zeus, you were unconscious for several moments." Several awful, awful moments.

He cursed and winced as the carriage hit a deep rut, jostling its occupants.

"We can't continue on, Alex! We must get you out and give you time to recuperate."

"Where? On the side of the open road? We will arrive in London soon enough; I shall rest at Devin House." As she humphed loudly, he added with a wink, "You can nurse me there more comfortably than here."

Suddenly, the painful facts that had been driven from her mind by concern for him rushed back with visceral clarity. She'd been so sure that the next time she saw him, if ever, she would not speak with him. So much for her resolve. She'd thought she couldn't possibly bring herself to acknowledge his lying, deceptive existence. And yet none of it mattered when she saw him lying unconscious, when she feared the very real possibility of losing him. Her capacity for self-deception was apparently bottomless. She looked out the window at green fields and wildflowers as she considered a complex onslaught of emotions, guilt foremost among them. He had come after her. When she admitted the truth about her marriage, he had forgiven her unreservedly. He hadn't made the truth public knowledge, which he easily could have done.

He'd said he loved her.

Yet she couldn't trust any of it anymore, could she? How much of it had been faked? Was it all just a cruel and elaborate ruse?

When she finally looked back at him, she noticed his eyes were closed, his body slumped.

"Alex! Alex, wake up!" She rushed to grab his hand and pat it. When her gentle ministrations didn't work, she slapped his cheek hard enough to sting her hand but not to rock his head. He raised his head a fraction, and his eyelids fluttered. "Alex, it's me. It's Nora. Can you hear me?"

He opened his eyes—thank God!—and she held his head in her hands, forcing him to look her in the eye. "Stay awake, Alex. Stay with me. Do you hear me? Stay!"

He nodded slowly.

"I'm sorry, Nora. I never wanted to lie to you."

"Leave that for now." She brushed hair away from his face, her heart seizing when he laid his cheek in her palm. "We'll discuss it later. Right now, we need to get you to London, and I need you to stay awake. Talk to me."

"About what?" he said sluggishly.

"Anything." She cast about for a subject, any subject that might keep him talking. "Tell me what possessed you to get on that demonic horse. You know better."

"Zeus is the fastest horse in the stable, by far. He was the only one who could catch up with you. Under regular circumstances, I would not take him, but I did not have a choice."

Didn't have a choice. How often had he used that reasoning? she wondered. Surely, that's the excuse he would give for deceiving her. And yet here he was, having braved an animal of which he was terrified and getting injured in the process. For her. What a difficult life, indeed, if he didn't have free will over any of the events that got him here.

The drive to London seemed endless and the roads abominably maintained. As they turned onto a smoother avenue, she noticed homes built more closely together. She kept him talking about nearly anything and everything, from his next planned speech in Parliament to the building of the railways to the actual costs of tea in China. She also managed not to touch him again. As much as it hurt her not to, she still could not trust him one whit. She'd get him to Devin House and see him properly cared for, and then she would sever their connections completely.

"Hit me," he said abruptly, interrupting her thoughts.

"What?"

"Hit me. As hard as you can." He looked clear-eyed and somber. Those eyes she'd found irresistible were a hard jade green, and she so wanted to give in. "It won't erase the awful things I've done to you, but it might make you feel better."

"You're certifiably insane."

"Do it. I deserve it."

"That is indisputable, but I cannot." She tore her gaze from his and folded her arms tightly across her chest. "You are already seriously injured. In any case, it would solve nothing, and the notion of touching you, even in violence, is too disgusting for words."

He closed his eyes, but she could not help feeling he wasn't done. They couldn't get to Devin House soon enough. And yet, she wasn't sure what made her heart ache worse—his utter perfidy or the imminent loss of him—and she hated herself for her weakness.

"Please, Mrs. Duchamp, you have been most kind throughout this journey," he said without a trace of irony and, he hoped, only a little begging, when they arrived at Devin House. "It would be a great favor if you could assist me in getting settled. I fear I am still unsteady, and you seem adept at handling emergencies."

She nodded tightly, and his heart thrilled at the tiny victory. He could not let her leave without offering her an explanation. Despite the many servants available, including his very capable butler Johnson, he made clear she was his guide and helper, and the others acceded to her directions. Soon enough, he was comfortably arranged on a sofa in the library with a copious tea placed before him.

"You must stay, Mrs. Duchamp, at least for tea. You have done so much and cannot have eaten in hours. It is the least I can offer as your incapacitated host." The footman left the library doors almost closed.

Again, she replied with a single, decisive nod, unsmiling. In all her attentiveness, she'd spoken directly to his staff and spared only minimal words for him. Perched on the edge of her chair, she served them both tea. She made both without sugar or milk and placed his tea and a biscuit within his reach; he struggled to remember when she might have learned his preferences—which she'd captured exactly—especially since he did not recall learning hers.

"Nora," he began, but she flinched at his use of her name. He closed his eyes against the sight, damning himself for his dishonesty. There was no other way but to spit out the truth before she abandoned him.

"It is my brother, Honoria. Withersby is threatening to expose my brother for sodomy, which I am sure you know is punishable by death." He said it in a rush, the words sounding strange even to him.

"Are you sure, then, that your brother is . . . has . . ."

"Fool that I was, I hired Withersby to keep track of my brother when he first left home. Andrew is so fragile and naïve, you see. My mother was beside herself with worry the first month he was gone. I just wanted to make sure he was safe and did not run into trouble. Three months gone, reports came in that Andrew had formed a very close relationship with one of his former school chums, that they went everywhere together, that they were inseparable, that they eschewed the company of women. Then came the reports of visits to bathhouses of nefarious reputation."

Her brows drew together. "But that's all still speculation."

"Somehow, Withersby managed to obtain a few photographs of them together. I have not seen all of them, but what I have seen is

suggestive enough to raise suspicion. And my brother cannot be subject to suspicion."

Her breathing was slow and deliberate. He watched her mobile
face as she considered.

"I fail to see," she said finally, "what that has to do with me and
Evans Books."

He forced himself to look her in the eye as he admitted, "Withersby ordered me to discredit you or else he would make public my
brother's disgrace. Andrew could be arrested, imprisoned, even
hanged, and the scandal would destroy my mother."

"Does your brother know all you do to protect him?"

"Of course not. I would never presume to talk with him about this
. . . proclivity. He is my brother, and it is my job to protect him. Without fanfare. Without acknowledgment."

"If you were my brother, I'd want to know what you know about
me. I'd want to be told what slander people sling about me."

"Funny, you care so much about what other people think."

"That's not true! I don't—" She caught herself in the midst of her
instinctive reply. And she thought about it. She always said it didn't
matter what other people thought of her . . . but it did. So much so
that she deliberately camouflaged herself in the middle ground, not
sharing herself, not standing out in any way, good or bad. She realized she'd rather be one of the faceless crowd because she couldn't
bear to put her best face forward and be found wanting. If she presented banality, there was no harm in being perceived as banal. If she
aspired to more, then she might be deemed a failure.

"Your devotion to your brother is admirable, my lord, but the fact
remains that you lied to me."

"Yes, but I swear to you, Honoria, that I had nothing to do with
the break-in. I was not a decoy. I was not using you."

"I would like to believe you, but now I can't trust anything coming from your lips."

"You must trust me, Nora. I did mean to investigate whether you
were the source of these papers, and I was ordered to stop you if you
were. But since the moment I met you, I knew I would not stop anything you wanted to do, even if I could. I would never deliberately
harm you. I have to protect my brother, but I will find a way to protect
you both. I can convince him to stay in Greece or some other wel-

coming nation for an indefinite period. He enjoys travel; I shall continue to fund him abroad and set him up in some honest work."

"You lied to me," she repeated.

"Yes." That was all he said. No apology. No expression of remorse. In the ensuing silence, he could see by her shifting expression that she accurately interpreted his tacit accusation. He wasn't the only one who'd lied.

"Yes, I lied too," she said, pacing to the far shelves, putting a display case and armchair between them. "But my lies were for self-protection. They weren't aimed at destroying you."

"Ah, but you have destroyed me, my love. You have utterly devastated me. You drive me to distraction. You are a cancer in my brain, and you lied too."

He walked to her and laid his palm on her soft cheek.

"And yet, once you gave me the truth," he said, "I sealed it within and kept your secret as my own."

She moved away, nodding, but then added, "So you say. So far. All this time, you've been spying on me, seducing me. You had me convinced that you wanted me. I knew . . . I *knew* it couldn't be real. You are quite the master thespian. And I am a desperate, dried-up fool. I hope touching me wasn't too much of a hardship."

"Do not do that. Do not dare doubt my affection for you. Every kiss was sincere. Every touch was honest. I love you." His frustration grew exponentially as he followed her, as the impossibility of his position sank in. There was no way she could trust him now.

"Sincerity? Honesty? Love? What do you know of any of that?"

"I know that one cannot possibly simulate *this*." He pulled her to him for a hard, frantic kiss. He focused all of his energy into this one kiss, hoping to communicate all his longing, all his regret, all his love from his body to hers. He desperately hoped her body would recognize the truth her brain wouldn't. She leaned into him, her arms around his neck pulling him closer. She opened to his kiss, and their tongues thrust and parried. His hands roamed her body with abandon, and he relished the sighs and moans coming from her throat.

But then, he felt her unmistakable rejection. She didn't pull away from him, didn't push against his chest to force him away. She didn't make a single sound of protest. She simply stopped. First her hands stopped moving, stopped clinging. Then, inch by inch, her body shut down. The tension he'd felt in her back and shoulders as she'd strained to embrace him tighter and tighter—all of that energy slowly dissipated until the fine muscles were again masked by soft flesh. Finally, her mouth, that unbearably sweet and mobile mouth, went slack too. It wasn't like holding a statue, which would be rigid and unyielding and defiant. It was rather like holding a dead quail, limp and lifeless and empty. He released her slowly, reluctantly. Even her face was devoid of life. At that moment, he'd have much preferred her eyes flashing fire bolts at him and her face contorted by fury. What he saw in her eyes instead was something horribly close to despair.

She backed away from him yet again, looking like a frightened doe. When she looked toward the large windows, he suspected she was trying to gauge whether she could safely drop to the ground if she went through one of them. When he reached his hand out to touch her face, he caught the faintest twitch of a grimace and stopped. She looked sad and worn. And he had done this to her.

"Every word, every touch, every—" Her voice broke. "It's all corrupted. Every memory is tainted with betrayal—mine as much as yours. It's all ruined, and I can't bear it. I believe it would be best for me to leave now," she said quietly, barely above a whisper.

"But, Nora—"

"I'm afraid I must insist, Lord Devin." Then he heard it. The barely controlled quavering in her voice. She was broken, and she didn't want him to see how severely.

"Listen to me—" he tried again.

She brought her eyes to meet his.

"Please," she said. "I beg of you. Just leave me be." He couldn't ignore how much it cost her. The Nora he had come to know never begged, not even in jest. And he had done this to her.

He bowed to her and said, "I am deeply sorry." He kissed her hand and released it. When she reached the door, she looked back, and his heart stopped.

"You deserve more than this," he said.

She nodded one last time and walked out, shutting the library doors firmly behind her.

When she was back in the Devin carriage on her way home, her body gave way and she sank to the floor. She sobbed uncontrollably.

From the very beginning, she told herself not to trust him. She'd known that his pretty words were empty tools of seduction. She'd known that every smile and flirtation and piercing comment was likely well rehearsed and as substantial as sugar floss. But then he'd really talked to her. And then he'd kissed her as if that were his whole reason for being on this earth. And then he'd declared that he loved her. And her instincts went awry. How could she trust herself now? Her judgment, so unfailing in business, utterly failed.

Even as she pulled up to Evans Books, she could not purge her thoughts of him. She relived his now-bittersweet kisses, relived what she'd let him do to her, what she'd so enthusiastically done with him. The vivid images in her mind made her want to—! She felt her gorge rising and made it out of the carriage just in time to cast her accounts into the gutter. The bile-filled effluvium was a bitter symbol of the sullied affection she'd been so stupid to indulge in the first place. When the spasms in her gut finally ceased, she stood, tears slipping down her cheeks.

"Honoria! Is that you? We weren't expecting you for at least a fortnight!" *Oh, no. Marissa.* She swiped her face with her sleeve in the hope that she could right herself before facing her friend. No such luck. The ever-ebullient Marissa wasn't one to stand on ceremony. No, Marissa came right around for a hug and peck on the cheek but froze at the sight of her face.

"Are you ill, Honoria? Let's get you inside, dear."

"I'm fine, dear. I will be fine." She clung to Marissa, now quite embarrassed by the show of weakness. "I couldn't stay away, but then the sight of the shop brought back such terrible memories of how I left it."

Her friend squeezed her hand and pulled her toward the shop.

"I remember it well. You'll be amazed at the progress we have made. Devin's workers are an efficient bunch, and I must say we ladies have acquitted ourselves rather nicely. Even Mr. Clarke got to employ his woodworking skills and now has grand plans for carving new accents for the shelves."

Honoria allowed herself to be guided into the building. When she saw the showroom, she slowly released the breath she didn't realize she'd been holding. It was indeed an astounding improvement. The floorboards were clean of debris, although covered in sawdust and shoeprints. The counter had been moved to a more logical spot in the room and completely rebuilt. She could tell they'd tried to restore as much of the original shelving as possible. Best yet, the room smelled of fresh pine.

She tried to blink away the stinging in her eyelids, tried to rein in the fresh tears. The workers tipped their heads in greeting but continued their diligence. The Needlework ladies swarmed around her to welcome her back. "We've missed you!" "You'd be so proud!" "You can always count on us!"

As usual, Marissa took charge.

"There will be plenty of time for chatter. Honoria's just had a long journey. She'll be wanting tea and quiet, I'm sure. In any case, it's about time for us to shut down the operation for today." She raised her voice a bit. "That goes for everyone. Let's pack up and get home to rest. We'll start fresh tomorrow morning."

Like Marissa, the sisters Helena and Elizabeth lingered after everyone else departed.

"I'll go make some tea," Helena said, just before she disappeared into the back. That was a bit of a surprise. Where was Minnie?

The other two ladies led Honoria up the stairs to her sitting room. She noticed they'd quickened their steps past her office downstairs. She had so many questions, but at the moment she dreaded the answers too much to ask. So instead she sank into a plush chair that she didn't recognize but found immediately comforting.

"Everyone has been so kind," she said as her eyes welled yet again. "I can't thank you all enough for doing so much for me."

Marissa perched on the arm of the chair and put a hand on her shoulder.

"We would do anything for you, Honoria. You know that."

Yet she didn't, or at least she hadn't. How could she have misjudged such good friends? She'd thought herself fundamentally alone in this world, and yet so many people now lavished her with care. So many people had put countless hours into repairs, not just downstairs in the shop but up here as well. Stripped of unnecessary decor—she would wait until later to ask what had been destroyed—the room seemed larger. The walls had been repainted in a soothing mint shade. It was humbling, all this effort just for her, while she'd been cavorting irresponsibly at a country house.

Before she could speak, Marissa added, "And don't you start on about how you should have been here, how we shouldn't have, how you've neglected your responsibilities, and all that nonsense. You always expect too much of yourself, and you never accept help! It was past time that you allow people to start taking care of you for a spell."

Helena entered with a loaded tray. "Here, here! Well said, Marissa! It's been quite fun, too, to have such a physical project. And those workmen are so amusing. One youngster keeps flirting with Elizabeth, teasing her about how well she wields a paintbrush, how masterful her stroke is."

To her astonishment, the matronly Mrs. Elizabeth Addison, five years a widow and the mother of seven, actually blushed, all the way from the edge where her blond coiffure met her forehead down to the lace at her collar.

"Oh, these whippersnappers are so outrageous," Elizabeth responded, "but they seem good at heart. I'm thinking of bringing my Vanessa to help us next week."

"Oh, no, sister. Vanessa would set these boys spinning!" Helena voiced what they all thought as everyone laughed. Even as a child, Elizabeth's youngest daughter had had a preternatural gift for wrapping men around her little finger. Now, at fifteen, she was learning the art of subtlety. "Let's save her powers for some future crisis," the girl's aunt added with a wink. "We have this well in hand and wouldn't want to cause any undue distractions."

It felt calming just to sit with these women, these friends. How had she been so blind to the camaraderie that surrounded her?

When Marissa asked how she wanted her tea, however, she straightened up and said, "Now, now, I'm fully capable of fixing my own tea. Comfort is one thing. Coddling is quite another. In fact, I am the hostess here. Sugar but no milk for you, correct?"

Marissa nodded, smiling, and graciously took the proffered cup and saucer. Her mouth quirked, a sure sign she was about to stir up the conversation.

"So, Honoria, when he visited to check on his crew's progress last week, your young Lord Devin said you'd be staying out in the country until the end of the month. What happened to cut your trip so short?" All three women seemed to crowd in upon her. Her young Lord Devin.

"Nothing happened, ladies." She avoided looking anyone in the eye. "I simply couldn't stay away. As lovely as Sharling Worth is, idleness doesn't suit me. Neither does running away from my problems." Well, most of the statement was true, anyhow.

Ever tenacious, Marissa continued with a grin. "I'm rather surprised Lord Devin let you leave. He seems quite . . . protective of you."

"Oh, yes," Helena interjected. "Why, just last week he had lots of questions about you—"

"What sort of questions?" Honoria interrupted. Of course, not satisfied with the damage he'd wrought thus far, he had to interrogate her closest associates. What had he let slip in reply? "What did he want to know? What did you tell him?"

Helena looked from Marissa to Elizabeth. For a long moment, none of the women spoke. She simply waited.

"Dear, it's nothing to get worked up about." Marissa spoke as if to a child, even going so far as to pat her hand. "For one thing, he asked about the pamphlets. I think he means to help you replace the press."

Elizabeth chimed in, "We talked a bit about the Needlework for the Needy activities. It seems his mother, Lady Devin, may wish to drum up support among her circle. How fancy would our little club be then!"

"Don't get your hopes up, ladies," she replied. "We should not be a nuisance to the Devins. In fact, I'm not comfortable accepting so much of their charity. They've done too much already."

"What happened at Sharling Worth, Honoria?" As always, Marissa went right to the heart of the matter.

She shook her head, unable to speak.

"You need to rest," Marissa decided. "But this discussion is deferred, not ended. You've been through a great deal of upheaval. And, obviously, Lord Devin is intimately involved." *Oh, Marissa, truer words and all that. Intimately* involved didn't begin to describe it. Still, she couldn't possibly admit to them how completely and humiliatingly she'd been fooled by him.

"This is my shop, Marissa, my home. Do not speak to me as if I'm a petulant child in need of a nap. I will decide how best to manage my business."

The sisters gaped at her before hurriedly gathering up the empty cups.

"We should be going," Elizabeth said quickly. "The children will be wondering what's kept me so late today. Come, Helena, we can share a hack." Elizabeth gave her a quick embrace and added, "Get some sleep, Honoria. We'll see you first thing tomorrow." Helena likewise gave her a quick peck on the cheek before sweeping out after her sister. The look Helena shot to Marissa just before she disappeared was not particularly subtle.

"Just one last thing, dear, and I'll leave you in peace for the night," Marissa finally said. "This business has gotten dangerous. There are more factors at play now than in a royal court intrigue. Do not allow yourself to be distracted from what—or who—is important."

For the first time, she noticed how worn Marissa looked. Her friend was always such a whirlwind of energy and opinions. Yet even her resources were getting stretched to their limit.

"What is important? That is the question of the moment, isn't it, Marissa? As you said, nothing will be decided tonight. Rest assured, there will be a reckoning, and soon."

"Take care of yourself, my friend. I have left a small welcoming gift in your closet. Keep it safe and close. I pray you never need it."

"Thank you." She kissed Marissa's cheek and saw her out. She had no answers, and she was barely holding together what little she actually had. But she saw now that she didn't have to do it alone.

Chapter Eighteen

When he was fifteen, Lord Devin thought he was a man because he'd bedded his first woman, a lush and energetic tavern wench recruited by school chums. When he was eighteen, he thought he was a man because his father died and he took on the role of Lord Devin, head of the family. When he was twenty-four, he thought he was a man because he'd become the kind of gentleman that other members in the House of Lords looked to before casting their votes. Now, at twenty-six, he knew he was a man because he finally understood what it means to love, without conditions or limits. He loved Honoria with everything in him, from the very marrow in his bones, and that meant he wanted her to be happy, and safe, even if her happiness didn't include him. Even if it meant acknowledging the threat he was to her and that she would be safer without him. He wanted her love, but he wouldn't begrudge her whatever choices she needed to make for her own sanity. He would kill any man who tried to hurt her—and at least incapacitate any woman who tried to do so—but he would not bring her any more misery himself. He would make things right for her.

His mother walked into the library that he now used as his office, a room she generally avoided.

"It is all right, you know. I have no objections to her, Alexander."

Honoria's words echoed in his mind.

"But you do not know her." He wanted his mother to harbor no illusions about Honoria, nor about him.

"Silly boy, I know you. And I knew from the first moment I met her that there was something between you. You hate my dinner parties. No, do not deny it. You always present yourself creditably well, but you have never enjoyed the formality or the small talk. Your clues to invite her to dinner were as subtle as a cannon. I was understandably curious about your motives. So unlike you. What I saw that night was not just what a lovely woman she is . . . and she is that. I saw in your eyes that you were smitten, even if you did not know it yet."

He ducked his head, feeling sheepish and suddenly much younger than he'd felt in years.

"I thought I was being so suave."

"That is how anyone but your mother would see it, yes." She responded with a quiet smile. "She is a fine woman. Fiercely independent, honest, and direct to a fault. She is not what I would have expected for you, but she is a good woman. And you love her. That is all I need to know."

"I . . . I have hurt her deeply. I . . . betrayed her trust in the worst way. What do I do, Mother?"

This was only the second time in his adult life that he'd asked his mother for something. It felt strange, but not unpleasant. She looked at him sternly for a few moments, without speaking. Then she walked up to him and began stroking his hair, like she'd done when he was a child.

"Trust is such a fragile thing. When given by someone like her, it can be stronger than steel and diamonds . . . and when shattered, it can be that impossible to rebuild. I cannot provide assurance, but I have faith in both of you. Have faith, my son, that the love you have for each other will overcome this . . . obstacle."

He didn't see how that would be possible. She had no idea how severely they'd lied to each other. Her faith sounded like a fairy tale, but he needed to believe it, even if it wasn't true.

"I never thought I could feel this way about anyone."

"You have led quite a self-contained life thus far. I had despaired of you marrying, but, more than that, I worry that you closed yourself off from what is most valuable in this life. That is why it is so clear that she is different. You would not lower your defenses for just anyone. And I am so very glad you have."

"I wish I had your confidence about her. About me. I do not deserve her affection. These feelings are entirely alien to me. She is as vital to me as breathing." He saw his mother's eyes glisten at that. "Was this what you felt with Father? I thought it was awful every time he left. But how could you stand it?"

His mother blanched, and he immediately regretted his question. They never discussed his father or his parents' marriage. Even now, his anger and guilt toward his father still simmered so close to the surface. And he didn't want to face his mother's whitewashed adoration.

"I am so sorry, Mother. I should not have asked something so personal."

"That is quite all right. I did feel awful every time he traveled. . . . It was . . . difficult. But our situation was different. We both made choices best suited to our life, our needs." Her tone was conciliatory, but she stood and ambled toward the door. She paused with her hand on the doorknob. "You are an honorable man. No matter what you have done to upset her, I'm sure you had the best of intentions. You can make this right. I am certain of it."

As she shut the door behind her, he could only hope her faith in him was deserved.

He sat at the desk trying to figure out how best to express himself to the one woman he wanted, the one woman whose forgiveness and esteem were now everything to him. But the words wouldn't come. So instead he began a note to Mrs. Marissa Clarke, member of Needlework for the Needy, offering his assistance in their endeavors in exchange for assistance in his own helpless muddle.

Chapter Nineteen

Evans Principle #i: Never forget that you are, first and foremost, a capable, honorable, responsible citizen of the world. You are an Evans. Your dignity is a legacy no one can take from you.

"My God." It was all she could say, all she could think.

The image was undeniable. The stacks of copies multiplied the image like an unholy kaleidoscope. The woman's hair, the tilt of her head, the line of her neck—Honoria recognized these almost as well as she would recognize herself, so familiar was she after years of close companionship. She had known Minnie since the girl's birth. From that time, she kept the tacit promise made by her parents to support and protect Minnie, as well as her brother. How the girl she remembered in pigtails and a pinafore became this spectacle, exposed, posed in horrifically explicit ways, she could not fathom. What she did know was that she had to speak with Minnie, who by this time was usually hard at work upstairs.

She jumped when she felt a hand at her back.

"Lord Devin, what are you doing here?"

"The repaired books arrived yesterday, along with the one you returned," he said quietly. "I came to settle my accounts. Since you weren't in the front room, I thought I would try back here."

He carefully took the photograph from her hand and placed it facedown on top of the stack, obscuring the images completely. His light touch gave her time to stabilize her racing thoughts.

"You know her perhaps better than anyone," he said. "She will need you to be strong. We will find the villains behind this, but right now you need to focus on her."

She nodded. Then he left the room, closing the door to the front room behind him without a sound. Only dimly did she realize that she hadn't greeted him, hadn't spoken to him at all.

She hurried up the stairs, frantic in her search for the girl. "Minnie? Where are you, dear? I'm here to help you! Minnie?" The rooms to all the doors remained open during the continued repairs, and she searched each one methodically for any signs. Finally, she found Minnie curled up on a narrow couch in a third-floor bedroom, one that would have been servants' quarters originally. As she took the poor child in her arms—*not a child any longer, Nora!*—she saw the photograph crushed in Minnie's fist and felt her most constant companion uncharacteristically pulling away from her, hiding her face.

"What happened, Minnie?" she asked gently. "You can tell me, dear. I know you. I know you are a good girl. Were you threatened? Were you forced? What did they do to you?"

"I'm so sorry, Mrs. Duchamp." Minnie's words were broken by body-shaking sobs. "I never wanted to hurt you. You've been like a sister to me." Her voice cracked. "But I truly had no choice."

"Why, Minnie? What have you done?"

"I trusted him. He seemed so honest, so caring. We met by accident. One day he offered to carry the groceries home for me. Another day, he bought me pastry. He was so kind. And then he turned lovey, and it felt so good."

Minnie shuddered, and Honoria took her hand for support.

"He would tell me how pretty I was, and he would kiss me in ways that made my stomach do somersaults. I was such a fool." Minnie's voice caught and tears slid down her cheek. "I thought he loved me."

She ripped her hand from Honoria's grasp and began pacing the room.

"He asked me for a special gift. He promised it would be safe, just between us. He swore I was the most beautiful woman he had ever seen. No one had ever treated me so. I would have done anything for him. I'm so ashamed."

"What did he do to you, Minnie? You must tell me. It will be easier if you say it quickly."

"There are other pictures. Photographs of things he made me do." Minnie began to sob harshly again. "It sickens me. I can't bear the shame." Unable to catch her breath, she stumbled on the rest of the story. "Then he started threatening to share the pictures unless I followed his directions. He said he would give them not just to his friends—he would spread them around Haymarket, post them on advertising walls between here and Mayfair. Unless I let him and his friends into the shop when you were away."

"Oh, Minnie." As she moved to embrace the poor, distraught girl, she heard a scuffle and male voices raised downstairs. Quickly, she moved to close and lock the door, meager protection that would be from whatever new threat had arrived.

Meager, indeed, as Erich exploded into the room, breaking the doorjamb and slamming the door against the wall so hard, plaster fell from the ceiling.

"Wilhelmina! Tell me it isn't true!"

Erich. Of course, this was what the situation needed. The young man rushed in, hair askew, a welt rising on his cheek, his shirt torn. Alex was close on his heels. Minnie folded into a corner and dropped her face into her hands as her body convulsed with weeping. Honoria bodily put herself between the siblings as she asked, "Erich, what's happened to you? Did Lord Devin do this to you?"

He tried to get past his employer, but she grabbed his face in her hands and forced him to look at her, not his sister.

"What happened, Erich?"

His eyes red, he barely registered her. He pushed her hands off as he said, "The boys down at the pub. One of them was passing around these sheets, snickering."

He threw photographs like the many on her desk. She quickly moved to gather them. In that moment, Erich charged toward his sister. Alex barely managed to catch him by the collar, causing him to nearly choke himself.

"We are trying, Mr. Hearsh, to figure out where these photographs came from and bring the source to justice," Alex said calmly, as he forced the youth to face him. How strange to hear Erich called by his proper name. An odd look passed between the two men, one that she could not decipher. "Your sister is understandably beside herself. As upsetting as this situation may be, cooler heads must prevail."

Before she could speak, Erich turned on his sister, kept at bay like a dog on a leash.

"Say it isn't true, Wilhelmina. Tell me that's not you. I took on three men at the pub to get those away from them. God only knows how many more there are. Tell me that's not you."

Minnie only curled more tightly into herself, sobbing hysterically.

"Clearly, we cannot solve anything right this minute," Honoria said, as she bent over the girl, wanting to shield her from all of this. "Minnie will stay here with me tonight. She needs rest to calm her. In the morning, we shall try to piece all of this together. Do you understand me, Erich?"

He gave a curt nod, looking not at all satisfied.

"Promise me you won't go back to the pub tonight."

He stared at her, narrowing his eyes.

"Promise me, Erich."

"Promise her, Mr. Hearsh, or I'll tie you up and lock you in a closet until morning." Devin's support was surprisingly comforting, bolstering her even as her own thoughts wanted to scatter.

"I won't go back to the pub tonight."

"Go home, dear. Get some sleep." She couldn't help but be moved by his distress. He must feel as responsible for his younger sister as she did. But in his state, he could not help her. "I'll see what I can find out from Minnie. You and I both know she is better than this. Whatever happened, she's better than that trash. We will help her through this. Together, we can find those responsible and make them pay. But that will not happen tonight."

That small measure of solidarity seemed to reach him. The tension in his scrawny body eased a little. He ran a trembling hand through his hair, leaving it askew, and walked over to Minnie slowly, quietly. As he took her hand gently, he said, "Min, all will be well. I guarantee it. Believe me, all will be well."

Minnie whispered something unintelligible in response, and then her brother stood and stiffly left the room.

Devin looked at her, a question in his eyes as he tipped his head toward the departing younger man. She nodded, and without exchanging words, he followed Erich, presumably to see him home safely and make arrangements for tomorrow.

Meanwhile, Honoria took over, treating Minnie as she might a sick child. She stroked the girl's hair for a bit and then led the way down to her own bedroom. Simple as it was, her room was still the most appointed in the house, and here she would watch over her charge all night, if need be.

Just as Honoria tipped over the knife edge of bone-deep exhaustion into sleep, Minnie spoke.

"I had to. Don't you see? The very idea of those photographs spread along the Strand. I could never show my face in public. I could be arrested. I didn't even know how it happened—how in one moment he was the prince of my dreams and the next—"

"What, Minnie? What did you do?"

"They wanted you out of the shop. They needed to know when you would be away for a significant amount of time and whether you would be in a public area where they could run into you."

"The break-in? You told the vandals where to find me?"

The girl nodded.

"I trusted you. I would have done anything for you, if you needed me to."

"I know, Miss Honoria. I'm so sorry. So sorry. You have to believe me. I can't stand myself for what I've done to you. But I had to!"

"No, Minnie. There are always choices, even if none of them are perfect. You had the choice, and you helped destroy the shop. You had the choice, and you smashed the printing press as badly as if you'd taken a sledgehammer to it with your own two hands. You had the choice, and you knew what he asked of you was wrong." She knew she was being hard-hearted, but this new betrayal crushed her.

"You don't understand. It isn't just about me. . . ."

Awareness rushed in, and Honoria gaped at Minnie's midsection in the dark. How had she missed the telltale spreading over the past few months? Minnie and Erich never starved, but they'd never suffered an overabundance of food either. She should have noticed sooner. She just never would have guessed; truly, people see what they expect to see.

"No, Minnie!"

Minnie looked truly agonized and could barely whisper.

"It's . . . I . . . I'm with child, miss. Oh, if my parents saw me now, they'd be so ashamed!"

"Oh, no!" She embraced the young woman whose sobs grew into great hiccupping, body-shaking misery. "Can you tell me, Min? Were you forced? Have you been harmed?"

"No, miss. I mean, I don't know. I wasn't abused, but I don't know my own mind. I am the soul of evil. When temptation came, I welcomed it. I knew it was wrong, but when he kissed me and touched me, I just wanted more. I couldn't control my lust, and he seemed overwhelmed by it too. I thought we must be in love."

Honoria couldn't trust herself to speak. What Minnie described was so very close, eerily close, to what she felt in Lord Devin's arms. Were women universally so stupid? Or were she and Minnie just such a monumentally pathetic pair?

"I thought . . . well, I thought he would marry me and I'd have a house of my own and a family. No offense to you, miss, but I thought he would free me from a life of service. Now I have to do what he says so he will claim my child and see to the baby's welfare."

"Minnie, think carefully. With all you know about him now, do you really believe he'll keep his word about taking responsibility for the child?"

Minnie's face fell as she answered, "I have to believe him. I have no choice. I have to believe he will do right by this babe, as long as I do what he says."

Honoria couldn't let it go.

"Has he kept any promise he has made to you thus far?"

Minnie shook her head slowly.

"Then you do have choices. You have choices to make about what you are going to do next to protect yourself, about how you are going to take care of yourself and your child. Assume you cannot count on him."

"No one will hire me like this. I have nowhere to go. I can't raise this child on my own."

"Oh, Minnie." She held the young woman tightly. "You will always have a home here, or at least for as long as I have a home here. Try to sleep. You need to rest, now more than ever. We will think this through tomorrow."

*   *   *

Day came much too soon, as did the heavy, solid footsteps of Lord Devin as he made his way through the house toward them. Funny how she already recognized his step. Funny how she *didn't* find it presumptuous for him to keep a key to the shop. When he entered, he looked almost as if he wanted to come to her, take her in his arms, but instead he halted at the far side of the bed. At that moment, she wanted desperately to go to him and take comfort in his embrace. She gripped the arms of her chair tightly. Minnie slept on.

"Mr. Hearsh will be here within the hour," he said, quietly. "He implied last night that he may know who is responsible for distributing the photographs."

"Have you met him before? The two of you seemed somehow acquainted."

"Our paths have crossed once or twice. He shall explain all to you when he arrives."

Since he didn't seem inclined to expand on that cryptic response, she went on to more pressing concerns. "You don't think he would go to confront the culprit alone, do you?"

He shook his head but appeared grim. "He needs our help. There is undoubtedly more than one person involved in this operation. In fact, I have already sent word to a friend in case we have need of him, or proper authorities."

"How can Erich know so much about this already?"

He seemed to brace himself before he spoke again. For some reason, it took him quite a while, during which he avoided looking directly at her. When his eyes met hers again, she knew what he would say.

"I said he would explain, but perhaps it is best that you hear this from me. Mr. Hearsh was the messenger who came to visit me at Sharling Worth."

She froze. Not Erich too.

"Withersby sent him to give me an ultimatum," Devin continued. "When you returned to London, it would be to close up shop for good. I do not know how long young Erich has been in his employ, but now I have no doubt that all of this is interrelated. That house you found when you followed the little girl—Peaseblossom House, it is called—is bound up in this. It must be the headquarters of these purveyors of obscenity, and I suspect it reaches much further than you or I could have predicted. Otherwise, their efforts to destroy you would not have gone this far."

She'd listened for as long as she could. Until the bile rose in her throat. Until her pulse hammered in her ears, and she couldn't breathe. Whatever else Lord Devin had to say must wait. She had to get out of that room, get out of his presence. She needed to find air before reason and reality collapsed entirely. She rushed past him and thanked heaven that he did nothing to stop her. If he so much as reached for her, she might strike him. She wanted, needed, to strike out at something. She ran down the stairs and out to the showroom.

It all seemed so farcical now. She'd devoted her entire life to this store, to establishing a safe and stable life around this store, and yet those closest to her had secretly been tearing it down, bit by bit. Those she'd trusted most destroyed everything she held dear. Suddenly, she couldn't bear the sight of this place, the only true home she'd ever known, the haven where she'd grown into an adult. She'd given up her soul to it. Now it turned out to be just another fantasy built on ashes and air.

She yanked the nearest books from the shelves and threw them across the room. So many had been beyond repair; the ones that remained no longer held any worth to her. She'd thought them all a kind of magic bound in leather and paper, but she'd been a fool. She began throwing books harder, faster. She couldn't clear shelves fast enough. Covers tore, pages scattered, and still none of it mattered anymore.

She caught a glimpse of Lord Devin from the corner of her eye. He stood in the doorway, watching. Waiting.

"I guess you told her, then." She whirled around to see Erich at the shop entrance. She backed away from him until she realized she was moving closer to Devin and stopped.

"What have you done, Erich?" she asked.

To his credit, he did not look away. He also did not look proud.

"I never meant to hurt you, Miss Honoria."

"I hope you understand that's of no purpose right now. What I need to know is what you did. Who are you working for? What do you know about their dealings?"

"I didn't know about the pictures, ma'am. Honest, I didn't." His fists were so tight, his knuckles went white. "I didn't know they got to

Min." He shook his head hard, as if still unbelieving. "Why would they bring her into it? I was getting the job done."

"Who are *they*, Erich?" Lord Devin asked. She shot him a quelling look. Only she had the right to interrogate Erich. She'd known him all his life. She was the one he'd betrayed.

"I don't know all of them, my lord. I spoke mainly with Mr. Withersby. He's the one who gave me assignments."

Devin continued his interrogation, damn it. "This will take quite some time if you keep giving us information piecemeal. Spill it all, man."

Erich's head snapped up, his hard gaze at Devin making him look suddenly older.

"Why don't you spill your own misdeeds, my lord? I'm trying to confess my sins, but it isn't easy. Maybe you ought to try it."

Devin refused to be baited. "Tell us what you know, and I will fill in from my experience. Mrs. Duchamp knows I am not blameless in this. You have some essential pieces of this puzzle, as do I. As does your sister. The sooner we can see all these pieces together, the sooner we can bring these villains to justice."

"Fine. I did whatever was needed of me. Mostly, I served as a courier, delivering messages and packages. I had no knowledge of any photographs or nasty activities. I visited Mr. Withersby three times a week at ten A.M. to find out my jobs. I was given addresses, sometimes written messages, sometimes just spoken ones. Sometimes small parcels. For all I knew, it was a private delivery service."

"What kind of messages did you convey?"

"More oft than not, they were deadlines like what I gave Lord Devin here. Some job needed to be completed by a certain time, and Mr. Withersby wasn't satisfied with the progress."

"There must have been signs," Honoria prompted. "Something. Anything."

"More recently, just before the shop was broken into, there were more parcels to deliver. And there were orders to deliver to glassmakers, chemists, sometimes paper mills. And Mr. Withersby started asking me more about the bookshop. He'd asked about it when I first started. After all, delivery is my job here." With a glance at Honoria, he added, "Was my job here, I s'pose."

She was sharply reminded of what was left here. Not much. And he was absolutely right. He could no longer work here. Neither could Minnie, truth be told. There was nothing left for them here. Suddenly, she felt very, very old.

"I must go check on Minnie," she said as she made her way to the back room. "We will continue this discussion later. Neither of you should leave anyway until we've sorted this out, or tried to anyway."

"Miss Honoria," Erich called after her, "may I go with you? I'd like to see my sister."

She raised a hand to beckon him toward the back. He looked as dejected as she felt, and her instinct was to comfort him, but her emotions were too raw, the pain of betrayal too keen.

"Lord Devin," she said, without looking at him, "please make yourself at home." She didn't mean it to be cruel, but she heard the ironic echo of his welcome when she'd stayed at Devin House the night of the break-in.

Chapter Twenty

Evans Principle #m: Have faith. In business, in people, in yourself, have faith.

Satisfied that Minnie was recovering sufficiently and that her brother would now be a caring help to her rather than a hindrance, she left them conferring quietly. She needed time—a moment to think things through. But Lord Devin waited downstairs—at her insistence, she recalled—and the reckoning was overdue.

He'd been tidying up. Instead of reshelving books, he'd stacked them in front of the empty cases. Prudent. She would have to sort through them to see which pieces were still intact, which volumes were still salvageable. At the thought, she laughed out loud, a harsh bark of a laugh. Nothing here could be saved here any longer.

He looked around the shop and said, "You deserve more than this, Nora."

"Deserve? You've said that before. As if the coincidence of my birth into a noble bloodline entitles me to more than someone else." She grabbed a fistful of pamphlets and thrust them in front of her. "By that logic, these children deserve all the misery and squalor they live in, simply because of the misfortune of their birth into poor families. The people in these stories—any of them would think them-selves in heaven to sleep in a featherbed rather than a pallet on the floor. To sleep in a bed of their own, not shared with the rest of their family, would be beyond belief. To have a bedroom of their own would be unthinkable." She was shaking the pamphlets at him. No— her whole body was shaking. "I have more than I need. If I deserve anything more, it's only inasmuch as they *all* deserve more."

"That is not what I mean." He ran his hand through his hair in frustration. "You run this shop because it was your father's. Because you feel responsible for continuing his legacy. Right now, you are the last of his line. What happens after you? What do you want, Nora? What do you want to accomplish in your life? What do you want to leave behind?"

Her silence compelled him further down the path. He longed to grab her, shake her out of her complacency.

"You are magnificent, and you do not even know it. You know your own mind, you have no fear when it comes to defending the de-fenseless, and you put everything you are into whatever you decide to do."

"None of that prettiness is to the purpose right now," she replied. "I need to figure out who is responsible for this filth and how to end it. Whatever you want of me, whatever you think of me, is on a far lower rung of priority. Get over yourself. Either help me or leave. Distraction and petty, solipsistic meditations do not constitute help."

His jaw clenched at her hard assessment of the situation, but he could not fault her for it. Her directness and devotion were among the things he loved most about her.

The doorbell chimed as someone entered. She hated that damned clanging. It might as well be a death knell.

"Mother said I would find you here! I must admit I scoffed at the idea that I could find you in a town bookstore." A young man in trav-eling dress, hair windswept, and breeches spattered with mud, bounded toward Lord Devin. A lavender scarf was thrown jauntily around his neck. His height, build, and coloring made his identity ir-refutable; even if he hadn't referred to their mother, he could only be Alex's brother.

"Andrew! My God, what are you doing here?" Alex rushed to him and they embraced heartily.

"The Continent got boring," Andrew said as they pulled apart. He tossed his hair and affected a jaded expression as he leaned against the nearest shelf. "And it is far too hot to go to Turkey or India."

"Did your . . . traveling companion . . . return with you?"

"Michael is probably in Germany or Austria by now. I had no idea you kept such close watch on my activities."

"Of course I would. I could not have my only brother traipsing around the world getting into trouble."

Honoria had excused their rudeness up to this point, attributing it to the unbridled joy of their reunion, but enough was enough. Her mind was awash with information and worry and responsibility, and she couldn't just stand there. Heaven forefend! "Gentlemen, pardon my rudeness, but I must part company and be about my business."

"Nora, my God, how could I be so thoughtless?"

She caught the arch of Andrew's brow at the sound of her name. She flushed at the implications of Alex's familiar tone. But Andrew was unruffled . . . and unsurprised, it seemed.

"So this is she," the newcomer observed.

"Pardon me?" She tensed.

"You must be Mrs. Honoria Duchamp. My mother has written me about you. She quite admires you, I think. She says you are all grace and charm and wit."

"Oh," Honoria said, faintly. "How kind of her." It felt strange to think of Lady Devin writing particularly about her, of anyone really taking enough notice of her to talk up her personal qualities to other people. In regards to the shop and its success, she rather hoped good word spread easily about her work and wares, but personally . . .

"And she mentioned that my brother has grown quite fond of you." He repeated himself for emphasis as he looked at his elder brother. "Quite. Fond. She says."

Honoria stared at him, training her eyes on him to avoid following his gaze. Again, Lady Devin's perceptiveness shocked her. So did the lady's bluntness.

Alex cut in.

"So it is clear that you know of Mrs. Duchamp. Allow me to complete the introductions. Honoria, may I present my idiot brother, Andrew."

"Need I remind you I took two firsts at Cambridge?"

"He is also quite a bore."

The change in Alex's demeanor made her head spin. How he

could suddenly appear so jovial when such serious matters needed attention brought a bitter taste to her mouth.

"Please do celebrate your joyous reunion, but I pray you will excuse me." She curtseyed before either of them could speak and left the room, her hands shaking.

With the prodigal son returned, Devin House became a whirlwind of activity as a suitable feast was prepared. Alex breathed a sigh of relief that he could now keep an eye on Andrew's activities and whereabouts and companions more directly and focus his energies instead on assisting Honoria. He might even be able to ask his brother to be more discreet, more self-aware, although he couldn't begin to imagine how that conversation might go.

After a suitable interval enabling Lady Devin to lavish chiding attention on her youngest child, Alex called him into the library for a serious talk. Andrew wandered around the room as if he'd never seen its contents before, although very little had changed in the past five years, certainly nothing since his departure for the Continent.

"Do sit down, Andrew." He grew increasingly annoyed when his brother ignored the request and instead continued to wander the room, scrutinizing knickknacks.

"What have I done now, oh, Alexander the Great?"

He merely raised a brow and waited for his younger brother to settle down.

"You know," his brother noted, "you always call me Andrew when I'm in some kind of trouble."

Well, that could not be denied. It was an automatic thing, he realized, calling both his younger siblings by their full names when the seriousness of the situation called for it.

"Mother does it too," Andrew added, soothingly.

"In any case, I must inform you that some unsavory rumors have surfaced about you during your sojourn abroad."

"I have never known you to give credence to idle gossip, brother."

"Unfortunately, this appears to be more than idling." That finally caught Andrew's attention.

"Is that so?" Eyes narrowed, his younger brother sat down to face him.

In that moment, he was shocked by how strongly Andrew resembled their father. That same wave of his hair, the tanned skin, the bright blue eyes, the strong chin pointed as if toward a new destination. Anger pierced through him, sharp and jarring.

"Surely, you must know that your behavior is under public scrutiny and that what you do always reflects on the Devin name."

"What are you suggesting, Alexander?" Andrew's voice grew deeper, harder. "Surely," he said with an edge, "you do not imply that I would knowingly besmirch the family's honor?"

"Andrew, there are photographs, photographs of you carousing with Mr. Michael Hadley at a Roman bathhouse and other... places."

Andrew's unbridled laughter shocked him. His brother should be ashamed, prostrate on the ground asking for forgiveness and protection; instead, he sat half out of his chair, doubled over with body-shaking guffaws.

"You have led such a sheltered life, Alex." But his sibling sobered quickly, presumably in reaction to the harsh look on his face. Truly, if eyes could shoot fire, the impudent fool should have needed dragon scales. "Pax, brother! I simply mean that Roman bathhouses are simply tourist attractions, not dens of iniquity. I wasn't there for an assignation, certainly not with Hadley, for God's sake! If it provides you any consolation, I am certain I can order an affidavit from a very talented courtesan I met in Florence. She sang my praises quite vocally, although it is possible she may have just been stroking my ego."

"Enough, you rascal. My interest in your romantic adventures is not prurient, you understand? The photographs are enough to prompt suspicion and rumor. I feared they would have been enough to convict you in absentia. Mother would have been devastated by the scandal."

His brother waved his hand dismissively. "Some enterprising photographer was showing off the newest developing techniques outside the bathhouse—he took photos of anyone who would let him. I don't recall posing for any, but I assure you it was common enough and completely innocuous. Besides, you underestimate the dear Mater. You know as well as I how progressive she can be."

"Politically progressive, she may be, but she would not survive the condemnation and imprisonment of her golden son, especially on charges of... immorality."

Andrew looked at him coolly, almost like a stranger.

"What bothered you more, Alex? That the Devin name was on the brink of ruin or that I might be a sodomite?"

He grimaced. No one had confronted him with the question before. Silence stretched between them as he thought hard.

"I guess I have my answer. Don't I, *brother*?" Andrew stood, his face red and drawn, his fists clenched at his sides.

"Wait, Andrew! Let me explain."

"What is there to explain? It is lucky I am not a lover of men, isn't it? It is even luckier that I consorted with a prostitute who would willingly attest to my masculine charms, correct? God help us if the situation were otherwise. *You* would never live down the shame, the sinfulness."

"Enough! Important questions require careful thought."

"No, Alexander. That which is truly important—your family—should require no thought whatsoever." When he shook his head, Andrew added, impatiently, "What if I or Mother objected to your Mrs. Duchamp? What would you do in that case?"

"I would tell you to go to hell. I would respectfully request that Mother mind her own business." His answer was immediate, instinctive. He got his brother's point. "Look, you know I would support you in every possible way. Without hesitation, I would stand up for you. Yet sodomy is still punishable by imprisonment or even death. If you were—I have no adequate wording for it—if you lived thus, any public shame would be nothing compared to the loss of you. That is why I hesitated, you dolt, because the thought of losing my only brother would break my heart! Even if he is an idiot."

Andrew nodded, his expression softening. They had never spoken so openly before.

Alex paused as a new line of inquiry occurred to him—"It all comes back to photographs." They needed to locate the photographers and their developing laboratory. Miss Hearsh's photographs had to originate somewhere. He was so preoccupied with sorting out how to do so that he nearly missed what Andrew was saying.

"... Michael has been struggling with his inclinations. He is a good person, and I only meant to support his self-discovery. I can assure you I am wholly interested in lovely ladies, although not, of course, your Mrs. Duchamp."

So there was one mystery solved. He felt Andrew's intense scrutiny and braced himself.

"What is she to you, Alex?"

That was no mystery.

"Everything, Drew. She is absolutely everything. And yet I have damn near destroyed her."

Andrew simply laid a hand on his shoulder. Sometime in the past year, his brother had learned when to talk and when to shut up and just stand by.

"I will fix this," he declared. He'd always been able to do so before, and he had no doubt he would do so now. Withersby, Honoria, the obscene photographs—he would solve all of it. He simply had to puzzle out how.

A short while later, a package arrived at Evans Books for Mrs. Honoria Duchamp. Dutifully, Minnie placed it on her desk with other mail and paperwork.

After closing up shop, which was really an empty gesture since the shop wasn't ready for customers and no one came, Honoria finally sat, dusty and filthy and overwhelmed by how much was left to do. The package's exterior gave no indication of who it was from. Still, once the wrapper fell away, the sender was clear. It would have been impossible for her not to know. Although she'd only seen it once, the leather and parchment of the volume were unmistakable. It was the First Folio. Between the cover and the first page was tucked a note:

Dear Mrs. Honoria Duchamp,
I cannot apologize enough. This is not payment. It is penance.
While I cannot ask your forgiveness nor hope to regain your
trust, I cannot deny my love for you. I owe you many things
that cannot be recompensed. This belongs to you.
—A

Honoria blinked quickly to fight the prickles in her eyes. It wouldn't do for such an historic and priceless work to be sullied by tears. She couldn't possibly keep it, nor could she forgive. Still, she tucked the note away in a desk drawer, looking forward to a time when reading it would not crush her heart and break her spirit yet again.

Chapter Twenty-one

Evans Principle 4b8a: Be fearless.

Honoria made her way to Peaseblossom House. She'd dressed as nondescriptly as possible, which wasn't difficult, given her limited wardrobe. With a large but simple cap covering her hair and her gray worsted suit, she could be any respectable working woman. It was inevitable, she supposed, ever since she first followed that little blond urchin. She'd stumbled upon a much larger, much deeper den of iniquity than she'd even suspected, and she could not let it stand. They'd threatened her livelihood, her life, and her loved ones. She would not be cowed.

Once Minnie described the building she'd been taken to, Honoria immediately recognized it as the one she followed the child to. Minnie was led through the same side door the child had gone through. Based on Minnie's description, she found the peaseblossom design carved into the shallow portico around what must be a servant entrance.

She made her way toward the back of the house, checking every window for a possible weak point of entry. To no avail. She slipped into the shadows and paused to reassess her plans. Finally, she accepted that she hadn't been thinking clearly. Surely no one so despicable would make it easy for someone to slip into their lair. They would be stealthy and protective; she needed to think more like them. After some quick thought, she decided to pass herself off as a poor, desperate widow willing to do anything for quick funds. She would simply go up to the front door and beg for employment. She rearranged her clothing to look a bit more disheveled and took a deep steadying breath.

Just as she was about to emerge from the shadows, however, a large hand covered her mouth from behind and she was pulled back into a hedge behind the house.

Immediately, her mind flashed back to the night of the break-in, the knife against her throat, the nauseating panic and helplessness. She struggled with all her might but could not break the hold. She tried to scream, but couldn't even breathe.

"Hush, Honoria!" Alex! She knew that voice, even in a whisper! Relief flooded through her, unclenching her muscles. Her body suddenly felt boneless, relying on his solidness to support her. Only then did tears slip from her eyelids, unbidden. He sucked in air when they slipped down her cheeks toward the hand still covering her mouth. He quickly loosened his grip and turned her around to face him.

"Did I hurt you?"

She shook her head but didn't trust herself to speak. Her hands shook. He seemed to read her mind when he said, low but fierce, "I'm so sorry, Nora. Forgive me for a thoughtless lout. It must have seemed just like that night at that shop." His hands stroked up and down her back soothingly. "Miss Hearsh told me how to find you. I only wanted to catch you before we were noticed."

She nodded and whispered, "All the windows within reach are locked. I'm going to pretend I'm a destitute woman looking for a means of support."

"No."

His forbidding tone only shored up her resolve.

"But, my lord, this house is crucial. I must find a way to get inside."

"No." This time, his voice and his firm grip on her arms brooked no objection. "We will summon the proper authorities. I will make a speech in the House of Lords next month. You will print all the damn pamphlets you want—we shall scatter them throughout Hyde Park! But you are not breaking into that building this evening," he said imperiously.

"That's all well and admirable, Lord Devin, but we still don't truly have clear evidence. It's simply Minnie's word, and you know anyone who sees those photographs won't believe her. The authorities won't do a thing. For heaven's sake, any local constables are likely already under their influence. I have every intention of printing a scathing exposé, but there are girls here now, *tonight*, who need my help. I won't leave without them."

He might look as unyielding as granite, but she refused to capitulate. And, apparently, he could see that. She would get what she wanted, whether he assisted or not.

"I will go in, not you," he conceded. "I shall pose as a new client."

"What if one of Withersby's men is in attendance? For that matter, what if other visitors recognize you?"

"Then consider that there is little we can do tonight. We need to plan and orchestrate an effective attack rather than barging into the lion's den armed only with bravado."

She stared at the balcony above them, the iron railing barely visible against the brick edifice. It was too still, too quiet.

"Something isn't right." She slipped from his grasp cautiously and crept to a window she could reach. "It's too quiet. There's no light. There should be some modicum of activity, don't you think?"

He moved past her toward the side entrance, pausing to listen, and then edged toward the front of the house. As he surreptitiously peeked around the corner toward the front entrance, he briefly gestured for her to follow, as if she would have stayed put. Even in the dim gaslight from the street, it was easy to see his surprise, followed quickly by the furrow of his brow, when he realized she'd been right behind him.

"The whole house appears dark, even the entryway. By this time of night, I would expect at least a few callers if this were the house of ill repute we suspect."

"I'm going in," she insisted, but he grabbed her arm, not gently, and trapped her back against the building.

"I meant what I said. If anyone enters that building this night, it will not be you. I am of a mind to toss you in a hack and have it drive you to Wales. Not so long ago, I watched helplessly as a mindless thug held a damned knife to your throat. God help me, it was the worst moment of my life, and nothing you can say will convince me to put you in harm's way again."

The anguish in his eyes was undeniable. She twined her arms around his neck and pulled him toward her for a quick, hard kiss.

"Then go on. They've likely absconded, which would be awful, but you can be the one to confirm it. If all is clear, we can search it together. If anyone remains, I'll run for help. Have we a deal?"

His kiss in response lingered, almost leisurely, as if he weren't a peer of the realm about to trespass onto hostile property. As if he had a right to. He smiled when he finally released her and drew a deep breath. And she could not fault him or object.

"We," he said. "Such a tiny but glorious word coming from your lips. We."

The tenderness in his eyes sent a thrill through her, though she couldn't trust herself any more than she could trust him.

"Yes, we. We will do this together. Now, go on. You first."

Cautious as he was, they quickly found that the house was indeed vacant. No one answered his knocks; there was no sign of activity at all. They tried the side door. Still nothing. Finally, they agreed to try one of the cellar windows at the back. When he asked her how she intended to gain entry, she simply flattened her skirts against the window and kicked as hard as she could, the sound muffled by layers of fabric. It was remarkably effective, a surprise even to her. The room within was likewise dark and silent. She slipped in feet-first to drop as quietly as possible to the earthen floor. They made their way through the house as swiftly as they could, considering the darkness. He led the way, clasping her hand, while she kept an eye trained behind them. They couldn't see any small clues in the darkness, but they could tell the house was abandoned in a rush. Food tins and threadbare blankets littered the cellar, chairs were tipped over or askew in the front parlor, as if a wave of people had tossed them about when it washed out the door. Strangely, the rooms upstairs held only the most basic items, a sofa in one room, a hip bath in another. No sign of photographic equipment or materials to develop films, no sign of children or duress. All that remained was the lingering but ephemeral scent of unwashed bodies and chemicals.

"We'll have to come back tomorrow and search properly," she finally said.

"I doubt it will do much good. There is nothing left here to find."

"But there must be. We simply can't see it yet. There must be some evidence of what was done here. More importantly, there must be some clue as to where they've gone!"

"It is impossible to tell at the moment. At best, we can try to gain legitimate entry in the morning. Whatever meager clues might remain, they are likely to still be here in daylight, when we could actually see them and not risk trampling them." He squeezed her hand, which he'd not released during the entire search of the house. "Now, shall we get some rest?"

"We?" she asked, unsure if she read his intentions correctly or simply projected her own desires onto his innocent question.

"With all the intrigue this evening, I find I am loath to leave your side. Wherever you wish to go, I shall be your guard. Where should we go? Evans Books or Devin House?"

"My shop," she said without hesitation. She needed to be on her own territory. "Please," she added.

Chapter Twenty-two

Evans Principle #z: Revel in your successes. Even the smallest of them is worth celebrating.

The next morning couldn't come soon enough. He hadn't slept a moment, keeping watch over her from an armchair by the bed. He guessed from her breathing that she hadn't slept either. As soon as they'd entered the shop, it was clear that she hadn't reasoned through her choices. There was only one bed—hers—and in a cramped bedroom with barely space for one of the chairs from the sitting room, wedged between the bed and the wardrobe. Until he brought in the chair, she seemed hesitant. He could see desire warring with duty—glazed with a layer of exhaustion. But he'd made a tacit vow to himself that this night would be all platonic innocence. His protection mattered, not his bodily urges . . . or hers. So he planted himself in the wooden chair, propped his stockinged feet on the edge of the mattress, and reassured her that she could sleep soundly without fear of disturbance.

The disappointment in her eyes nearly broke his resolve.

Before he could move, she slipped under the covers fully clothed. She reached for his hand, which he gave readily. Perhaps she was as desperate as he to maintain contact. Hours passed as they simply held hands. Infinitesimally, the room brightened as the gray dawn approached. At the sound of the first street vendors, they both gave up the pretense of sleep.

The sound of a door and light, hurried footsteps had them both standing and tense in a moment. Minnie's voice gave Honoria only a tiny modicum of ease. It wasn't an intruder, but her voice still conveyed alarm.

"Miss Honoria! You must help! Miss Honoria, are you in? Please help!"

They both rushed down the stairs to meet the poor, breathless girl. She must have run much of the way from the apartment she and Erich shared.

"What is the matter, Miss Hearsh?"

She hated that both she and Minnie were in such a state, both so close to hysteria, so in need of Alex's authoritative direction.

"It's Erich! He's gone after them! He left me a note this morning! You must help him!"

"Who, Minnie? Did he say exactly who he went after? We tried Peaseblossom House yesterday, but it's been deserted. Where did he go?"

"His note only said that he has gone to make things right. Here! Please tell me you can figure out where he's gone!"

Alex scanned the note quickly before handing it to her. What Minnie said was no understatement. Erich's writing left no clues, only a terse vow. It sounded like a good-bye from someone on a suicidal mission.

"The only connection I have left is Withersby. I will see him immediately," he said, tense and determined.

"I am going with you," Honoria said, just as firmly.

"If I thought I could convince you otherwise, I would. Just give me a few moments to send word to some friends, powerful friends, and to my brother."

After sending a handful of notes out with his footmen and making sure Minnie was secure in the shop, they set off for Withersby's office. Honoria felt no inclination to inform Devin of the pistol hidden in her skirt, the gift Marissa had left in her closet. With any luck, it would not be needed.

She entered Withersby's office alone, marching past his assistant's desk with a quick "Your employer will want to see me." Abruptly, she halted just inside the door when she found the man she assumed to be Mr. Withersby prone on his desk, face and chest bloodied, being attended to by a physician. His assistant closed the door behind her.

"Is he—?" she hesitated. "Is he seriously injured?"

"Mr. Withersby has taken quite a beating. I expect he'll be in a bit of pain, but I've found no broken bones or internal injuries to speak of. Are you a family member? He'll need some care and attention for the next few days."

She swallowed the caustic response that flashed through her mind and simply said, "No, I don't know him. I came here on business."

"I am afraid he is in no condition to conduct business. You shall have to call again when he has recovered."

"I'm afraid that is insupportable. I need to speak with him immediately, regarding a matter of utmost seriousness and urgency."

"I cannot allow that, madam."

Honoria drew herself up and determined that it was time to speak plainly.

"I have reason to believe Mr. Withersby was attacked because he has knowledge of a group profiting from the production and distribution of obscene photography, particularly featuring children." At the physician's horrified expression, she nodded grimly. "Furthermore, the subjects used for this iniquity are being held captive, forced to endure untold manner of degradation. And I believe Mr. Withersby can tell me where to find these unfortunates and these monstrous villains. He must say so."

The man looked from her to Mr. Withersby, who had yet to show any sign that he was aware of the conversation. Except Withersby's hand had moved, she was sure. His right hand now lay over his heart, fingers curled under in a loose fist. When she looked back at the physician, his face was pale.

"He is, um, indisposed, madam, as you can plainly see. He—I— uh, I cannot allow you to subject him to any unpleasantness."

Only then did it occur to her that this physician might be embroiled in this degenerate business as well. She went to open the door, noticing the doctor's obvious relief at her assumed departure, and signaled Lord Devin to join her. It was with some satisfaction that she caught the panicked recognition on the man's face, before he bowed awkwardly. With a sense of pride, she stood by Alex's side, feeling a deep sense of partnership in this effort. Lying on the desk, Withersby moaned once but made no move.

"Dr. Horwith, I believe. You may recall we met last year when Mr. Withersby's sister suddenly took ill while visiting him here at the office."

The physician nodded slowly, darting glances at his patient.

"So, sir," Devin continued. "Approximately how long have you served as Mr. Withersby's private assistant?"

Of course. They might not be able to get Withersby to cooperate, but such an operation might need the services of a physician occasionally. Her stomach rolled as her mind shied away from the dark possibilities of what might cause need for a physician under those circumstances. But if he knew anything about these pornographers and their victims, the two of them would drag it out of him. For heaven's sake, she would resort to acts that would damn her soul if it would help them rescue the forsaken.

Reluctant as he may have been at first, Dr. Horwith proved to be remarkably helpful and direct, almost as if he'd been longing to confess his sins. While she didn't discount the possibility of a trap, his manner appeared in earnest and his admissions rather graphic. Besides, Devin seemed unperturbed, which was enough to reassure her that things were well in hand. That is, until they arrived at the dubious address in Whitechapel.

Dr. Horwith secured them entrance, claiming Devin was a foreign physician studying venereal diseases and she his assistant. A servant, a young girl whose face was dirtied by perhaps ash or, Honoria feared, old bruises, hurried them into an empty sitting room, claiming someone was badly injured and in need of immediate attention.

It took her a moment to realize that the pile of rags on the floor was, in fact, Erich. She rushed to his side and found his face bloody and swollen almost past recognition. If it hadn't been for a birthmark on his neck that was remarkably untouched, she might not have been able to confirm it was him. His entire body was disturbingly slack. When the servant brought a bowl of water and some linens, she gently cleaned his face and was relieved to hear him groan, to be assured that he was alive, at least for the moment. There was hope.

That fleeting hope died a sharp stabbing death when a stampede of heavy footfalls approached the room. Devin placed himself directly in front of her and therefore in front of Erich. It was a gesture for which she would be forever grateful, assuming they survived whatever was approaching.

Five men entered the room. From her kneeling position by Erich and partially obscured by Devin, she could not see much of them. The two in front seemed roughly dressed and were carrying clubs. Two near the door were dressed more formally; they could have entered the House of Lords without a stir. Of the fifth man, all she could see were muddy trousers and boots. Then she felt, somehow, Devin tense—and she heard the fifth man speak.

"Never thought I'd have the bad luck to see you again, milord."

The man who broke into the shop. They'd come full circle. If there was any need for confirmation that they were in the right place, this was it. A dark, red emotion surged through her, causing her scalp to tingle. A copper-tinged bitterness flooded her mouth. She gripped the handle of the pistol in her skirt pocket, determined that he would not live to leave this building.

Without conscious thought, she stood. Devin tried to pull her close behind him, shielding her body with his, but she refused to be subdued. Instead, she stepped in front of him, touching his sleeve as if to keep him in place, and said, "You cannot get away with your depravity. I will see to it that you are prosecuted to the fullest extent of the law for your abuse and indecent exploitation of women and children."

"Ah, this day is lookin' up," said the hooligan from her memory.

She fought hard to suppress the tremor of revulsion that ran through her. The thugs remained emotionless while the well-dressed men behind them laughed.

"My dear woman," said the man on the left, the one with a blazing golden waistcoat finely embroidered, "you say that as if you believe you will be allowed to leave here alive. Surely, following the trail of bodies like bread crumbs, you must realize there is only one possible conclusion."

"We are not the only ones who know about this place, about your ... business," she said. "Several authorities have been notified. I'm sure they are making their way here as we speak."

"That is unfortunate. For you." The Golden Boy looked to the other gentleman and said, "Mr. Smith, please make ready to welcome any additional guests." The other man quietly stepped out. She feared what these degenerates might have in store to defend against intruders.

"Gentlemen." Alex drew their attention away from her as he walked slowly toward the center of the room. What on earth was he doing?

"Watch yer step, pup. I already owe you and mean to collect very soon."

"Gentlemen," he repeated in an unbelievably reasonable tone, seeming to ignore the brute and address only the leaders behind him, "there must be a way for us to resolve this without bloodshed or assault. Surely, you realize how impossible it would be for you to dispatch a viscount and a respectable merchant without drawing intense scrutiny. As the lady has said, our visit here is widely known. In fact, I have a dossier being held in trust that documents what we can prove of your activities. Sales records from chemist shops throughout the region suggest a pattern and identify a regular purchaser."

As stunned as she was by his revelation, it was nothing compared to Golden Boy's reaction. His face drained of color.

"That is impossible," the man said as he took a step back toward the door. His voice squeaked. The ruffians turned back to him and then to each other for guidance. Clearly, they were disconcerted by their leader's show of weakness.

"It is not only possible, Lord Feldspar. It is a fact. Your name and that of your associate, along with a hefty file of documentation, have been delivered to Bow Street. The Lexington Company will not be pleased to hear that you have used company funds or staff for such depravity. Silver nitrate is common enough, but when combined with the glassware, paper, and other materials that can be traced back to the same account, the evidence is clear enough."

When the no-longer-golden Lord Feldspar turned tail and ran out the door, his guards followed close on his tail, hollering that he pay them before he escaped.

With their lives no longer in imminent danger, Honoria's legs suddenly gave way. The dull thud of the pistol as she sank to the floor drew Alex's attention.

"Are you all right, Nora? What was that?"

"Ridiculous is what it was. Mrs. Clarke loaned me a pistol. Despite having never fired one before in my life, I thought it might prove useful in this situation." She gave a sad laugh.

"It could very well have, if Lord Feldspar or his associates had responded differently. Come. Can you stand? We should see if we can find the unfortunates being held captive. My brother should be here soon with reinforcements."

Chapter Twenty-three

Evans Principle (I've given up counting, dear daughter): The deepest truths, the clearest answers, can almost always be found in a book.

Two months passed as chaos slowly resolved into order. Reflecting on what they had accomplished together, Honoria felt pride tinged with ambivalence. Alex's inquiries with local chemical suppliers and other vendors proved critical, and he'd performed his investigation without her knowledge. He'd been the one to inquire about the new collodion process for creating photographs, the process they'd seen on display at the Great Exhibition. He'd done all of it without seeking her assistance, which she had to admit hurt, but he'd also done it without expecting any praise or attention from her. He'd done it not as a way to woo her but simply because it needed to be done.

Arrests were made, though not of those truly responsible. Lowly scapegoats, including Mr. Withersby and Lord Feldspar, bore the brunt. Untold cartons of children's photographs and exposures were carted out. Untold lists of clients were seized, but, again, only a few lowly figures on the list were publicly identified and charged. The most severe offenders, likely also the most powerful and wealthy, re-

mained unpunished. There was also no telling how many photographs had already been released. Buyers would not dare identify
themselves or volunteer information. There was also no telling how
many other such outfits might exist, especially considering how easily they could change locations if needed.

At least these women and children were saved.

Lord Devin did indeed present what many praised as an impas-
sioned speech in the House of Lords about the insidious distribution
of obscene materials. Under Honoria's guidance, the Needlework
ladies together produced a series of accounts relating the mistreatment the women and children of Peaseblossom House experienced
and their subsequent reentry into decent society. It was rumored that
novelist and publisher Charles Dickens, after reading some of the accounts and learning that the biggest culprits had not been brought to
justice, nearly went into apoplexy. Still, the victims who'd been imprisoned and abused were now free. For the most part, the girls and
boys found stable homes. A few returned to relieved families, and the
ones who had nowhere left to go found a home in a Devin estate a
few miles outside of London, which was rechristened Temple Haven.

During those two months, Alex's drive and influence and stature
in public were magnificent to behold. She wasn't the only one to note
it either. At least two news articles praised his newfound extroversion
as remarkable, calling him "a changed man" and "a modern leader."
She marveled at how different he was from when they first met.

Yet throughout this period, they barely spoke. Written correspondence served their purposes most of the time. On the few occasions
when she saw him in public, he'd been cordial, formal. They never
touched, barely looked at each other. It was to be expected, of course,
after exposing such criminal obscenity and mistreatment, that they
should present unimpeachable public personas. Still, she missed him—
his hand on her shoulder, his low chuckle as it rumbled through her.

As she shelved some new acquisitions, made possible by the tremendous surge in customers after the public scrutiny of the Peaseblossom scandal, she noticed a fine rain had begun outside. Even rain
sparked her longing.

So mired was she in melancholy and regret over what could not be
that she almost didn't hear the door open, chiming to announce a new
customer. She brushed off her skirts as she prepared to greet the new-

comer but paused as an all-too-familiar and piquant fragrance reached around the corner of the bookshelf. Her breath caught, anticipating, grasping toward even the most ephemeral traces of him.

"Mrs. Duchamp. May I speak with you?"

"Lord Devin." She made to curtsy, but he took her hand instead. Her heartbeat sped as she looked up at him. He was dressed impeccably, a large emerald pin glittering in his simply tied cravat. But it was the clear, bright look in his eyes, soft as moss, that took her breath away. She would never be free of whatever this influence was. She nodded, barely cognizant of what question she was answering, and then took a moment to make sure the shop was empty before locking up and offering him tea. If they were going to speak, they would be civilized about it.

Preparing tea and making pleasantries could not forestall Lord Devin, however, who began his campaign as soon as she settled into her armchair.

"As you can yourself attest, I already have a fine and upstanding mother, one who, in fact, is the very paragon of maternity, grace, and parental guidance. I do not seek another mother."

She hadn't prepared for such a direct frontal assault. She froze in the act of bringing her teacup to her lips.

"My psyche is not in any way bruised or malformed," he continued. "I simply desire you as a woman. There is nothing wrong with that. Your intellect and selflessness and vitality and, yes, your beauty are ageless. You inflame my passion in ways no other woman ever has. I love you. Now marry me."

She finally managed to put the teacup down before spilling tea all over herself. The porcelain clattered as she shakily set the cup in its saucer.

"This is impossible. It will not work, Lord Devin." Her formality made him wince. "Your social capital would be ruined. I do not fit in that world."

"What does that matter? What a happy excuse for me to play the hermit, visiting the House of Lords to pass reform bills and spending the rest of my time firmly ensconced in your arms."

She put a finger to his lips to interrupt him, but his eyes plainly identified exactly where he intended to house himself on her person.

"That won't do, and you know it."

" 'Had we but world enough, and time, / This coyness, lady, were no crime.' Marry me, Nora."

She was standing now, putting her chair between them. She shut her eyes. Of course, he would quote poetry to her. Of course, he would speak its uniquely intimate language to her. Her knees buckled, but she leaned on the chair for support.

"I," she said imperiously, "am too old to be coy. And you hit upon exactly the problem. We do not have enough time. 'Time's winged chariot' chases us down."

"What is it, Nora? What is your real objection to marrying me? Do I disappoint you in some way?"

"No! It's not you, dear boy—"

"Stop that!" He leaned toward her, shoulders taut as if he were about to spring forward. "Stop using condescension to distance yourself from me. You keep throwing these excuses between us as if they are insurmountable, but none of them matters."

"Our ages are not trivial. Our stations are not trivial. Of course, they matter. We do not live in a bubble, frozen in time in our own private Eden. You are really so much younger than I. It matters. For heaven's sake, I was your age when Her Royal Highness Queen Victoria ascended the throne. You couldn't have been out of short pants yet. Think of the talk. The speculation—either about your perverse attractions or my perverse mercenary intent. The scandal would be unbearable."

"Speculation be damned. I love you and you love me, I know it. Our ages do not matter. You glow with life. If our ages were reversed, no one would think to question it."

That was all well and good, but whatever light he thought she exuded wouldn't last forever. In ten years, or perhaps twenty if she were really lucky, she would be gray and decrepit, likely senile as well. He, on the other hand, would still be bursting with vitality, almost certainly even more devastatingly handsome than he was at this moment. Love would become an undue burden. And, even if it took twenty years to happen, she could not bear to grow so dependent on him only to watch as his ardor devolved into annoyance and pity. Her heart physically hurt at the image of them in her mind's eye, years hence: his still-powerful stride and ramrod spine in stark contrast to her gnarled and weary demeanor.

She floundered for a compromise and faced him to recite: " 'Come *live* with me and be my *love*.' " She touched his cheek as she continued. " 'And we will all the pleasures prove / That hills and valleys, dale and field, / And all the craggy mountains yield.' " She took one of his hands and laid it on her body.

His eyes roamed over her hills and valleys. But he didn't miss the message.

"That is not *yes*. You are offering to be my mistress instead?"

"I am. You offered this option yourself some time ago, as you may recall."

He nodded. The Folio.

"That offer expired long ago," he said. "And I tried to give you the Folio without obligation, to no avail. Why will you not marry me?"

"Marriage is out of the question. But we can surely still enjoy each other's company a while without such a binding contract."

"That would be enough for you?"

"Absolutely." She hoped.

"What if it is not enough for me?"

"I am well aware that you should wish to continue your line." She chose her words carefully. "You are expected to marry well and procreate. I would accept what I can have, assuming all parties were amenable to an arrangement."

He gaped at her for a moment before indignation transformed his features.

"How can you suggest that? How can you think that, with all I feel for you, I could marry another and divide my affections? Divide my body?"

"Don't you see? For you, I can be all pleasure and no obligation."

"You see marriage to me as obligation?"

No! Her heart cried out.

"Yes." She'd lived a lie for so many years, it should be easy to lie now. But the word choked her. He refused to see. Marriage would be an obligation—for him. It would become an unbearable obligation, trapping him with a withering prune, at best. She could very well decline as her father had, eventually losing his memory of who he was and how to function. She could not allow him to shackle himself thus. He simply could not see how he would suffer under such a commitment.

"I see," he said coldly. "More fool I. Of course, you prize your independence, meager and fragile as it might be, more than a life of comfort and affection with me. Far be it for me to *obligate* you any further. I shall see myself out."

When the door latched behind him, she sank to the floor, her legs trembling too much to stay upright. *This is best for him*, she promised herself. Hurting him now would not be nearly as cruel as accepting his proposal.

Chapter Twenty-four

He hadn't been to the club in ages. He hoped getting back into his usual routine would help him regain his usual equanimity, help block Mrs. Honoria Duchamp, heroine of the downtrodden—correction: *Miss* Honoria *Evans*, the only woman with the power to devastate him—from his infernally distracted mind. So far, a few drinks, a few rounds of billiards, and he was starting, ever so slightly, to feel like his old self again.

"Hey, Devin, old boy! You've finally deigned to grace us with your presence again?" It was Carlton Ashleigh, a chum from his Eton days. And, of course, trailing close behind him were the Anderson brothers and the ever cynical John Hartley. After hearty handshakes and pats on the back all around, he ordered a round of drinks for his circle and settled into amiable conversation about sports and the railways and travel.

Just when he thought he'd managed to forget about Miss Honoria Evans, Ashleigh poked him in the side and said in a low voice, "I hear you've finally taken up a mistress, Devin. About bloody time."

He opened his mouth to object, to deny, but didn't get the chance.

"Didn't you hear, though," interjected Hartley, "that he got this wrong as well? Attached himself to an old crone when there's any number of young, nubile widows and actresses and, heck, seamstresses he could choose from. A bluestocking and a reformer, to boot. I would have thought such a one would have a steel trap for a quim."

Without thought, he leapt up and had John pinned against the nearest wall, his arm against the man's throat.

"One should not speak of issues one knows nothing about. Moreover, one should never speak of a gentlewoman, any gentlewoman, so coarsely." He heard himself growl, actually growl, but could not regret it.

Hartley's surprise was evident as he held both hands up in mute surrender, perhaps because the poor fool couldn't take a breath to speak. Equally surprised by his own ferocity, Alex stepped away.

"I apologize, Lord Devin. Truly, it was in jest."

He nodded. Still, he would kill the next man who spoke of Nora thus. But even as he fumed, he saw that what she had said was accurate. Whatever their connection, their relationship, it would not be recognized by the world for what it was. Whatever affection she had for him—and he was sure she held strong feelings for him, despite her protestations—their association was tainted by the wider world. He would be condoned (clearly, he would be praised) for having a mistress; she would be castigated for being said mistress. No one would believe that he courted her, that he genuinely wanted her. But it mattered. For her sake. He did court her (after a fashion), he did try to woo her (after a fashion), and he most definitely wanted her with every fiber of his being.

And he wanted everyone else to recognize that she was worthy of such attentions.

Chapter Twenty-five

Evans Principle #more: Keep your ears, your eyes, and your heart open. When the best opportunities arise, you will know.

She recognized the Devin carriage as it stopped in front of the store. Yet, when she steeled herself to face Lord Devin, she was surprised to see Lady Devin alight, followed just as inexplicably by Mr. and Mrs. Browning. She rushed to the door to assist their entry.

"It's an honor to have you all in my modest shop." She curtsied to them, not out of expectation but out of heartfelt respect. "Mrs. Browning, Mr. Browning, if you wish, I would be happy to show you the shelves where I house your work."

"Please, allow me to get you some tea," she offered, once they were all comfortably situated. "I'll only be a few moments."

"I will come with you, dear," said Lady Devin, following her.

"Oh, no, I wouldn't dream of it. You're my guest. Please have a seat."

"I insist, Honoria. Contrary to what you might expect, I know my way around a kitchen. And I will not be refused. Now lead the way."

She began to dread any and all conversations that took place over tea.

"Nora, I am certain I have told you before that my cousin in Paris found herself a widow somewhat late in life and ultimately remarried," Lady Devin said as she counted teacups and saucers. "What I refrained from mentioning, and what even my children do not know, is that she remarried a Frenchman much younger than she. The French, she told me, are far less stuffy than our English compatriots about what constitutes love." Her voice dipped low. "She tells me she derives exponentially greater pleasures from her current match than she ever did in her youth. She says it is not so uncommon in France for the women to reach their sexual peak later than the men. I tell you, she so recommends the experience that she almost makes me want to take a discreet lover or two in order to test her theories." She winked like a naughty schoolgirl. "Almost."

Honoria's face flamed at Lady Devin's suggestiveness, at the slightest possibility that Lady Devin might suspect what pleasures her son was capable of giving.

Still, without shyness, Lady Devin continued. "What I am trying not so subtly to convey to you, my dear, is that my son loves you with a depth and intensity I have never seen. You make him happy. Or at least, you made him happy. These days, he swings between being a ghost and a bear, miserable either way. If he makes you as happy, then all the rest of it be damned."

Shocked by Lady Devin's plain speaking, Honoria didn't want to say what she had to say next. As terrible as it felt to lower Lady Devin's esteem for her, she had to reveal the truth.

"Lady Devin, you have a right to know. I don't deserve your son. I don't deserve his affection—or your kindness. The woman you see before you is built on a lie, a lie all the worse because it feeds on the pain and pity of others."

Lady Devin withdrew her hand.

"I am not a widow." Honoria paused, silent as the grave. "I was never married. I perpetrated a fraud to qualify for my uncle's inheritance and keep my father's bookshop running." God, but ever since she'd first admitted the truth to Alex, the almost-forgotten gut-wrenching desperation that spurred that old deception had reawakened. The pain simmered afresh just below the surface of her skin. Way back when, she'd thought it a brilliant scheme, the only way out. "It was the only way I could protect my father's legacy and stay out of the poorhouse myself." She felt deflated, unable to fill back up with air. "You were so kind to share with me your loss, under the belief that yours was kindred to my own. And I am so sorry I abused that sacred trust. I am not equal to such kindness."

To her inexpressible relief, Lady Devin reached out to her again.

"My dear, you may not have had a husband, but I know you have felt loss at your core. The loss of your parents, your only family, devastated you. I can see that it devastates you still today. You have harmed no one with this prevarication, except perhaps yourself. I do not presume to know what it is like to be in such dire straits. But I plainly see that you are a fine, upstanding woman. And I see that you love my son as much as he loves you. And you are, in every way, deserving of it."

Honoria couldn't lie to Lady Devin anymore, couldn't deny the feelings she so keenly perceived. *You are, in every way, deserving of it.* She fervently wished she could believe it. She carried the tray down the stairs with Lady Devin following close behind and carrying an extra plate of biscuits.

Once Mr. Browning was sure that his wife was comfortable and that he'd spent a polite amount of time with them, he excused himself. The affectionate look he gave his wife before he walked out the door spoke volumes.

Mrs. Browning's eyes were kind and gentle as they looked around the room. Her manner was open as the three women conversed about many things. Yet it was clear that she and Lady Devin had come here on a mission.

"You know something of my life story, I suppose," Mrs. Browning said. "It is no secret that Robert and I have faced some obstacles. My failing health, my brother's death, my father's decree that none of the Barrett children marry—I had nothing but my work until Robert's letters began to arrive.

"Look upon me, Honoria, and listen well. My limbs are useless, but my heart is strong. I am six years older than Robert, and I don't care. I love him with everything I am. And with all that loving *me* entails, he does so, unconditionally. We have both accomplished so much more together than we ever had apart." She looked pointedly down at her body. "Even at my advanced age, God has blessed us with a miraculous son. Do you think I have not feared loss? Do you think, at every juncture, I have not considered the safer path? Love is not for the timid, but I see that you are no coward. Embrace the gift that is before you and hold it to you for as long as you can."

Nora battled in vain to prevent brimming tears from spilling down her cheeks.

"I leave you with this reminder, which you are not, under any circumstances, to sell!" Elizabeth handed her a slim volume, her own *Sonnets from the Portuguese*, published just last year.

As with many other new arrivals to the shop, Honoria remembered skimming it quickly all those months ago upon release, and they'd struck her as sweet and pretty. She'd recommended it as a wedding gift more than once. She'd memorized several of the sonnets and easily remembered the one that gave her the sharpest pain now.

She began to recite Mrs. Browning's words quietly: " 'How do I love thee? Let me count the ways: / I love thee to the depth and breadth and height / my soul can reach . . .' " By the time she reached the end of the sonnet, she was openly sobbing: " '—and if God choose, / I shall but love thee better after death.' " She looked up at Mrs. Browning and leaned in to grasp her hands.

"What if I cannot?" she asked, trembling.

"If I can, Honoria, you can." Mrs. Browning squeezed her hands hard. "But you must make the choice. And then you must commit to it with your whole heart. No one can convince you. Only you can make that decision."

Chapter Twenty-six

Evans Principle # 8,526:
Believe in happy endings, dearest Honoria, because you deserve one.
                                                    Signed,
                                                    with everlasting love,
                                                    your father.

Masquerade balls had become cliché in London society, or so Honoria had read in the society papers time and again. The grandeur of the elaborate costumes had become just another competition of strutting peacocks, male and female, trying to outdo each other and themselves with their cleverness and innuendo. And the mystery of masked identities had become a tired game. Everyone knew everyone else. By now, most everyone knew who was using the masquerade for illicit trysts with whom. Even the occasional surprising reveal wasn't really all that surprising. Some young miss, once an ugly duckling, would be revealed like the climax of a magic trick, complete with dramatic hand flourishes, to have grown into a ravishing, elegant, heart-achingly beautiful swan of womanhood.

Yet, as blasé as the ton had become about them, when invitations to Lady Devin's masquerade ball began arriving at their doorsteps, people took notice. They set about planning and sketching and coordinating, and speculating about whose costumes would be most (and least) impressive.

She had never been to a masquerade ball. So, for her, the entire experience was novel and, if she were being honest, very entertaining. Her dress, again something borrowed from Amelia's old wardrobe, didn't fit her character, but it was the prettiest of all the very pretty options. And, since she was masked, who could judge that she was too old to be a butterfly, fleeting as their lifespans are? She'd been mesmerized by the striking combination of orange and blue, lined with delicate black patterns, but she declined to wear the wings that went with the dress. Some things were simply too out of character. The elaborate mask edged with tiny gossamer wings and the fanning pagoda sleeves would have to suffice.

As enthralling as the ball was at the start, its appeal eventually faded. Her natural aversion to large groups and small talk soon outpaced the novelty. Still, she was rather fascinated by the effects of masquerade: she'd been approached by no less than four nice young men so far, each clearly curious about her identity and clearly assuming she was just another young miss to flirt with. Although she'd arrived unescorted, she hadn't been alone since the moment she stepped into the ballroom.

She quickly became tired of the attention, of being constantly on guard, and so, when one of the flock asked, for the tenth time, clutching her hand . . . "What is your name? Can't you give us a clue?"

She blurted out, without thinking, "Mrs. Honoria Duchamp. Mystery solved and now you can move along." She was horrified by her rudeness and felt sure she'd never be invited to one of these extravaganzas again—which, she thought in turn, suited her just fine. She thought identifying herself as a Mrs. would dampen their ardor, but the boys didn't move along. If anything, their circle tightened, wolves closing in on a kill.

"Oh!" one said knowingly. "So you are Lord Devin's newest paramour." He leered.

She felt her face go red, felt her ire shoot up to dangerous levels. What had he said about her? He wouldn't have talked about her so cavalierly, she was sure. But these boys . . .

"I shall have to update my view of dowagers for you are surely the most delightfully sensual creature I have encountered this evening," said another young upstart, who then had the audacity to put his hands, his scrawny, presumptuous hands, on her waist.

"Take your hands off of me," she said, shocked. She batted his hands away, but that only seemed to tighten the group again. Surely, they wouldn't do anything in a crowded ballroom. She could easily raise her voice to draw attention to their . . . antics . . . but she couldn't seem to find her voice. Her mouth went dry, her throat closed, as their collective stench of cigarettes and brandy washed over her in such close quarters. Why didn't anyone notice this absurd clustering, anyway? Surely, a pack of leering, sniveling brats would draw some attention. But then she noticed she'd somehow ended up at the border of a dark alcove, accented with heavy drapes. The very thought that she could be in any danger here was ridiculous—crowds of people nearby, brightly lit, except for the alcoves built into this wall. She simply needed to relocate.

"You can't deprive us of your company. We wouldn't dream of it."

One whelp lounging against a wall a few feet away said, just loud enough to carry the distance, "When you've tired of Lord Devin, please do consider me as his successor." Yet his tone clearly indicated *when he is tired of you.*

"You . . . gentlemen . . . should take more care when speaking with the woman I intend to make my wife."

Five jaws, including hers, dropped. Her sense of relief at hearing his voice was palpable—she could give the sensation a color and shape and scent. She felt it wrap around her like a thick, wool blanket. Just hearing that commanding tone of his, she knew she was safe. So very relieved was she that it took a few moments for his actual words to sink in. Even then, she couldn't quite believe what she'd heard. It was one thing for him to talk idly about marriage in private, both of them knowing it could never happen. It was quite another for him to state his marital intentions publicly, which was fundamentally as binding as saying "I do" in front of the minister. For him to state his intent to marry an old and crotchety nobody, well, the news was destined to spread throughout the room like wildfire within the next three minutes. And the reactions would be awful.

"And, you," he said, pointing to the one who'd, moments ago, offensively put his hands on her waist, "would do well to keep your hands to yourself. While you still have them."

There he stood, proud and dashing in black and white, holding a simple white mask, no doubt as a nod to his mother's theme. And yet his eyes held a fury she hadn't seen before.

Most of the young bucks around her started to stammer and rushed through whispered apologies before scattering—bolting, really—to the far edges of the room.

The last of them, the one who'd been holding up the wall, calmly shook Lord Devin's hand and said, "You were right, Devin. You were absolutely right. I envy you." He then made a graceful bow to Honoria and ambled away.

"Thank you, Hartley," Lord Devin replied.

Once they were out of earshot, he looked directly at Honoria and said, "Avoid that one. Stay away from them all, but particularly that one."

"But, of the bunch, he seemed the...nicest, the most sincere, which I'll grant wouldn't be much of an accomplishment in that particular sampling of British manhood."

"That is precisely why you need to avoid him."

"I must admit, I normally find machismo ridiculous, but I'm rather enjoying this little display of possessiveness. It's..."

"It's what?"

"Adorable."

"Nora..." A warning.

"Endearing?"

"That is slightly better."

"Irresistible." She touched his cheek and looked at him, suddenly serious and breathless. "You're irresistible."

His eyes darkened but he said nothing.

"How did you know it was me?" she asked. "Did you recognize your sister's dress?"

"No, it was not the dress. It was your hair. I recognized those precious silver strands immediately." He winked as she batted him with her fan. Then his eyes swept downward, assessing. "I have never seen that dress before. In fact, this couldn't possibly have been my sister's. The cut would never have fit her, and you can tell how exact it is from the way the pattern lines up."

"Oh, but then..." Now that he'd pointed them out, the seams were flawlessly aligned to maintain the continuity of the pattern. This couldn't have been altered at the last minute; the designs and construction required painstaking attention. She fell silent as she realized how very much Lady Devin had given—and continued—to give her. Her face burned.

"What could you possibly be thinking, making a pronouncement like that?" she finally caught her breath enough to ask.

"I simply spoke the truth," he said. She wouldn't have thought his gaze could get more intense, but it did. "I intend to make you my wife—or to convince you to take me for your husband—or however you wish to phrase it. I intend to spend the rest of our days loving and being loved by you." He must have seen the fear in her eyes as she glanced around the room. "It may seem like disdain, but in fact they are terrified of you—not of you as a person but of what you represent—the ebb and flow of your family's status, the fact that your father willingly relinquished his social standing to become a merchant, and now your subsequent reentry into society as my wife. If you can fall and rise so easily, their rise can just as abruptly fall away. In a blink, they can lose all the pomp and privilege they so blithely enjoy. When you stand before them, they cannot deny the threat that looms over them. But their anxiety is none of your concern."

He took her hand and led her to the orchestra. She felt a tremor run through his body into hers and saw a combination of resolve and surrender in his eyes.

"None of that matters," he continued. "What matters is you—you and I. And anyone who disapproves can go hang," he whispered in her ear. "I intend to show everyone, without a doubt, that I am utterly undone by you."

She didn't notice his cello until he left her side to climb the steps and sit in the midst of the musicians. He nodded to the conductor. The entire audience, whose interest was already piqued by the couple, became mesmerized by the opening strands of Haydn. A low whisper ran through the crowd, spreading word of Lord Devin's performance, remarkable not only for its magnificence but more importantly for its existence at all. Peers didn't perform before an audience; that was something ladies did in a drawing room. Men might join in for entertainment; virtuosos might play sold-out performances in a proper hall to demonstrate their expertise; but this was something entirely different. He laid bare his soul. She felt his passion as the notes vibrated through her. His arms, his body, all of his energy so clearly went into the notes he played. And when his eyes weren't closed, anyone could see they were locked on her, on this Butterfly Lady. As the music swelled, the sharp tilts of his head with the rhythm made his hair brush along his face, leaving it in disarray. She could even distinguish his cello from the other instruments, coursing through her, raising her to the same emotional crescendo she saw in him. As the final movement came to a close, there was an audible collective sigh, including her own, before the audience erupted with applause and shouts of "Bravo!" The sight of him expressing himself so fully and so honestly through his music—and in public, no less—left her speechless. He did this for her.

As if that performance were only a prelude, Lord Devin made his way down from the dais. Contrary to his natural air of authority and aplomb, he looked unsure, unsteady, and, in fact, he missed the last step down from the stage. His momentum pitched him forward toward her. Their resulting embrace, abrupt and forceful, sent a gasp through the crowd. Her hands braced his chest, as his arms wrapped around her to anchor himself. With a bark of laughter, he righted himself, shook his head as if to clear it, and then solemnly, regally took both of her hands in his. In full view of the party, he then got down on both knees, her supplicant.

"Marry me," he said simply and then took a deep breath.

"Yes."

His response came out in a rush of air. "It does not matter what anyone else thinks or says. We can leave it all behind. We can be— wait. What?"

"I said yes." She couldn't help but smile at his incredulity. He seemed so often to know what she needed before she did that she was relieved to be able to surprise him. "Yes, I shall marry you," she said, louder, slower, and clearer, to make sure he truly heard it.

Ultimately, she experienced no earth-shaking epiphany. No thunderbolt of realization. No stinging arrow from Cupid's bow. Slowly, inexorably, all the messages people had been giving her simply melted into her, in particular the refrain he'd been singing over and over, that he loved her. And she loved him. How simple. She faced her fears and replaced them with a deep, unequivocal conviction. Yes, she would share the rest of her life with him, whatever that entailed. She smiled at his sudden loss of speech, at the brightness of his eyes as tears welled.

He wasn't the only one stunned into silence. The entire room was too quiet. This was what they could look forward to from London society.

He stood, nodded to the conductor, who led the orchestra into a waltz, and calmly escorted her to the balcony.

"Why?" His question startled her. It seemed so incongruous with his hand stroking her cheek.

"Why what?"

"Why did you change your mind?" His eyes searched her face.

"Well, because you love me."

"And?"

"What do you mean 'and'?"

"Come now," he said, looking surprisingly shy. "You already know I love you. That did not seem to be enough before. So what else?"

"And . . . because you and I somehow fit." At his raised brow, she added, "Not only in the way you're thinking, you scoundrel, but in a larger sense." His mouth twisted even more suggestively, and she swatted his chest. "You know what I mean. I'd long ago decided that there was no such thing as a soul mate. It wasn't simply that I'd given up on marriage. I could happily live as a redundant woman, eking out an independent life. Yet you make me see how my life could be shared, how I can be stronger and accomplish more with a true partner."

"And?" he asked in a whisper. He kissed her gloved knuckles, his eyes fixed on hers, almost pleading.

"Oh, dear. You poor man. I suppose I haven't said it yet, have I?"

"No," he said, his voice low and tense. If the line of his shoulders and the working of his jaw were any indication, he might break apart any second from the anxiety. "No, you have not. Ever."

She said she'd marry him. Could he doubt her feelings? Could he think she would agree to marry him for anything less than complete devotion? She laid her palm against his cheek, such a simple touch.

"You seem to have so little need for words, so little regard for sentimentality. Could one little declaration mean so much to you?"

He nodded, his eyes fierce, his throat bobbing as he swallowed. His warmth spread through her glove and continued through her body. She smiled up at him, opening herself to him.

"And," she said, low but firm, "I love you. I've wanted you from the day you first walked into my shop. I think I've loved you since your mother's dinner party," she admitted. "I do have reservations, but I love you, and now, just this once, I will be selfish—"

That was all she could manage to say before his lips took hers. Chaste and gentle, this kiss still managed to set her heart soaring and her mind whirling. Only their hands and lips touched, and yet she felt they were already one.

"Well," he said, long moments later, as he composed himself, "I had a whole speech prepared to sway you."

"You could have fooled me. In any case, you can present it to me later." She laughed and then said quietly, "I shall grow old, you know."

"So shall I. God willing, we shall do so together."

"But I will grow old much sooner than you. I could become an invalid. I could become demented. I will most certainly lose whatever physical charms attract you to me."

"Nora, I love you. I love everything you are . . . but, most of all, I simply love you. Whatever happens, I will always love you. I will be by your side and revel in every moment."

When they reentered the ballroom, Lady Devin was already waiting and swiftly embraced Honoria enthusiastically.

Society would accept his decision. And so, without warning, he reset the stage, determined to elicit the joyous response his new fiancée deserved. He led her up to the dais and addressed the guests.

"My dear friends, I believe it is reasonable for me to say that my mother's balls, while infrequent, are occasions of grand celebration." Cheers of "Here, here!" rang out in salute of his mother. "Tonight is an especially auspicious occasion. Mrs. Honoria Duchamp, you are everything I could ever want in a woman. I love you with everything I am. Will you do me the honor of becoming my wife?"

Yes, the proposal had already been made, but he'd apparently determined that this was the way it should be made, with outrageously dignified pomp.

She stood her ground, eyes only for him.

"Yes, my Lord Devin, nothing would make me happier. A thousand times yes."

He squeezed her hand as his mother and friends applauded.

Slowly, the sound grew as the entire assemblage followed suit. Or most of it. A few dour souls made their way to the exit, but their censure would not darken the moment. Several of Lady Devin's friends came up to give their felicitations, and it turned out to be the ball of Nora's dreams.

In his arms, she felt whole. She felt cherished. She felt seen. And she felt as if, just for once, she could be the heroine of a grand, epic story indeed.

Epilogue

It was Lord Devin's favorite time of day. As the gray sky deepened into twilight, he strolled into the bookshop, placed the CLOSED sign in the window, and locked the front door. He could hear his lovely wife humming in the back office, no doubt closing the day's accounts. He'd suggested she hire an accounting clerk, but she insisted on handling the ledger herself. She simply didn't trust anyone else to do it well enough, and finding someone as meticulous as she would indeed be difficult. They'd had his personal accountant run an audit covering the past five years. When it was complete, the man immediately offered Honoria a job with his firm, so impressed he was with her acumen. But, of course, nothing could woo her from the bookshop.

Speaking of wooing her from the bookshop, he was surprised at what an inordinately long time it was taking for Honoria to settle this day's ledger. There she sat at the desk, head down in concentration, pencil moving continuously, pausing every few moments as she calculated. Surely there hadn't been so large a spike in sales on a random Thursday. When he said as much, she simply raised a finger to her lips. He couldn't even begin to explain why, but he found even the most infinitesimal of her movements charming. The pursing of her lips, the touch of her finger, the lilt of her eyebrow. Utterly fascinating.

And yet he knew from experience that, if he distracted her from this task, it would take even longer for them to get home and explore more fascinating and enjoyable endeavors.

So he wandered the office, scanning the ever-changing stacks and ever-stable knickknacks—the miniature of her parents, a pressing of the first flower he ever gave her. He'd grown quite fond of this room . . . and that desk. In fact, he had several extremely fond and vivid memories of that desk. Such as the evening soon after their engagement when he'd accosted her after closing, finding her on one of the ladders and then doing what he'd dreamed of since he'd first laid eyes on her. He dove under her skirt and petticoats as she stood above him and found *her*. One thing quickly led to another, and he'd laid her out on that very desk and tasted her womanhood, feasted on her deeply and thoroughly, as she moaned and squealed and cried out.

He finally sat down in the plump leather chair across from Nora and waited. Such recollection had a way of building like a snowball rolling down a mountain. He couldn't stop himself from remembering another evening soon after that when he'd arrived late, delayed by friends at his club, and found Nora waiting impatiently. Hungrily. She'd pushed him up against the desk—right there!—roughly freed him from his trousers and then knelt before him, insatiable and relentless.

He grinned.

The problem with such memories, he thought as he shifted uncomfortably, was that there was only one satisfactory end result. And Nora was still too buried in the ledger for him to prompt her toward such results. He needed to distract himself before the tightness of his trousers and the throbbing of his groin made him a nuisance. So he forced himself to examine the items on his side of the desk very, very carefully.

"Here is an old friend," he said. "*One Thousand and One Nights*! What an odd coincidence to find this portentous fellow lying about."

"Hmm," she said idly. "Yes, I acquired another copy recently. I was reminded of it today and wanted to check something."

"Do tell."

"Such a wonderful work. Do you remember the ending?"

"Let us see. Well, of course, the king falls in love with our ines-timable heroine Scheherazade and ultimately decides he cannot pos-sibly kill her."

"Mmm-hmm. There was another detail I'd forgotten. . . ."

"Which is?"

Without raising her head, she held up her hand again, in the midst of calculations.

So he flipped through the last few pages of the book in his hands. Within those pages, an idea took root in his mind, growing from a whisper to a roar, a glorious and all-encompassing roar. Could it be? Dare he hope?

When he closed the book and looked back at Honoria, she was looking at him with great affection. He swallowed hard and moved toward her.

"My lady wife, is there some message you wish me to glean from this volume?"

"Yes."

He rounded the desk and leaned in.

"I would rather not mistake your meaning. So could you give it to me plainly?"

"Certainly, my lord and husband. Our Scheherazade, brave and clever and beautiful, was very busy in all those long nights. Some-how after all those nights of drama and fancy, she not only found her-self beloved and secure—but also in a rather happy but delicate condition."

Barely breathing, he asked, "And why would you be reminded of her romantic denouement today?"

"Because, my love, it's taken us far fewer than a thousand and one nights, more like one hundred and fifty nights, at least according to rough estimate by the doctor and midwife I saw this morning."

His heart leapt, apparently into his throat, for he found himself unable to speak. He held her face gently, reverently in his hands. She truly did glow. And he wondered, not for the first time, what he could have possibly done to earn such a charmed life.

"You are *enceinte*? I did not think such a thing could be possible," he said, finally. "Are you sure? Are you all right? Is it safe?"

"I am fine. I'm so much more than fine, love. I'm over the moon, and my heart is dancing among the stars." She sobered a little. "The doctor says it could be rough going, bearing a child at this age. But it's not unheard of. I'm strong in mind and body, and I have you with me."

"I love you," he whispered.

"I know," she replied. "I know . . . we need better words for love." And, when she kissed him, gently, he knew that this was one of those things for which no words could possibly suffice.

About the Author

Amara Royce writes historical romances that combine her passion for 19th-century literature and history with her addiction to happily-ever-afters. She earned a Ph.D. in English, specializing in 19th-century British literature, from Lehigh University, and a master's degree in English from Villanova University. She now teaches English literature and composition at a community college in Pennsylvania. When Amara isn't writing, she's either grading papers or reveling in her own happily-ever-after with her remarkably patient family.

www.amararoyce.com